Praise for the book

Giving brings a joy and purpose that no amount of wealth can offer. Rashmi Bansal, in her book, 'Live to Give' beautifully captures an idea that I deeply resonate with, that we are trustees for the wealth we create.
-Anu Aga, Former Chairperson, Thermax Limited

These are some great stories about people who took to philanthropy at different stages of life and for different purposes... they have made a difference... with deep passion and incredible commitment.
-Ashish and Vasvi Bharatram, SRF Group

My tryst with philanthropy started 25 years ago. I've learned from nonprofits, changemakers, fellow givers, and I keep learning. If 'Live to Give' can inspire even one of us to give more, sooner, and smarter, it's made an impact.
-Deep Kalra, Founder & Chairman, MakeMyTrip

'Live to Give' is a great initiative of AIP for the Indian philanthropic ecosystem. I see the emergence of a set of young and thoughtful philanthropists driven by a sense of purpose, making a culture of giving both a habit and deep responsibility.
-Deepak Parekh, Chairman, H T Parekh Foundation

Real success and real purpose in life comes not just from making money but in giving it away in your lifetime. Read these inspired tales about the heroes of our times – they not only gave but gave smartly.

-Gurcharan Das, Author

True impact lies in building institutions that endure. 'Live to Give' celebrates those who give with vision and resolve.

-GV Prasad, Co-chairman and Managing Director, Dr. Reddy's Laboratories

In 'Live to Give', storytelling becomes a mirror–showing how wealth, when guided by purpose, transforms lives and ecosystems. Each story affirms what I've long believed: passion must lead purpose.

-Harish Yarlagadda, Founder, Malaxmi Group

'Live to Give' is about the quiet strength of those who choose to care, even when no one is watching. These stories don't just inspire; they stir your conscience, challenge your thinking, and awaken a deeper sense of purpose.

- Jalaj and Vita Dani, Co-founders, Dani Foundation

Philanthropy is a bold act of imagining and co-creating a better future. 'Live to Give' is a rare recognition of these givers and their mindsets - hoping to inspire many more to give more and better and sooner!

-Mekin Maheshwari, Founder and CEO, Udhyam Learning Foundation

In our culture, giving isn't a grand gesture....
it's simply what one does when life has been generous.
'Live to Give' captures this belief... that true giving
isn't about spotlight or scale, but about quietly
showing up where it matters.

-Motilal Oswal, Founder and CEO, Motilal Oswal Financial Services Ltd

Reading 'Live to Give' reminded me why this space
means so much to me. I was especially moved by how
the spirit of generosity flows through families
and across generations - something I have been
fortunate to witness in my own life.

-Rati Forbes, Director, Forbes Marshall Group

A much-needed collection of stories that shine a light
on India's many paths to giving. I hope it inspires not
just generosity, but thoughtful, sustained action
for the greater good.

-Sanjeev Bikhchandani,
Founder, Info Edge (India) Limited

Philanthropy must create pathways to dignity
and opportunity. This book celebrates those
who give to uplift lives.

-Satish Reddy, Chairman, Dr. Reddy's Foundation

Heartful giving becomes mindful connection - inspiring
compassion and a future rooted in unity and love.

-Tanya Bali, Chief Catalyst,
Neonates Foundation of India

Live *to* Give

Inspiring stories of Wealth with Purpose

RASHMI BANSAL

The facts and opinions in this work are provided by the subject of each profile and the publisher is in no way liable for the same.

Content by Bushfire Publishers LLP (2025)

First edition by **Bushfire Publishers (2025)**
(venture by Rashmi Bansal)
Core House, Off CG Road, Near Parimal Garden
Ahmedabad 380006

Bushfire and the Bushfire logo are the trademarks of Bushfire Publishers LLP, or its affiliates.

PB Book ISBN : 978-81-947679-7-8
E Book ISBN: 978-81-947679-4-7

Book and Cover Design: Bhavi Mehta
Page design: Madanmohan Anumalla

Printed at Thomson Press (I) Ltd.

Dedicated to dear Sharad

You live to give. No greed, no glory.

Foreword

One regret I have about my philanthropy is that I did not start early enough. So, it is wonderful to see that so many others started much earlier in their life than I did. Many of these people have contributed to this book. This group of people brings in many perspectives and yet there is a common core.

That common core is a belief that wealth is a privilege bestowed on us. It is a privilege because such wealth is created only through society and societal institutions. Thus, we must see ourselves only as trustees of this wealth, not its owners. Mahatma Gandhi has said this and this belief is an integral part of Indian culture. Realizing this gives us the responsibility of doing our best to use our wealth towards societal good.

In my view, this is both a responsibility and duty for people who have this privilege. But at the same time it is equally important to recognize that the sense of responsibility and duty must emerge from within and cannot be mandated or forced from the outside. When the urge to discharge this responsibility comes from within it is deeply fulfilling, and also becomes a lot more effective.

This urge from within that I am referring to is not some mysterious force. Like any other human tendency and behaviour, it is shaped by the environment around. Development of empathy through genuine connection with the wider world, most importantly with the real lives of human beings, most of whom do not have the privileges that we have, is essential. We must try to develop these real connections; it wouldn't happen through the fleeting glimpses of such lives from our cars. We must have some mechanism to develop a real connection.

Experience and examples of others are the other things that we can seek — which one can relate to. This book is directly useful for that.

As you read through this book you will come across a range of styles for philanthropy and even within those varying perspectives. This provides a rich range of possibilities of learning, which is crucial because each one of us has to discover ones own approach. I have discovered my own over time. Let me share the three things that I have learnt.

First, social issues are far more complex than business. People who have wealth have made it in business. And then through their philanthropy they are dealing with society and its issues. This is as though very good football players are now starting to play five-day cricket test matches.

The difference between the two games is not just the length of each match but also the rules of the game, the objectives of the activities, and the effect of the conditions. Business and societal change are even more different. Simply stated, I have learnt that philanthropic work is a different world from business; we must not try to play football in a cricket match.

Second, in our country, and I can't speak for any other country because I have no philanthropic experience outside India, all improvement and change is dependent on on-the-ground presence and institutions. No amount of good policies or smart strategizing is effective unless the central and foundational part is adequate and engaged human capacity at the panchayat, ward and block level. Even a district is too large as a unit of action. In fact it is exactly the reverse – once there is sound human capacity on the ground, and grassroots institutions, then any policy can be made effective and all strategies can seem smart.

Third, for our philanthropy to be really useful, we must have greater humility than our wealth. Our success in business must be set aside. We must try to learn afresh. Very often it is also a situation where we need to have the humility, along with the wisdom, to accept that the most important learning is to appreciate and empathize, not to deploy our intellectual might for solutions — because there are others who can do it better than us so long as we have the humility to let them do what they do.

After 25 years of being actively engaged in philanthropy, I still learn more each day, because I meet so many people who seem average but are doing extraordinary things. It is deeply fulfilling and also very enjoyable.

This book is another mode of learning. I am sure you will find each piece in this anthology interesting and useful. I wish all of you the very best in your own philanthropic efforts.

Azim Premji

August 2025

We Believe

Philanthropy in India is undergoing a quiet yet profound transformation. No longer confined to acts of charity or purely driven by a moral imperative, it is becoming a conscious choice—an expression of empathy, conviction, and strategic intent. Today, more wealth creators are asking not just how much to give, but how best to give.

Philanthropists today are choosing to engage deeply, build institutions, support changemakers, and invest in solutions that shape India's future.

'Live to Give' captures this spirit with honesty, heart, and hope. Through sixteen compelling stories, the book reveals the diverse motivations, methods, and missions of Indian philanthropists who are using their resources, time, and intellect to serve the public good. These are individuals who have chosen to walk the path of giving while living—who see philanthropy not as a side project, but as a second calling.

Some lead with their hearts, working hands-on to heal and uplift. Others bring the power of strategic thinking to build institutions and solve problems at scale. Still others give with quiet trust, enabling changemakers and strengthening ecosystems. There is no single right way.

Whether giving is led by Prana, Gyaan, or Daan—each path is purposeful, and each story is a testament to the many ways one can give.

As Core-Founders of AIP, we believe strategic philanthropy is one of the most powerful tools for nation-building. It allows us to address root causes, build resilient institutions, and create sustained change. It also allows us to listen—to communities, to changemakers, and to each other.

That is why we built AIP—to foster a vibrant peer network, to inspire, influence and inform giving, and to help India's wealth creators give more, give sooner, and give better.

We thank Rashmi Bansal for bringing these journeys to life with clarity and emotional depth – reminding us that behind every act of giving is a story of purpose.

This book also reflects our civilizational values of seva, daan, and samaaj, while embracing the tools of modern change making. It shows that there is no single way to give—only a shared commitment to give with purpose. Let us build a culture of giving... Let us live to give.

Signed:

Amit Chandra

Ashish Dhawan

Harish Shah

Rohini Nilekani

Vishal Tulsyan

The Core Founders, AIP | August 2025

Author's Note

I have a love-hate relationship with my country. There is no other place I would rather live; at the same time, living here makes me despair.

Why can't things be better?

Why can't we progress faster?

Every day, these questions come up as we go about our lives. We rant on WhatsApp groups, in coffee shops, at dinner parties, and conclude – 'kya kar sakte hain, kuch nahin.'

Let's just earn enough money to insulate ourselves.

This is a book about those who think differently. They're saying, yes, India has problems, lots of problems.

I am going to pick up one of them and do something about it!

Instead of sitting back and savoring success, they're rolling up their sleeves. Using their minds, their hearts and their funds, to boldly go into the uncharted and unknown.

Markets rise and fall, valuations decline; in the end you see - nothing is 'mine'.

May your actions bear fruit, may your wealth provide shade. Like the Giving Tree, may your kindness cascade.

May your roots find depth, may your branches stretch wide. May you give without measure – no ego, no pride.

Rashmi Bansal

CONTENTS

Prana Gyaan Daan

Prana

Working hands-on, with patience,
and a strong in-house team.
Driven strongly by the heart.

Gyaan

Philanthropy as problem-solving,
with a burning desire to achieve scale.
Driven strongly by the mind.

Gyaan

Philanthropy as problem-solving,
with a burning desire to achieve scale.
Driven strongly by the mind.

Daan

Carefully selecting and funding changemakers,
with a hands-off approach.
Driven strongly by trust.

Note to readers: As you read, you may notice an asterisk (*) in some chapters. This indicates that the beneficiary's name has been changed to protect privacy.

Prana

Working hands-on, with patience,
and a large in-house team.
Driven strongly by the heart.

"Start early
and start small,
that's what
we did."

So Many Starfish

KUMARI AND S.D. SHIBULAL

Shibulal Family Philanthropic Initiatives (SFPI)

They began by giving two scholarships at Shibu's childhood school in Kerala. 25 years later, the Vidyadhan program supports 10,000 students in 21 states.

The odds were stacked against Kumari. She was born in a tiny village in Kerala with no electricity or roads, to parents who tilled the land to make ends meet. It was a time when girls were barely educated and married off early. That would have been Kumari Daniel's fate, had it not been for her strong-willed mother.

At harvest time, when kids bunked classes to lend a hand to their parents, Mary Daniel made sure that Kumari stayed in school. She scraped together a little extra money by selling eggs – 10 paisa an egg – and instead of buying a new pot, or a sari, or a few treats, she used that money to send her daughter for tuitions in English.

Kumari excelled and got a government scholarship of 15 rupees a month to attend PUC, in a college 30 kms away. As there was no bus, she would need to stay in a hostel. What about the fees? Her parents took a loan on heavy interest to cobble together the funds, even as relatives whispered that the money could be better used to buy gold.

"I got my first pair of sandals when I went to college," Kumari recalls. Till then, like everyone else in the village, she walked barefoot.

Kumari Daniel became one of the few girls from Ramamangalam village to complete B.Sc.

Education transformed her life, her thinking, her possibilities. So, when she and her husband S.D. Shibulal had the means, they decided to 'do something'. There was no plan laid out on an Excel sheet. It started with giving just two scholarships.

25 years later, the Shibulal Family Philanthropic Initiatives (SFPI) supports more than 10,000 students in 21 states with Vidyadhan scholarships. What stands out is the painstaking personal involvement with which the program has been conceived, designed and implemented.

Kumari insisted on doing the selections herself. Covering the state of Kerala meant 10 days on the road, from Trivandrum to Kasargod, with 20-25 interviews a day. The kids were shabbily dressed, shy, underconfident. No one had ever given them such importance.

"Sometimes I felt it was a younger version of me, sitting on the other side..."

The understanding in her eyes made all the difference.

This is the story of those raw diamonds, born to shine bright. Holding the light.

Pehchaan sako to har insaan mein jyoti hai
Heerey ki parakh johri ko hoti hai.

You know those Bollywood love stories of the 70s – 'rich boy, poor girl, yeh shaadi nahin ho sakti'! Well, this one is all that, and more.

In the cool environs of Maharaja's College, Cochin, on the banks of the Vembanad Lake, a young man walked down the corridors in bell-bottoms and a shirt with long, pointed collars. They were much in fashion at the time. He was in the second year of college, the mess secretary, a bit aloof and considered to be 'full of himself'.

Kumari's first impression of Sarojini Damodaran Shibulal was not positive. She was in Class 12, living away from home for the first time, careful about every rupee she spent. Her parents had sacrificed so much for her to be here. No - she was not interested in casual friendships with boys.

Friends had warned her, for good measure. "Stay away, he's not our type."

Her quietness, her firm demeanour, her indifference to a senior with so much swag, was intriguing. The more Shibulal tried to befriend her, the more firm her resolve. However, he persisted; they began talking and became friends. Indeed, Shibu was different, not just in his dressing, but in his thinking. Bold and ambitious, yet kind and caring.

Just before graduating, Shibu asked Kumari, "Can we be 'friends for life'?"

She froze, not knowing what he meant or how to respond. He took her silence as 'yes'.

Love blossomed via inland letters, as Shibu completed his Masters at S. N. College, Kollam and then moved to Bombay, to take up his first job at BEST (Bombay Electricity Supply and Transport).

A year later, he felt settled in the new city and travelled back to Kerala, to request Kumari's parents for her hand in marriage.

"What does the boy do?" asked her father.

"He is a programmer. His job is making travel arrangements," Kumari replied confidently.

They were not too impressed and further, he was a Hindu while they were Christian. However, they did not stand in the young couple's way.

On April 14, 1979, Kumari travelled by train for the first time, with a boy who had not yet put a taali around her neck. Soon after, they had a court marriage in the presence of three people. The groom proceeded to office right after the ceremony. Work always came first.

In 1980, Shibulal shifted to Patni Computer Systems; six months later he was invited to join the founding team of Infosys. Kumari pawned her mangalsutra so that her husband could contribute his share.

They moved to the US, along with others in the founding team. They lived in shared apartments, taking turns to cook.

A birthday dinner at Pizza Hut was a luxury. On weekends, Shibu went to the video game arcade, with 25 cents from his wife. Those were years of hardship, which eased with the Infosys IPO in 1993.

It was only in the late '90s, when the stock market went through the roof, that the founders became rich. Rich beyond their wildest dreams.

Now, they felt a moral responsibility to 'do something'.

But what? Where? How?

PHILANTHROPIC JOURNEY

In a modest brick house in Alleppey, the aroma of jackfruit stew wafted from the kitchen. Professor S. Ramanand's stomach growled. It had been a long day at S.D. College but he knew that amma would not serve dinner, until her beloved Shibu arrived. That's how it had been, since their college days.

The two had lived together in Kollam while doing their Master's, with amma looking after them. Post-college, Ramanand stayed anchored to Kerala, while Shibu had a burning desire to make his mark in the world.

The two friends remained close, and one year, during Ramanand's annual visit to Mumbai, Shibu confided in him.

He was thinking of leaving his job, to join a bunch of people starting a new company. Go for it, said Ramanand.

Shibu's plan had worked splendidly. Amma now took childish pleasure in boasting to the neighbours.

"I used to make payasam for the Infosys CEO."

On a midsummer evening in 1999, Shibu shared his ruminations on 'giving back' with his childhood friend. He shared a story which had deeply touched him.

An old man was walking along the shore. The beach was littered with starfish, washed up by the tide. The man noticed a boy bending down, to throw a starfish into the sea.

He asked the boy why he was making an effort, there were thousands of starfish lying on the beach.

"Your action will hardly make a difference!" the old man exclaimed.

The boy picked up yet another starfish and threw it far into the ocean.

He smiled and replied, "It made a difference to that one!"

After brainstorming, they reached a decision – let us start with our own school. The common practice was to award scholarships to meritorious students but Shibu had a different view. It is better to support a needy student who wishes to pursue higher education. A starfish who may otherwise remain on the beach.

"Yes, let us start with two scholarships for needy students," agreed Kumari.

So, they approached the headmaster of T.D. High School, Alleppey and asked him to recommend eligible candidates. Follow-up would be needed over the next 5-7 years, until the recipients completed their studies.

That job was entrusted to Ramanand, who also became a trustee of the Sarojini Damodaran Foundation, formed in 1999.

There was no specific goal or plan. The number of scholarships grew organically, from four to six, to ten. There were so many deserving students, it felt wrong to turn them away. Gradually, the Akshaya scholarship program spread to other schools, first in Alleppey, and then in neighbouring districts.

In 2005, Ramanand came to the Shibulal's with some disturbing feedback.

"I am hearing from people that headmasters are being partial. They are not recommending the most needy students to us."

After some thought, Shibulal said, "Let us bypass the headmasters and conduct our own entrance exam."

Ramanand was taken aback – this was rather ambitious! However, he saw merit in the idea and plunged into the nitty-gritties. Setting the paper was relatively easy, but a state-wide exam meant at least five test centres.

How would they conduct it fairly and efficiently, in different locations?

TRAVELLING THE PATH

Where there's a will, there's a way. The Sarojini Damodaran Foundation had also set up a program to recognise and award organic farmers. This program had a representative in every district of Kerala. So these farmers, and some retired persons, were roped in as volunteers. And this worked out well.

In year one, 500 students appeared for the exam; 300 were shortlisted for interviews.

They were sons and daughters of daily wagers, who could ill-afford to take a day off. Yet, each one was proudly accompanied by a parent. Kumari insisted that each candidate was given transport cost and a daily allowance. A small gesture which went a long way.

> *"Very humble, soft spoken, genuine. That was my first impression of Kumari ma'am."*
>
> *– Venugopal Shenoy, scholarship recipient*

In 2006, when the Shibulals relocated to India from the US, Kumari began playing a more active role in selections. Coming from a humble background herself, she knew that it was not easy for such children to face an interview panel. Hence, Kumari insisted on being present, and adopting a kinder, gentler approach.

"I wanted to make sure the children did not feel intimidated while talking to a stranger."

Venugopal Shenoy, son of a small-time sweet-maker in Alleppey, vividly recalls the first time he met Kumari ma'am. A student of SDV Secondary School, Venu also delivered sweets to local shops and helped his father with money collection.

'How can I get my family out of this daily struggle', he asked himself. *By studying, making something of myself.*

It was a muggy August afternoon when Venu rushed back from his daily market visit to take a quick bath, wear his 'good clothes' and attend the scholarship interview. After verification of documents, tea and biscuits were served to Venu and his father.

Finally, he was called inside for the interview. There were four people on the panel – three gentlemen and a lady in a silk sari.

The lady said, "I am Kumari, wife of S. D. Shibulal."

Venu was awestruck. He had read an article on Shibulal in the Manorama newspaper. The man was a billionaire. Why had his wife come all the way to Alleppey to interview a 10th pass student like me, he wondered?

But her soft-spoken voice and kind demeanour made him comfortable. She briefly related her own story; it sounded similar to his own. Then, the interview panel asked questions about his schooling and family background.

"What is your aim in life?" they queried, after initial chit-chat.

Venu replied, "To become an officer in Indian Air Force."

All this while Kumari had been silent. When she finally spoke, she raised an important question: 'What is your Plan B?'

"I will become an aeronautical engineer or a pilot," came the prompt reply.

Venu's clarity of purpose and 'will to win' impressed the panel.

The interview lasted 30-40 minutes. It would change the entire course of young Venu's life. Although he did not make it to the Air Force, Venu completed his B.Tech. at a local college and went on to secure a well-paying job. Today, he is a successful IT professional living in Bangalore, with his young family and aging mother.

"It is only because of Shibu sir and Kumari ma'am that I have reached so far in life," says Venu.

He is one of hundreds of young people for whom the program has been a game-changer. While giving a scholarship sounds simple enough, doing anything at scale is a challenge. This was no different.

HAIL SCALE

As numbers increased drastically, the panel travelled across the length and breadth of Kerala, meeting up to 100 candidates a day. Kumari travelled with them.

The interviews were brief – 5 to 7 minutes – but enough to gauge the motivation level and neediness of the candidate.

It was a hectic couple of weeks for Kumari, while Shibu managed the home front. Their daughter Shruti was studying in the US but their son Shreyas was still in school.

"Every night, I was exhausted, yet exhilarated," recalls Kumari.

As the program expanded, so did admin work. Ramanand roped in a new set of volunteers – a 'Karma Sena'. These were the past recipients of the scholarship who were studying in and around Alleppey. They assisted with admin work, corrected papers and helped organise the annual scholarship distribution event.

> *"99% of our focus is on children, of which 90% is in education."*
>
> *– S.D. Shibulal*

"Ramanand Sir also used to hold soft skill development classes for us – public speaking, self-motivation, those kind of things," says Venu. The exposure he got being part of the Karma Sena helped his all-round personality development, and came handy when he went for job interviews.

By 2009, more than 8000 students wanted to appear for the test. So, a crucial decision was taken – the process went online. That year, the number of applications went down drastically. Internet was not easily accessible and many were not comfortable with the online medium.

"We wondered, have we done the right thing?"

With the rapid penetration of mobile internet, the issue got resolved. Since the numbers were huge, filters were applied to identify the most deserving and most needy students and call only those candidates for the test.

From 1000 test takers, 400 were called for interview, of which 150 would be in the final shortlist.

In the last phase, there was a mandatory home visit, to verify the candidate's economic status and family details. Ultimately, 100 scholarships were disbursed, covering education up to graduation or even post-graduation. Which meant a 5-7 year commitment for each student.

Kumari and the local band of volunteers had indeed taken the program far. In 2014, when S.D. Shibulal stepped down from the CEO position and officially retired from Infosys, he turned a critical gaze on his philanthropic foundation and asked the million-rupee question, "How can we do more?"

SHIFTING GEARS

Meera Rajeevan had spent 22 years in IT but in 2014, when her younger son went to college, she decided to quit.

"I had always wanted to join the social sector and it felt like this was the right time."

When she put in her papers, Shibulal heard her out. The next day, he made her an offer: "Work with me. I want to scale the scholarship program."

Till that time, Meera had no idea about the foundation or its work but she had complete trust in her former boss. Shibulal recognised the value of a high quality professional and sweetened the offer. He let Meera work from Thrissur, so that she could look after her parents.

"It was a leap of faith from both sides," grins Meera.

She joined in November 2014 and her brief was two-fold. Firstly, to scale the Akshaya program, now called Vidyadhan, in terms of numbers and locations. Secondly, to get like-minded people and corporates to sponsor candidates so that more and more students could be supported.

There was a third dimension which concerned Meera – scaling the childrens' level of ambition.

When she asked youngsters, 'What do you want to do in life?' the standard reply was 'doctor' or 'IAS officer'. They had no other role models.

She went back and told Shibulal, "We must invest in training and mentoring".

A five day residential training program was thus introduced, during the vacation period. The focus was on life skills and bringing people from diverse backgrounds to address the students. These sessions were indeed very effective in helping the children think bigger and dream bigger.

In 2015, the program made its first foray into a new state – Karnataka, which had 30 districts and three times the number of students completing class 10. Moreover, there was no volunteer network. Hence, it was decided to shortlist students after Class 12, based on their board exam marks or CET rank.

Kannada speakers were enlisted to do telephonic screening of applicants. The most deserving students were invited to Bangalore for an interview. This was an eye-opener for Meera. Coming from a corporate background, she had a hiring and performance review mindset. This was diametrically opposite to the foundation's approach.

Kumari's instructions to the panel were clear: no stress interviews. These are children, we must treat them with respect, not demoralise them. Many of them will be shy or poor communicators. Encourage them to speak. Their English may be poor, but let them try to express. If they are uncomfortable, mother tongue is okay.

This gentle approach worked like magic. Meera was amazed to see how a hesitant child would open up in just a few minutes. A case in point was Viji*, who confided that her mother was always shouting at her. On further probing, Meera learnt that her father was schizophrenic; the mother was his caregiver and also the family's sole breadwinner.

Another poignant case was a girl with more than 90% marks who was an orphan. Her father had killed her mother and was now in jail. Even in stable homes, many of the fathers were drunks or wastrels, with the mothers toiling to put food on the table and send the children to school.

"I developed empathy and how to assess need, by asking open-ended questions."

What kind of house do you live in?

What work does your father do?

What kind of school do you attend?

For example, a Kannada medium government school indicated a very needy child. A daily wager's son or daughter got extra weightage. If agriculture was the main source of income, one year the crop may be bountiful, the next year a failure. One acre in Kerala is huge but in Karnataka, in a dry area, it is nothing.

Taking into account a number of such factors, one could assess each child's real financial position, beyond the standard income certificate.

"This is a different version of Shibu from what he was at Infosys. More empathetic, more patient."

– Meera Rajeevan, CEO, SFPI

In 2016, Vishwanath, a Kannada-speaking MSW graduate joined the team. An entrance exam was introduced, similar to the one conducted in Kerala. The exam tested subject knowledge, logic and General Knowledge. In addition, each candidate had to write one page about themselves. Those who did well were invited for an interview, followed by a house visit.

The Kerala formula was thus replicated and found to work. This opened the doors to entering new states. It also meant leaving one's comfort zone – South India – and embracing new challenges.

For example, in Odisha, it took three years to scale up, as ads in the newspaper only brought in applications from the cities. The foundation was able to connect with the rural and tribal belt only after tying up with local NGOs.

Local language knowledge was a must, hence state co-ordinators were appointed. While retaining their essence, the interview process was codified. A model was used to calculate neediness score, in addition to academic score.

However, everything can never be captured on a spreadsheet, so state co-ordinators had some discretion.

For example, in Gujarat female applicants were less, so they got priority. In Karnataka and Telangana, students from backward districts got additional weightage. Meera would often travel to remote locations to oversee the first set of interviews.

From time to time, Kumari would also join.

"Initially, I was hesitant as facilities in remote areas are poor but Kumari ma'am is so down to earth."

No matter what the food or bathroom situation, she never once complained. However, these visits did sensitise Kumari to the level of desperation in the hinterland.

In some parts of India, a 'house' might just be four sticks and a plastic sheet. A sight one would never see in Kerala.

Due to Covid, the test went online and numbers skyrocketed. In 2024, there were 95,000 applicants from 21 states with 3000 candidates getting selected.

By 2025, the number of students in the program reached 13,000, with cumulative scholarships crossing 63,000.

The dropout rate is just 0.5%. This is because of the active efforts of the team to keep track of and mentor each child, when needed. If a child who scored 95% suddenly drops to 40%, there could be a death or an illness in the family, or some other mitigating circumstance.

As head of the program, Meera Rajeevan personally looks into each and every dropout case. Her zest and commitment to Vidyadhan remains steadfast.

"In corporate, I never liked doing the same thing," she admits.

"But I have been here for 10 years now and it has been an amazing journey... it humbles you every time."

SHOW ME THE MONEY

The question arises, how much does it cost to run this program? Each student gets Rs 10,000 to Rs 1 lakh per annum, depending on the course of study. This adds up to a sizeable sum.

No doubt, the foundation could keep funding this program but Shibu's thinking went beyond this.

What if Vidyadhan could disburse 1 lakh scholarships? Many companies and wealthy individuals would gladly sponsor a needy child, if they were sure that he or she was genuinely deserving.

"Let us open up our program so that others can sponsor our children," was the brief given to Meera.

This gave birth to the 'Each One, Teach One' program in 2015. In the pilot phase, outreach was through family and friends. Flex India became the first corporate sponsor to sign on. They had operations in Maharashtra and Tamil Nadu and wanted children from both states.

"We decided to enter Maharashtra, due to this push."

Today, more than 2,000 Vidyadhan scholarships are sponsored by UST, Elite Foods, LTI, NASSCOM Foundation, and many others. For companies, it's a win-win. Vidyadhan does the legwork – identification, verification and monitoring of the children. The sponsor will fund and, in some cases, provide mentoring.

In most NGOs, 20-30% of donor money goes towards admin cost. At Vidyadhan, the foundation absorbs all expenses – team salary, training and overheads. So 100% of your CSR money goes to the child. The donor can even browse profiles of children on a dedicated portal and select whom to sponsor

"We started as a project... then it became a program... and now, Vidyadhan is a platform," says Shibu.

By allowing others to use it, Vidyadhan can scale faster.

While building the platform, Shibu's vision was that 1 lakh people would come forward to support 1 child each. That did not happen but, he remains optimistic.

The new target is to get 100 companies to sponsor 1000 children each, and who knows, in the near future, the magic number may be within reach.

It is also heart-warming to see a large number of past Vidyadhan students, who are well settled in jobs, now funding scholarships. Either individually, or in a group. In fact, Prof Ramanand exhorts even current scholars to share 2% of the scholarship amount back to the foundation. The Rs 5 lakh thus collected funds a few additional students.

"In Malayalam, we say 'orumayude nanma', which means goodness of the collective," he says.

More than a dozen Vidyadhan scholars have joined the foundation after completing their studies. They are not only bright but truly committed.

It has been 25 years since those first two scholarships were disbursed. Kumari continues to take hands-on, personal interest while Shibulal conducts quarterly reviews. He is occupied with running a startup accelerator, as well as several other philanthropic initiatives.

THE OFFSHOOT

We return to the story of the starfish being thrown back into the sea – it's a wonderful analogy for the Vidyadhan program. But what about the starfish who were too weak to survive?

Again, one might say, I cannot save them all, but Kumari and Shibulal saw it differently.

In 2002, the criteria for disbursing scholarships was lowered drastically, to reach out to truly needy children. At the end of two years, a disturbing trend was noticed – 50% of the scholarship recipients had dropped out of school. The Shibulals were troubled – what could possibly be going so wrong?

The problem was not with the scholarship, it was the child's circumstances. The 'ultra-poor', earning less than $2 a day, have no fixed address or permanent job. As they go from city to city in search of livelihood, keeping a child in school is not even possible at times.

"We are happy to see more girls applying, they are smarter, more motivated than boys."

- Kumari Shibulal

These were the weaker starfish whom the Shibulals decided to transfer to a pond, and nurture with extra love and care. That pond is 'Ankur', a residential program for the ultra-poor set up in 2004. It started in a rented house in Jayanagar, under the supervision of Asha Thomas and Aparna Goenka, former employees of Infosys.

"At that time it was pretty bold – we took children at the age of three," says Shibu.

The program had two children in its first year, two in the second year, ten in the third year and slowly, kept expanding. By 2008 there were 40 children but it was far more complex to run than the scholarship program. Taking complete responsibility for a child was a huge commitment, and difficult to scale.

The real problem surfaced when they started attending local schools - they were treated differently. This affected the very purpose of the program – it was just not acceptable. But how do you change the general mindset of society? Kumari and Shibulal took a bold step.

"We will start our own school for these kids, based on our value system."

The Shibulals set up Samhita Academy in 2009, with a school building, staff quarters and hostel built on a 6 acre campus in Bannerghatta. By this time, there were 45 Ankur children, all of whom shifted to these new living quarters and joined Samhita Academy, which functioned from nursery to Class 4.

As the Ankur children grew, so did the school and its intake. Kids from well-to-do families vied for admissions, but this mixing of social classes came with its unique challenges.

The Ankur children were mostly from the interiors of Karnataka, and they were not selected on merit. The criteria was 'who has the maximum need'. Only a basic assessment of current educational level was conducted; even a child who spoke no English at all was eligible to join the program.

So how would Deven, whose family lived in a mud hut and struggled to make ends meet, integrate with Devika, the only child of high-flying IIM graduates?

It was indeed a unique social experiment. But would it work?

IN FULL BLOOM

14 year old Nandu* had been with Ankur since age four. He had been a quiet, above average student, who liked playing cricket. The year he started Class 9, his behaviour became erratic. His homeroom teacher said she noticed this change soon after he came back to the hostel after spending summer vacation in his village.

Nandu would often have angry outbursts, and he even stopped doing the one thing he loved – playing cricket. It was difficult to understand, at first, what was going on in his mind. But finally he confided that he hated going home and staying in a squalid one room house, where his alcoholic father created a ruckus every night.

"Teacher asked us to say what we did in vacation," said Nandu. "Everyone is saying I went to foreign or I went to Shimla, what will I say?"

Nandu declared that next year, he would rather stay back in the hostel than go 'home'. This is my home, he said.

While this sense of belonging was indeed beautiful, Kumari and Shibulal felt a nagging doubt. Was it morally right to take a child into Ankur at such a young age?

After much debate and discussion, the Ankur program was re-engineered in 2016. Instead of age 3, children would now join at age 10, after they had bonded sufficiently with their parents. But, you will say, taking a Kannada-medium child into a CBSE school in Class 5 is 'mission impossible'.

This is where the 'bridge' curriculum developed by Ankur comes in. Children join in December and spend 6 months developing English language skills, starting from phonics, to reading, writing and comprehension. By June, when they join the school, they are able to follow what's happening in class.

Those who have grown up in difficult circumstances carry hidden trauma, which hinders them in numerous ways. When confronted with issues, the management did not sweep them under the carpet.

They acknowledged the problems, and came up with solutions. Today Ankur is run on 'four pillars' – the first and foremost one is emotional wellbeing. Then comes intellectual development, safety and medical fitness.

"Today, our children are calm and confident," says Colonel Krishna Menon, Director Ankur. "But this did not happen overnight."

By Class 11, the Ankur kids are completely on par with any of the day scholars. They are participating in public speaking, sports and taking on leadership positions in the school.

"There is no 'us' and 'them' – this makes us very happy and proud," says Jyothi S, Principal, Samhita Academy.

The story doesn't end with school – the Ankur model is from Class 5, till the day the child secures a job. Today, 170 children in the hostel attend Samhita Academy, 62 are going to college and 14 are either in jobs or in the process of getting placed.

Ankur is indeed a success, by any qualitative or quantitative metrics. However, the model is hard to replicate. The school is self-sustaining but the cost of running a hostel with caring wardens, mentors and medical facilities is substantial.

The money spent on a single Ankur child for a month would be enough to fund a Vidyadhan scholar for a year. Hence, although there are more than 500 applications, only 20 students are admitted to Ankur every year.

For Kumari and Shibulal, it is more than a program. These kids have a permanent place in their hearts.

On a sunny October morning, a group of well-dressed young men and women gathered for breakfast at the Shibulal residence. Over medu wada and sambhar they laughed loudly and urged 'uncle' and 'auntie' to share anecdotes from the days when they were kids and sat on their laps.

"I have just started a new job – see my visiting card!" said one.

Kumari's eyes welled up. These were her kids, all grown up, settled, so wise and mature. They are doctors and engineers, teachers and managers. Professionals, citizens, good human beings.

The starfish who made it back to the sea.
It made a difference, a difference to me.

Post Script:

Kumari and Shibulal discuss their life and philanthropic initiatives in greater detail in a set of books scheduled to be published in 2025. These books contain little known anecdotes of their shared journey and the learnings, failures, and successes of their experiments.

For more on The Shibulal Family Philanthropic Initiatives scan:

ADVICE TO YOUNG PHILANTHROPISTS

If you wait for the 'right moment' it will not happen.

Your personal needs are never-ending. If you wait for everything to get settled down, you will keep waiting. If you wait for retirement, it's too late.

So, as soon as you feel like doing something, go ahead, it will happen somehow.

Start early and start small, that's what we did. That allows you to experiment and come to certain conclusions.

You need to be patient if you want to create sustainable impact because, you know, transforming lives is not easy. There are no shortcuts.

And you have to accept some amount of failure, right? Because that's part of life. You cannot assume that 100% of what you do is going to work...

When it comes to scale, you need the same systems and process-thinking as a business entity. But the ROI you look at is very different and so are the time frames.

"You have to find your passion, what pulls your heartstrings and follow that."

Main Shayar to Nahin

SANJIV SARAF

Rekhta Foundation

This maverick philanthropist is investing his time, money and expertise to bring new life to age-old Indian languages.

Sanjiv Saraf was born into a Marwari business family. In 1955, his grandfather Durgaprasad Saraf set up India's first ferro-alloys plant – FACOR. In less than a decade, it became one of India's largest exporters. It was only logical that one day, Sanjiv would join the business.

Far removed from the world of minerals and metals, an abiding influence on young Sanjiv was his father's love for Urdu poetry. His childhood home in Bhubaneshwar was filled with the voices of Begum Akhtar, Farida Khanum, Mehdi Hasan and Ghulam Ali, playing on a 33-1/3 inch gramophone. The words did not make sense, yet Sanjiv felt a soul connection.

"Emotions are expressed so well in Urdu, even as a young boy I was deeply touched."

From Scindia School, Sanjiv took an unusual path for a boy from a business family – he joined IIT Kharagpur. He did return to work with FACOR but was restless to do something more. So, at age 26, Sanjiv Saraf set up a company called Polyplex, which manufactured biaxially oriented polyester film.

The year was 1986, when License Raj prevailed – there were challenges galore. The company almost went bankrupt in the first three years of its existence but over the next decade, Polyplex became a force to reckon with.

Over the years, Sanjiv set up the online legal portal Manupatra and ventured into hydro-electric power, but by 2011, business was no longer exciting for him.

Ek ajeeb si bechaini ka ehsaas hone laga tha.

One evening, as Sanjiv sat in his study enjoying a glass of single malt, listening to his favourite ghazals, a soft voice whispered from within.

"You have worked enough for money, it's time to feed the soul."

At 53, Sanjiv decided to hire a tutor and formally learn Urdu. Little did he know that decision would result in the creation of Rekhta. A unique effort to preserve and popularise the Urdu language. What started with a website expanded into a massive offline event and cultural phenomenon.

Now, Sanjiv is applying the same principles to propagate Marwari, Rajasthani, Gujarati, Hindi and working on Punjabi and Sindhi as well.

Philanthropists tend to focus their efforts on health and education – where the need is obvious and visible. Sanjiv Saraf has chosen a different path.

"This is my passion," he shrugs. "Ya phir keh lo junoon."

To use one's passion to make a difference is what the soul hungers for.

Mire junoon ka natiija zaroor niklega
isi siyaah samundar se noor niklega.

On a pleasantly cool Delhi evening in 2011, at a social soiree, Najeeb Jung, Vice-Chancellor of Jamia Milia Islamia University, felt someone approach him.

"Can I have a moment, please?" said a soft-spoken man in a bandhgala.

One meets countless strangers at such gatherings but this particular mulaqaat remains etched in Najeeb Jung's mind. Because it was so unusual a request.

"I want to learn Urdu... Can you help me find a teacher?"

Najeeb Jung looked the man up and down. Why in the world would a smartly-dressed businessman with the surname 'Saraf' want to learn Urdu? Nevertheless, Jung saheb connected him with the head of his Urdu department.

An Urdu tutor was duly assigned to visit the Polyplex CEO's well-appointed, fifth floor office twice a week. Sanjiv's executive assistant looked on, bemused. Dharmendra Saha was a young engineer who had joined Polyplex to work on renewable energy projects. He knew that his boss was a bit of a maverick.

"He liked to do New York Times crosswords; I thought this was a similar pastime."

Indeed, learning Urdu is a bit like a brain exercise. Learning the unfamiliar right-to-left script takes a lot of practice, and patience. That challenge kept Sanjiv occupied far longer than he had anticipated.

After achieving some level of literacy, Sanjiv started searching for reading material. But Urdu books were not available online and websites had limited she'rs, wo bhi aadhey-adhurey.

Exasperated, Sanjiv said to his E.A., "Dharmendra, let's make a website!"

It was a side project, a whimsical demand from his boss, which the E.A humoured. He calculated that it would take about six months to select the kalaams of 50-100 well-known Urdu poets and upload them. Accordingly, Dharmendra onboarded a freelance developer for a fee of Rs 1 lakh.

Back then Urdu poetry was shared online either as a jpeg image or in Roman script. When Sanjiv consulted professors at Jamia Milia they said, 'Urdu to Urdu mein likhni chahiye'.

But not many people can read the script, a poetry lover pointed out. Aap kripya Devnagari mein bhi likh dijiye.

As the wishlist kept expanding, so did the scope of the project. Bring it on, said Sanjiv. Let's think bigger...

KAR KE DIKHAANA HAI

Experts are important, but they are overly attached to 'how things are'. Neither Dharmendra nor the developer knew Urdu. So, they came with no preconceived notions. For the two engineers, this was simply a software project with distinct technical requirements.

For example, the calligraphic Urdu script posed a challenge.

"Bhai, there is no Unicode font for this language!" said the developer in exasperation.

The only existing software was InPage, created by an Indian company in 1994. It was being used by Urdu publishers across the world. The software's 'nastaliq' style was incorporated into the website, as it gave a feel close to calligraphy. By this time, the workload was so high that the developer had joined the project full-time.

In 2012, Sanjiv set up the Rekhta foundation. Rekhta is the old name for Urdu and means 'scattered', which is apt. It is an amalgamation of Farsi, Turki, Khadi Boli, Prakrit and Braj. The 16th century ruler Quli Qutb Shah is considered the first Urdu poet, but it was Mir Taqi Mir – and later, Mirza Ghalib – who made it into an art-form.

Sanjiv's original vision was to select the 'best' shayari of well-known shayars and make it available online. But who would decide what was best? And more importantly, vouch for authenticity? Verses were often lost, or changed, as they were passed down orally.

Scholars had opposing views, leading to heated discussions in Sanjiv's office.

Poet Farhat Ehsaas was persuaded to come on board as Editor-in-Chief, overseeing content. Meanwhile, IT people and typists came in to handle ever-increasing uploads. 12 people now worked full-time on Rekhta, including Sanjiv's erstwhile E.A. The 'hobby project' was rapidly becoming more important to Sanjiv Saraf than his plastic packaging conglomerate.

The Rekhta website was launched on January 11, 2013, with selected shayari from 300 poets. It could be enjoyed in all three scripts (Urdu, Hindi, Roman). Sanjiv's collection of Urdu books had also been scanned and uploaded on the site. As the authors were long dead, there were no copyright issues.

The project was lauded by readers and scholars alike.

"Bahut oomdaa kaam kiya hai aapne," was the refrain.

Indeed, Sanjiv was quite pleased with his creation. Surely a few shaukeens would find their way to the website and benefit from all the hard work that had been put in. The IT team assured him that they would get around 200 visitors a day. They could not imagine how off the mark they were!

In less than a month, Rekhta was attracting 2000 visitors a day. The visitors were not just savants – they were ordinary people. Because the site made the language accessible to all. For example, when a user clicked on an Urdu word, a pop-up appeared with the meaning in English.

Thus, even a newbie could enjoy the nuances of Urdu poetry.

A modest personal project had exceeded all expectations and gone beyond national boundaries.

WHERE'S THE JOSH?

The Rekhta website quickly developed into a community of sorts. One of the desires expressed by users was to make spoken poetry accessible to more people.

Speaking at Sham e Rekhta 2014, Sanjiv Saraf described the mehfil as a 'chhoti si koshish' to showcase the adab and andaaz of Urdu.

Indeed, until then, a poetry reading would attract maximum 50 people. The inevitable topic of discussion was 'Urdu ka surat-e-haal' (the downtrodden state of Urdu). Sanjiv disliked this negative way of thinking.

He decided that the following year, Rekhta would not organise a mehfil but a completely new kind of festival.

> *"We will celebrate all forms – qawwali, ghazal, poetry, drama and dance."*

'Jashn-e-Rekhta' was held for the first time on 14th and 15th March, 2015 at India International Centre. Speakers and poets were happy to attend. Even the renowned Javed Akhtar gladly participated. However, the organisers were worried about the other side – would there be enough audience?

Sanjiv sent out an email to his employees: 'You are 'requested' to attend Jashn-e-Rekhta organised by our company'.

What happened next took everyone by surprise. A tsunami of Urdu lovers descended on India International Centre. The tranquil IAS retiree club buzzed with excitement and shayarana andaaz. The event was a huge and unqualified success, with over 18,000 footfalls over two days.

Jashn-e-Rekhta gave Sanjiv the courage to follow his heart and throw himself into the work of the foundation. He handed over the operations of Polyplex to his friend and colleague, Pranay Kothari. What started as a passion project had organically morphed into a full-time commitment.

Sanjiv rolled up his sleeves and worked on Rekhta with the same zeal that helped him build profit-making enterprises. Earlier, the raw material was plastic and steel, ab lafzon aur jazbaaton ka maamla tha. But to succeed and scale up, the work had to follow due processes, and managerial principles.

For example, early on, Sanjiv separated Rekhta (the behind-the-scenes work) and Jashn-e-Rekhta (the event with visibility and glamour). The two facets of the organisation were handled by dedicated teams, so that each could focus and excel in their respective areas. This was a wise decision, as Jashn-e-Rekhta acquired a life of its own and the website also grew exponentially.

In 2016, India International Centre refused to host the festival – 'you need a bigger venue', they said. So, the event was held at the Indira Gandhi National Centre for the Arts (IGNCA). Colourful shamianas gave a mela feel, with young people coming in large numbers. The attendance kept growing and by 2019, the event had to be shifted to the much larger Major Dhyanchand Stadium.

"It was thrilling that we could fill up such a large venue...!"

The festival came to a halt during Covid but returned with a bang in 2022, attracting more than 1 lakh enthusiasts. Crowd control became such a concern that it became imperative to charge a nominal entrance fee. Nevertheless, the crowd at Jashn-e-Rekhta 2023 was immense and exuberant, with a footfall exceeding 300,000.

In 2024, Jashn-e-Rekhta was moved to the Jawaharlal Nehru Stadium, as an even larger space was needed.

If this festival were the only thing Rekhta had instituted, it would be a rich enough legacy. But as far as Sanjiv is concerned, it is only the tip of the iceberg.

CREATING A LEGACY

While the festival gets the eyeballs, quietly, without fanfare, the majority of Rekhta staff has been working on the preservation of rare and precious Urdu books.

These books lay forgotten in dust-laden libraries. Why not scan these copies and create a virtual library? The trouble was, getting permissions.

"Aapki madad kari, to idhar kaun aayega?" said the custodians.

It took two years of effort to convince the first library – run by the Anjuman-I-Taraqqi-I foundation – to let Rekhta digitise its collection of 11,000 books. However, they had a condition: books could not be taken outside the library.

So Rekhta installed a machine on their premises, as well as dedicated staff, to carefully scan the delicate tomes.

That exercise took four years; in the meantime, the work of convincing more libraries continued. Sanjiv reached out to Najeeb Jung, then Lieutenant Governor of Delhi, regarding one of the oldest public libraries in India – the Lala Hardayal Municipal

Heritage Library in Chandni Chowk. The library was a treasure trove of manuscripts, which, sadly, were in very poor condition. Yet when Rekhta sought to digitise, there was major resistance from the library's custodians. Najeeb Jung overruled them.

"Go ahead", he said to Rekhta, "Yeh kaam zaroori hai."

It was dry, painstaking work. The kind of work that takes time, effort and money. 60 machines were installed across 27 cities in India, 90 people scanned books and created metadata entries for them. Uploading large images meant heavy investments in server space and IT infrastructure.

Today, the Rekhta website attracts 150,000 daily visitors, but the 'ebook' section gets very few views. It is accessed only by serious scholars and shagirds. But this is the lasting legacy of Rekhta. Three lakh books, which would have been lost to the world, have been preserved for posterity.

And this work continues unceasingly.

SPREADING THE LOVE

As Rekhta grew, people began asking Sanjiv a question.

"Aap Urdu ke liye itna karte ho, what about other languages?"

He could have shrugged his shoulders and said - maine is desh ki sabhi bhashaon ka theka thode na liya hai! But this is where the man's entrepreneurial spirit kicked in.

A great deal of original thought and execution had gone into designing the Rekhta website. In 2018, he had an epiphany: 'What we have done with Urdu can be done with any other language.'

The key lay in the union of language with technology, and that could be expanded. The first experiment in this direction was Sufinama, launched in 2019. It is a website dedicated to the tradition of Sufism, which brought the dohas of Kabir, songs of Meerabai, the abhangas of Eknath, and the poetry of Lal Ded onto a single platform.

Then came Covid, which proved to be a blessing in disguise. Since events were not possible, the single-minded focus of the organisation shifted to new projects.

Hindwi.org, dedicated to Hindi literature, was launched on 31st July, 2020, the 140th birth anniversary of Munshi Premchand. This was followed by a one-of-its-kind trilingual Rekhta Dictionary (Urdu-Hindi-English).

> *"A small step for Rekhta, a giant leap for Gujarati language and literature."*
>
> *- Udayan Thakker, poet and translator*

"I also addressed the request from Rajasthani brethren by doing something with Marwari," smiles Sanjiv.

The website Anjas.org is his effort to preserve Rajasthani literature and oral tradition. It was launched in October 2022 with a two-day cultural festival at Garh Govind, Jodhpur.

The newest baby on the block is Rekhtagujarati.org, inspired by Tushar Mehta, the Solicitor General of India, who is passionate about both Urdu and Gujarati literature. The website was launched in Ahmedabad in February 2024 by Shri Morari Bapu and is receiving a fantastic response from the Gujarati diaspora.

It is important to note that every new language has its challenges. Unlike Urdu, one cannot scan complete books in Hindi due to copyright issues. In the case of Rajasthani, there is no official 'state language' – there are multiple dialects like Marwari, Mewari, and Bikaneri – which complicates matters.

However, where there's a will, there are many ways. It also takes money.

"Sanjiv has a big heart," says Prithvi Haldea, close friend, Urdu lover and Chief Trustee, Ibaadat Foundation. "I know many who have interest, have money but not the jigraa to spend it."

Currently, Rekhta Foundation has 260 full-time employees who occupy a six-storey building within Polyplex. It is partly funded by Polyplex CSR money but mostly by Sanjiv's personal philanthropic money, with assistance from like-minded friends and philanthropic organisations.

"In Arabic there is a blessing," says Sanjiv. "May your expenses increase. Because, as they increase, God will provide for you."

Indeed, this has been the case with Polyplex. The company is 'doing much better' after Sanjiv's handover, with net profit jumping from Rs 27 crore in FY '16 to Rs 491 crore in FY '22.

Moreover, Polyplex recently sold a 24.3% stake to Dubai-based AGP Holdco Ltd, giving Sanjiv greater flexibility in expanding his philanthropic activities.

But the scope of Rekhta's work is ever-increasing, and it will take more than money to build a critical mass around each language.

NAYI MANZILEIN

So here's Sanjiv's proposition: Every language needs a champion. Rekhta has the know-how, technology backbone, learning curve and processes.

He is happy to 'open source' this model i.e. share it with any individual or organisation. But the partners must be willing to channelise monetary resources, as well as junoon and jazbaat, into the project.

Will Rekhta succeed in incubating Rekhta-like online and offline communities for many more Indian languages? Sanjiv certainly believes so. Surely there is a Sindhi overseas, or an enterprising Punjabi, Kannadiga or Maharashtrian business group willing to invest time and money in a project of such significance.

All they need to do is reach out and make the commitment.

From a passion project Rekhta is evolving into an institution, which aims to be self-sufficient and broad-based in scope.

And, while building Rekhta, Sanjiv Saraf serendipitously met his wife, Huma Khalil. Born in an illustrious, literary family, Huma is an author, director, scriptwriter and, since the last three years, a Rekhta trustee.

"A shared passion and commitment to Urdu brought us together," says Sanjiv.

It is a joyful personal and professional partnership. Huma oversees the Urdu content of Rekhta, all aspects of Jashn-e-Rekhta and the audiovisual initiatives of the foundation. This gives Sanjiv the time and space to work on new projects.

Sanjiv and Huma spend most of their time in Dubai, with the team in Noida taking full ownership.

Among them is former E.A. Dharmendra Saha, who is proud of using his time and energy to create lasting value. Dharmendra is no longer a mechanical engineer but an engineer of dictionaries and language projects. He is part of the team which has used the internet to reimagine the cultural and literary concept.

"We treat each word as a unit, linking it to multiple languages," he says.

Take a word like 'tadap' - it exists in Hindi, Kumaoni, Garhwali, Braj, Avadhi, Kannauji, Maithili and so on. In all these languages 'tadap' means agitation or anxiety in the heart. But in Magahi 'tadap' also means to jump (as in 'deewar tadap jaana').

Connecting a word to multiple languages makes our understanding of Indian languages richer; it also shines a light on how much we have in common. It is an example of 'cultural innovation' made possible by philanthropy.

"I feel blessed to be part of something beyond balance sheet or P & L," says Dharmendra.

That sentiment is shared by all at Rekhta. As well as those whose lives it has touched in 160 countries. Online, offline, and deep in the heart.

Sanjiv quotes Majrooh Sultanpuri...

Main akela hi chala tha janib-e-manzil magar
Log saath aate gaye, kaarvan banta gaya.

For more on Rekhta Foundation scan:

ADVICE TO YOUNG PHILANTHROPISTS

You have to find your passion, what pulls your heartstrings and follow that.

Money is important but so is your personal involvement. If there is blood and sweat and there is no money, then the vehicle will not move forward. Fuel is a must.

But if there is only fuel and no passion, no involvement, then also vehicle will not move forward. There is no direction. Then you can go round in circles and go nowhere.

A single person can't do anything. You have to have a team of committed people who will work with you, who share your vision, your passion and work with you.

This is an unlimited field. The more you do, the less it is.

"I work in rural Bihar to keep my connectivity with my village."

Doing it My Way

SANJIV KUMAR

Parivartan Bihar

He believes that India will develop when her villages do. This experiment in Bihar's Siwan district demonstrates how it can be done.

The accent is unmistakeable. Bihar is in his blood and Sanjiv Kumar proudly flaunts it. As a practicing lawyer in the Patna High Court, his father had moved to the city. But summer holidays were always spent in the village. Climbing trees, swimming in the pond and gorging on malda mangoes.

His ancestors were zamindars, with vast fields and orchards in Narendrapur village of Siwan district. But Sanjiv's upbringing was very different. Both his parents were communists who believed in egalitarianism. Sanjiv was exposed to many radical ideas, as well as literature and culture, in their drawing room.

After a stint in State Bank of India, Sanjiv moved to Delhi and entered the real estate business. Visits to Narendrapur were few and far between. Then, in 1990, his grandmother passed away. Sanjiv's father Shri Fanish Singh opened a primary health facility in the village, in the name of Late Ramkishori Devi.

"Main kuch karna chahta hoon, kya tum log saath doge?" Babuji asked.

There was no high school in Narendrapur, so, Sanjiv's father took the lead in setting one up. He bought the land while Sanjiv bore the deficit in running cost (Rs 20 per child, per month).

Then, quite by accident, Sanjiv set up a branch of the famed Delhi Public School in Patna, followed by four other DPS franchises. He could have run an education empire but just when it was about to take off, a voice within said 'no'.

Instead, he rolled up his sleeves and decided to do something for his own village. In 2011, 'Parivartan' was born. 14 years later, it is a unique experiment in rural development with a physical campus running multiple programs. Transforming the farmers, the children, and most of all, the women in 39 nearby villages.

On a bright winter morning you will see girls gleefully playing kabaddi. You will hear the clickety clack of looms, and cheerful conversations of women workers. Once confined to the chaar-diwaari of home, now earning both money and respect.

Parivartan is constantly evolving and adapting to the needs of the community. With the entry of his only daughter, Setika, came fresh energy and ideas.

"There was no pressure," says Sanjiv, "the decision was hers."

At a time when everyone talks of scale, Sanjiv has no desire to expand his footprint. But he is more than happy to share his learnings in community-based development, should anyone wish to replicate this model in their home district.

Kehte hain ek Bihari, sau pe bhaari.
Dekhte raho, parivartan hai jaari.

The journey from Patna to Narendrapur seemed endless. As his car navigated yet another stretch of barely existing road, Sanjiv Kumar felt his bones rattle.

"Anjar-panjar dheeley ho jawey," was his usual complaint when he reached his ancestral home. The last stretch leading into the village was particularly bad. But surprise, surprise! The narrow path had been widened and made pucca. Sanjiv entered the house beaming... Babuji had done it again.

That evening over litti-chokha, father and son discussed matters close to their heart. At age 58, Babuji had embarked on a PhD (a comparative study of Premchand and Gorky). But his pet project was the uddhaar of Narendrapur. Every time he visited, Sanjiv would learn of yet another initiative – whether it was planting trees or fixing the water supply.

"I admired Babuji's enthusiasm. Haath pe haath dharey baithna, wo unka style na tha."

Sanjiv was too busy growing his own business to get deeply involved. Whenever Babuji asked, he would contribute money. He was rapidly making strides in the area of real estate and construction when, quite by accident, he entered a whole new business – education.

In the late 90s, every parent in Delhi wanted their child to study at Delhi Public School, R.K. Puram. Sanjiv Kumar was no different. His daughter Setika would surely attend DPS, he thought. Unfortunately, she did not get selected. Instead, the management offered him a DPS franchise for Patna.

Sanjiv admits he has no idea what he was getting into.

"I thought I will construct the building and they will run the school," he says.

"I felt that if I do something here, my connection with my village will remain."

Bihar was then a badland; parents sent their 4th and 5th class kids to boarding schools, as there was nothing of any standard in Patna. So, when DPS announced it was entering the city, there was a mad rush for admissions. Sanjiv Kumar was stunned. Expectations were so high, would he be able to deliver?

His educational background was ordinary – Hindi medium school, Hindi medium college.

"My English is weak even today," he grins.

What's more, DPS only lent its brand name, and some broad guidelines. After that, you were on your own. Sanjiv took it up as a challenge. Kyunki, DPS ka naam hai, par Patna mein jawaabdaari to meri hai.

And he got completely involved, spending 20 days a month in Patna. He dived into every aspect, from pedagogy to teacher training. DPS Patna started in 1998 and was a huge success.

In 2003, Sanjiv started a DPS in Pune, the following year came DPS Ludhiana. That's when a question arose in his mind.

"Why are there no high quality schools in smaller towns?"

It was a business opportunity waiting to be tapped.

FINDING A DIRECTION

In 2005, Sanjiv conceived Takshila School. But parents in smaller towns were not willing to pay the fees of a DPS. So, how would those schools deliver quality?

Flipping through the pages of a business magazine, Sanjiv found his answer. Airlines followed a 'hub and spoke' model. It was perfect for his schools.

"DPS will be the hub, with Takshila schools in cities nearby!"

In 2007, he started building schools in Gaya (near Patna), in Ahmednagar (near Pune) and in Hoshiarpur (near Ludhiana). At the time, the fee of DPS was Rs 1200 p.m., while Takshila would charge Rs 699 p.m.

A year later, three schools were ready and the admission process had started. And then, Sanjiv Kumar had a realisation.

To scale the model, he would need to set up at least a dozen schools and run them in two shifts. Additionally, his vision was to make the school infrastructure accessible to all. For example, opening the library for public use, or the computer centre for training, after school hours.

What's more, Takshila was not envisioned as a for-profit. The surplus from the DPS schools was to be ploughed into the new venture, so that it would eventually break even. And none of it would happen without his intense involvement. The weak link in the system was clear – his own management bandwidth.

"I am a very hands-on person. I realised it will be very difficult for me to handle this..."

In February 2008, Sanjiv sold the three schools and recovered his cost of investment. That Diwali, on one of his rare visits to Narendrapur, Sanjiv was walking in the fields.

He asked the young men accompanying him, "Tum ka karat ho?"

They all replied, "Kuch nahin bhaiyya, aisa hi idhar udhar jo kaam mil jaawe."

Boys married young, had children and eked out a living, with little hope of a better future. That night Sanjiv tossed and turned on his bed. Gandhiji's words rang in his ears: 'To develop the nation it is necessary to develop the villages first.'

India had ignored this advice and done the bare minimum for its 6.5 lakh villages. And then there was Babuji. With limited resources, he had done so much for his beloved Narendrapur. 'Haath pe haath dharey rehne se koi fayda nahin,' he could imagine Babuji saying.

It felt necessary and it felt right. It was time for action.

THE TRANSFORMATION

What comes first – the chicken or the egg? Well, to begin with, you need a farm. That was Sanjiv's thinking – to first create a built space. And not one small building but a sprawling campus with functionality and aesthetics. A space with an inviting atmosphere, jahan hawa kuch badli hui si hai.

In 2009, he embarked on the uphill task of purchasing land from 43 separate families and consolidating it. What's more, part of the zameen once housed the village graveyard. That made it easier to acquire, so the worry was yahan kaun aaeyga? But Sanjiv had complete confidence.

"My belief is that if you give it all, a dream will materialise..."

So when people gawked at the construction and asked - what will happen? - Sanjiv's muskurate hue reply was 'something will happen'. It was tough to imagine though, given the ground reality - two hours of electricity a day, zero telecom, barely any road connectivity.

There were countless problems each day but Sanjiv took it in his stride. Having grown up in Bihar, it was nothing new or surprising. It did not feel like a problem.

As infrastructure was taking shape, in parallel, Sanjiv started exploring 'what to do'. He commissioned a baseline survey in a five kilometre radius around Narendrapur. The idea was to get a snapshot of the prevailing socio-economic conditions, as well as some crucial data. Such as number of households, employment status, and so on.

Around this time, Sanjiv happened to meet Dr Rajeshwar Mishra, an old acquaintance of his father. A professor of social psychology, Dr Mishra had extensive field experience.

"Your survey is too academic," he said to Sanjiv.

Dr Mishra advised him to begin with community building activities involving rural youth. This resulted in a program called YFC (Youth For Change). The idea was to identify local boys and girls, train them and get them placed in government programs, such as ICDS. Meanwhile, Sanjiv was also considering setting up an ITI (Industrial Training Institute).

Then, in the course of his travels, he met Rukmini Banerji, CEO of Pratham. This led to the idea of a partnership.

"We will be more than happy to work with you," said Pratham founder Madhav Chavan.

In 2011, when the hardware was complete, the 'software' was ready to be installed. Pratham introduced three courses with job linkages. For hospitality, the students went to the Taj group for training and placement; for the electrician course there was a tie-up with L&T. Getting such opportunities in Siwan district was rare and precious.

When Chandan Kumar* heard about the training, he was skeptical. The son of a marginal farmer, he barely scraped through school and made a living doing odd jobs.

"Kauno hamaare liye aaj tak kuch nahin kiye," he shrugged.

Why would this sanstha be any different? But what did he have to lose... Chalo, dekh kar aatey hain.

It was the best decision of his life. Chandan was among the first batch of trainees who went on to work with the Taj Group. Today, he is well-settled in the hotel industry and thanks to that, his family back in the village has prospered as well.

> *"Do not go with a ready solution, engage with the community first, learn what is possible."*
>
> *- Dr Rajeshwar Mishra, advisor to Parivartan*

The livelihood program was extremely successful. In fact, by 2016, there were no young men and women left to train. Pratham proposed to widen the catchment area. Why not bring youth from other parts of Bihar? It sounded only logical but Sanjiv was not interested in geographical expansion.

"I started Parivartan to uplift my village. Usi ke aas paas mera focus rehna chahiye."

In December 2016, the Pratham centre closed down. 480 students had completed the skill development certification, 50% of them had taken the placement. But livelihood was only one of the areas Parivartan wanted to work in.

Basic needs are important but the poverty of the mind goes much deeper.

The ultimate goal is mental transformation.

TOUCHING LIVES

The standard NGO model is to pick a cause and work in that one area. It could be education, or agriculture, or woman empowerment. The Parivartan approach is different. At inception, Sanjiv decided, we will work in 39 villages in Siwan and work towards holistic development.

"By 2013 we had six verticals and worked with every member of the family unit."

While younger men left to work in the big city, those who stayed behind were marginal farmers, who struggled to make ends meet. Parivartan recruited agricultural experts to help them adopt new practices. With training and hand-holding, more than 450 farmers have rejuvenated their land.

When it comes to education. Parivartan works with anganwadis and schools to upskill both teachers and students.

Sports is another powerful tool in Parivartan's arsenal. Sanjiv recalls the time he used to visit from Patna - young people in the village gathered in the evening to play volleyball.

"Aur bhi bahut saari baatein hoti thi," he recalls. "I wanted to revive that culture."'

Parivartan's Community Sports program Umang is about bringing kids together. Khel khel mein, they learn important life skills such as discipline, punctuality and hygiene. A second program called 'Sports for Excellence' is aimed at those with the potential to rise to higher levels.

Rigorous training was provided in cycling, kabaddi, football and athletics, with top perfomers being sent to district and state tournaments. But early on, this program faced resistance – there was zero participation from girls.

"Parents had all kinds of objections," recalls Alok Kumar Singh, program co-ordinator.

The worry was, if girls play football, they will break their legs, unse shaadi kaun karega.

Well, the only way to eliminate fear is to look it straight in the eye. The Parivartan team persuaded a few girls from the village to start playing. But kicking a football in salwar kameez and chappals was not ideal.

So, Parivartan went back and talked to the parents. Reluctantly, they allowed the girls to wear track suits.

Today, the team - all of them in half pants - is cheered on by the entire community. It's not about what they are wearing but what they are scoring. Several girls are in the state kabaddi team, a couple have even made it to the nationals. What's more, sports has even resulted in jobs.

"People now give sports the same value that they give to education," says Alok.

At a deeper level, the status of the girl child is slowly but steadily being raised. Whether it's going to school or playing a sport, agar ladka kar sakta hai, to ladki kyun nahin.

However, the most challenging segment to work with was women. Confined to their homes, with little agency over their lives, often ill-treated. How do you win their trust?

Dr Mishra suggested that Parivartan collaborate with an existing state government program called Mahila Samakhya.

Following this model, 2800 women were organised into 168 groups. These groups were further subdivided into tolas, and muhallas. Sahyoginis were identified in each panchayat, to conduct weekly meetings. The goal was to raise awareness in five areas: education, health, domestic violence, financial empowerment, panchayat.

Magar sirf baaton se haalat badalte nahin. Chahiye kuch nayi manzilein, kuch nayi soch.

A NEW ERA

Setika Singh was an undergraduate student at University of Warwick when she heard that her father was setting up something called Parivartan. She had grown up in Delhi but, like her father, spent many summers in their ancestral village, enjoying the small pleasures of rural life.

As an economics major, Setika interned at different organizations, from J. P. Morgan and Barclays to the NGO Pratham, which produces the Annual State of Education Report (ASER). As an intern, Setika was sent to Ayodhya with the Pratham team, to conduct an audit. She enjoyed the project thoroughly.

"That's when I decided, this is what I want to pursue in some form or the other."

Setika went back to the UK, for a degree in Social Policy and Development from the London School of Economics. In 2014, she returned to India but did not join Parivartan.

"First, work somewhere to understand what it takes to run an organization," said Sanjiv.

Setika joined the NGO Magic Bus as Executive Assistant (E.A.) to the CEO, Pratik Kumar. It was an exciting time, as the 'sports for development' model expanded to Nepal and Myanmar. Setika absorbed it all. What's more Magic Bus then helped Parivartan set up its own community sports vertical.

After a year and a half with Magic Bus, Sanjiv felt that his daughter was ready to take on a larger responsibility. So in 2016, Setika joined Parivartan as Executive Director. The differences between what the London School of Economics taught you about development and, the reality of working in rural Bihar now became starkly evident.

One of the key skills that is not taught in a classroom is how to engage with the community. To help people, you must talk with them, understand them. But how do you win the trust of a woman in ghoonghat, with little exposure to the world? This took time to learn, but Setika was determined to do it.

"I have seen Setika patiently and calmly absorb the nuances of the rural society," says Dr Rajeshwar Mishra, who was her mentor in this period.

At the same time, Setika brought to Parivartan new ideas and new thinking. Her father did not believe in documentation. He was a man in a hurry, always itching to 'start doing something'. Baad mein dekhenge, dum hai ya nahin.

In contrast, Setika believed in a measured approach. Let's first assess the situation, make a plan and then start working.

As you can imagine, there were arguments before launching any program, before hiring people, and even on whether or not to have an annual report.

"We disagreed a lot," says Sanjiv. "I gave my views but as Executive Director, I let Setika have the final say."

Thus, for the first time in 2017, Parivartan published an annual report. A formal curriculum was charted for each program and an impact assessment report was commissioned. Over time, father and daughter have developed respect for each other's viewpoints and see the arguments as useful debates. Which help Parivartan evolve.

"Everyone has seen us fight," laughs Setika. "But they know it's nothing to worry about. We are both so passionate when it comes to Parivartan."

But even as she was involved in all aspects of the organisation, there was one program which Setika was drawn to. Kuch kaam ho raha tha, but a lot more could be done.

This could be her dream project. Something to call her own.

THREADS OF CHANGE

Jamaal Haata, a traditional weaver's village in Siwan district where weaving had completely stopped. As there was no market for handwoven cloth. When Sanjiv heard this, he decided that Jamaal Haata would supply the material needed for uniforms at all 4 of his DPS schools.

Not only that, he decided to train women from other villages to start weaving. So, he persuaded Satish Poludas, founder of Kora Design Collective, to join hands with Parivartan. An NID graduate, Satish specialised in working with handloom collectives, mostly in Andhra Pradesh. However, at Parivartan, he faced a unique challenge.

The women of Siwan were not traditional weavers, they would have to be taught from scratch. Most of them had never stepped out of their homes to do any kind of work before. Besides, their hands were already full, looking after their farms, livestock and families. Would they even want a job?

"I encouraged Setika to join the development sector but the final decision was hers."

Despite all these questions, and more, the project did start. Two master weavers were employed to teach women pre-loom and post-loom processes. The first 3 months were spent just getting into rhythm, which is fundamental to successful weaving. Slowly and steadily, the women got the hang of it.

"We work in four hour shifts, so they can fit in weaving, around their household chores," says Satish.

This means when one weaver leaves for the day, the next must take over. Initially, there was resistance - how can I sit at the loom vacated by a woman from a lower caste? But gradually, the unit became so bonded and the work so joyful, it ceased to matter. This is when Setika decided to take the handloom project to the next level.

So far, the sarees woven by these women were not being sold commercially. They were purchased by Sanjiv Kumar, and gifted to the teachers at his four DPS schools, once a year. This large order consumed at least six months of the total weaving capacity. Which was a blessing for sure but Setika aspired for more.

Setika's dream was a brand woven by the women of Bihar, proudly worn across India. The result was Sabrangi – a brand with its own design ethos, quality standards and digital marketing effort. It's not easy for a non-profit to don a for-profit hat, so the brand is making slow but steady progress.

"While I enjoyed all my work at Parivartan, once I started Sabrangi, I found my space, something I enjoy," says Setika.

Today, women are cycling to work, laughing and chatting with each other freely. Even sharing their problems. When they go back home with money, they have a little more decision-making power. Many of them spend a large chunk of their earnings on their children's education.

Agar isey kehte hain parivartan, how can a hundred Parivartans bloom?

TAKING IT FORWARD

One of the unique aspects of Parivartan is that it is completely self-funded. The money that Sanjiv Kumar makes from running four franchises of Delhi Public School is ploughed into his non-profit.

The total capital expenditure is around Rs 15 crore, while annual revenue expenditure stands at Rs 1.5 crore.

To make the operation sustainable, no matter what, Sanjiv has created a corpus of over Rs 40 crore. The money generated as interest thus covers the annual budget of the NGO.

This financial security gives the NGO freedom from being observed by a donor, or monitored by an external agency.

For example, in 2020, Parivartan reduced the number of core villages under its wing from 39 to 21, whereas most NGOs actively pursue scale, in order to attract donors.

Parivartan also works in unorthodox areas, where 'iska kya fayda hua' is difficult to quantify. These include community theatre, art and culture. The Parivartan library provides 4,000+ books in English and Hindi, while 'Kislay' builds language, confidence, and craft skills in children via storytelling and arts, in partnership with local schools.

"This is our way of creating an enabling environment."

Can impact assessment capture the nuances of these activities in a report? Setika admits that when they attempted the exercise, it was not satisfactory. The consultants who were hired could not understand why Parivartan undertook so many diverse initiatives.

Nevertheless, both father and daughter strongly believe in Parivartan and its model of integrated rural development, where multiple verticals work seamlessly together. In fact, they say that this model is open to all. Students, researchers, NGOs, donors and development experts – all are welcome at Parivartan.

See, adapt, khud karke dikhao.
India is in its villages, aap idhar aao.

For more on Parivartan Bihar scan:

ADVICE TO YOUNG PHILANTHROPISTS

Choose something in which you have an interest. In my case, the vision was to develop 'my village, my area', and I moved forward with that in mind.

If you are not sure of your interest, look at the various kinds of development work happening in the country. Find an area that you feel strongly about, or truly care for.

But giving money is not enough, this is a very important point to note. The leadership issue, how to run philanthropy, that is one area where the new generation should fill the gap. There are many projects but for those projects to work effectively and deeply you need to get involved.

Also, I believe that people should do concentrated work. The country should be divided into units in terms of focus on development.

We also need to look at the environment because without clean air and water, there is no future for us all.

"I realised early on that we must work ground-up."

It Takes A Village

SWATHI KANTAMANI

Natco Trust

She took the reins of the family philanthropic trust and gave it new life and direction, working with the poorest of the poor in Telangana.

Swathi Kantamani was born and brought up in Vizag, in a family which prized academics. Her grandfather was the vice-chancellor of Andhra University while her father studied at Rishi Valley School and wanted his children to study there as well. That's where Swathi actually grew up from age 8 to 18.

"Both at home, and at school, I learnt that money is fine but intellect is what matters."

At Rishi Valley, the focus was on finding your passion, and cultivating compassion. Every week students were sent to do plantation work in nearby villages. This was Swathi's first glimpse of a world beyond her little bubble.

Returning to Vizag for her undergrad was a culture shock. Feeling intellectually stifled, Swathi shifted to the University of Hyderabad for her master's. Then, she met Rajeev at a family friend's home. It was an arranged marriage but they 'lucked out', with Swathi coming into her own.

Right after the wedding, Swathi's father-in-law, V. C. Nannapaneni, Chairman and MD, Natco Pharma, invited her to work with Natco Trust. But, at age 24, she had other dreams. Besides, Swathi didn't want to parachute into a role because she had married into the promoter's family.

In the quest to establish her own identity, Swathi applied to Oxford for a master's in English Literature and was accepted. After returning to India, she joined a publishing company and also began taking an interest in the activities of Natco Trust.

At first, out of curiosity, and then, because there was so much to learn. Working at the grassroots in the poorest of communities suddenly seemed much more meaningful than editing books.

In 2007, when her father-in-law once again invited her to join Natco Trust, Swathi said 'yes'. Bringing new life and new energy into its functioning.

From upgrading Natco High School in Kothur, to initiating the mobile health clinic and Bal Vikas Kendra, Swathi's operating principle was simple: 'do not assume you know what people need, ask them'.

Working in the remote tandas (tribal hamlets) of Nagarjuna Sagar has not been easy. But it has brought development to the doorstep of those who need it the most.

Child marriage was once common in these parts, it is now rare. Families aspire to send their girls for higher education. This kind of transformation is possible only when there is a long-term commitment.

"The family tops up the annual budget whenever needed, ensuring that ongoing programs never suffer."

The world is a village, the village is a world
In that sacred space, may goodness unfurl.

On a foggy Saturday morning, Swathi Kantamani's alarm rang loudly. It was five am. Half an hour later, Swathi was hurtling down the highway to Nagarjuna Sagar, the location of Natco Pharma's earliest plant.

After a quick stop at the plant for idlis and coffee, the vehicle headed to a remote village, off the highway. With every kilometre, the road got worse; Swathi could feel her bones rattle with each bump.

The vehicle stopped near a raggedy cluster of huts. Swathi alighted, and so did the other lady in the vehicle - the project manager at Natco Trust. One of the programs they had embarked on was donating an R.O. plant to villages which lacked safe drinking water.

To run an R.O. plant, you need groundwater; to bring water up, you need a pump. Here, the pump itself was out of order. So the project had to be completely re-evaluated. Going to the field and seeing the conditions that Natco Trust was working in was a complete eye-opener.

On the ride back to Hyderabad, Swathi was in a reflective mood. When she took up English literature, the standard question was – what use is this? More so, African-American women's writing, the subject of her master's thesis. But a common thread runs through this literature - deprivation, poverty, lack of access.

"Subconsciously, I was attracted to a theme... similar to the work the Trust was doing."

So, it became a routine, when the project manager went on a field visit on a Saturday, Swathi joined her. Mostly as an observer, just listening and absorbing. The tribal hamlets they visited were extremely poor and yet, the people were intelligent and living with as much dignity as possible.

This one time, Natco Trust went to a village with the idea of building a school or vocational training centre. A meeting had been arranged at the panchayat office at nine in the morning. No one turned up. Why would they lose such a precious opportunity, Swathi wondered.

"Visiting the field really energises me. It gives me the insight I need for a project."

Gradually, a few home truths became clear. You cannot say that 'I will do something' and 'they will benefit'. The village knows what the village needs, listen to them. Being an extremely backward area, the residents of Nagarjuna Sagar tanda were in need of basic facilities such as health and nutrition.

"I realised that we really need to partner with the community and get a buy-in."

These weekend visits got Swathi thinking about her own goals and priorities. Working at a publishing house was interesting but she wasn't breaking any new ground. It had once been her dream but now she could not help thinking – 'what I do here, does it really mean something'?

At the same time, Swathi had questions about Natco Trust. The intention was noble but was it really achieving anything? The work was mostly ad-hoc, there was no long-term vision. When there was a request, the Trust would go and do what was necessary but there was no follow-up whatsoever.

Even as these thoughts were swirling in Swathi's mind, her father-in-law once again asked, "Will you take over Natco Trust?" This time, she said 'yes'.

There was so much that could be done, and here was an opportunity to do it!

A NEW VISION

Natco Trust came into existence in 1995, soon after the company was formed. But when Swathi took over in 2007, there were no records of the work that had been done.

Apart from ad-hoc giving, the only on-going project was a high school established in Rangapur, which was the Chairman's native village near Kothur.

"One of the phrases he'd always use is 'our people', that is our guiding principle."

The school was as old as the trust itself, and it was open not just to workers of the Natco plant in Kothur, but any child from the village. In fact, the fees were highly subsidized for all. However, setting up a school and running it well are two different things. In 2007, Natco High School had a number of issues.

When Swathi walked in for the first time, the stench of urine assaulted her nostrils, from the main gate of the school. That was how poorly toilets were being maintained.

"I decided that was the first thing that needed to be fixed!"

The building was dilapidated, the science lab not in use and children were not allowed to touch the books in the library. There was hardly any difference between Natco High School and a sarkaari paathshala, and this state of affairs was not acceptable. So, the initial focus was on improving infrastructure, making the school look and feel better.

Children began taking pride – "Oh, this is our school! Such a nice building is made for us?"

But that was just the start. The deeper issue was mindset. Since most of the children came from impoverished homes, there was an attitude among the teachers ki inka to kuch nahin ho sakta hai. So why put in effort?

For the first few months, Swathi went to school every day, talked to the teachers. To share a new vision for the school and its learning outcomes. Yes, these are first generation learners but it doesn't mean they cannot learn. As teachers, you must believe in them, nurture them, treat them with respect.

Initially, there was resistance, and some teachers were even asked to leave.

"Who are you? We will complain to your father-in-law!" one of them threatened.

But the family was firmly behind Swathi, so by and by, everyone fell in line. Teachers began to sit down and prepare their lessons. An educational startup – XSEED – was brought in to equip teachers with tools to make their teaching more interactive and fun. Consequently, students took more interest, and began performing better.

However, teachers still faced many behavioural issues, especially with teenage boys. Use of foul language and physical fights were common among class 9 and 10 students. While teachers underwent training, counselling sessions were introduced for students and their parents.

"Swathi ma'am personally conducted the training sessions," recalls V Suryanarayana, who has been with Natco Trust since 2009.

It took three years and a lot of hands-on involvement to execute a complete turnaround. Natco High School found an excellent principal, and things stabilised. The Chairman was pleased with the school's new avatar, and all the goodwill it was bringing. Hence, in 2011, a second school was set up in Gollamudipadu village near Guntur.

However, the need for education is tremendous and one entity cannot keep setting up schools. Hence, as an experiment, Natco Trust adopted a government school situated near its head office in Banjara Hills. The school had dilapidated infrastructure and catered to 150-200 children from the nearby slums.

Repeated trips to the collector's office finally resulted in an MOU. Natco Trust partnered with the government to improve the infrastructure of the school, starting with the building. Further, the trust paid for the salaries of Vidya volunteers, whose role was to help teachers do their jobs better.

"We also do after-school tuitions and provide the staff who keep the school clean and safe."

Today, Government School, Borabanda runs two shifts a day, with 3000 children enrolled in English, Telugu and Urdu medium. The number of kids who complete grade 10 and go for further studies has shot up dramatically.

It is a public-private partnership (PPP) that has reaped good dividends.

IN THE BACK OF BEYOND

Natco's Nagarjuna Sagar plant is located in picturesque surroundings, which can be mistaken for a picnic spot. However, just a few kilometres from the plant are the tandas (tribal hamlets), where people lived a bare minimum existence.

Bringing development to their doorstep was the ambitious goal of Natco Trust.

"If we can't do it, then no one else can," was Swathi's belief.

After extensive consultation with the villagers, the trust embarked upon a project to improve the groundwater situation. Because the land is arid, it was scarce. What's more, there were high levels of fluoride and sediment. Once the drinking water situation improved, the next concern was nutrition for pregnant and lactating women.

On one of her regular field visits, Swathi was approached by a group of women.

"Amma, we never went to school, we want to learn little bit something," they said.

So the trust began basic literacy classes in the evenings, teaching adult women how to read and sign their names.

"I am so happy, amma," said one student. "I can read now, so I know which bus to take."

"The heart brings you in and then you need to use your head more."

In Thangilla tanda, there was a request for an aanganwadi, which led to Natco Trust establishing a Bal Vikas Kendra. The land was donated by the villagers; they also helped in digging the foundation, in the spirit of 'shramdaan'. The building was designed by an architect from Hyderabad, with as much care as an important urban project.

Another pressing problem in the tandas was the lack of health facilities. Being remote and poorly connected, doctors were unwilling to serve the area. So, instead of setting up clinics, Natco Trust decided to provide a mobile health van. This van, manned by a young post-graduate doctor, would be assigned to a cluster of villages.

The van would have fixed days in the month to visit each village. This facility greatly improved access to healthcare, especially for senior citizens. Over 30% of the villagers were diagnosed with common illnesses such as hypertension and diabetes. Now, they also had access to medicine.

This became one of the first on-going projects, with measurable impact, as opposed to the as-and-when-needed approach.

There were many problems to tackle but the budget was limited.

"So, we decided to focus 95% of our effort on health and education."

Initially, the trust started after-school tuitions, to strengthen fundamentals. But the question was, after kids complete class 5, then what? There was no secondary school for miles. Logically, you would say, oh we should construct a school. But would that solve the problem of dropout?

In a tribal family, a child was better off at work, contributing to the family income. Apart from that, child marriage was common. At the age of 10 or 11, girls would reach puberty and be married off.

Keeping in mind these social dynamics, the trust came up with a brilliant, out-of-the-box solution.

The Telangana government runs fully residential Gurukul schools - along the lines of Navodaya Vidyalaya - for underprivileged children. Admission is through an entrance exam held in Class 4. Every Gurukul student gets free education till Class 12.

What a wonderful opportunity for children in the tandas - 'let's prepare them for this'!

In 2013, the trust set up a coaching centre in Jaltanda to tutor Class 3 and 4 students, with one volunteer, and government school teachers willing to work after-hours. In the very first year, one child named Sundar* got a Gurukul seat. His parents reluctantly sent him to this unknown place...

When Sundar came back to the village after two months, he had a completely different aura. The boy held his head high and talked about things no one had heard of. Sundar became the talk of the tanda.

Now, villagers were receptive when the Natco volunteer approached them. 'If Sundar could do it, my child can do it too,' was the hope in every parent's heart.

The trust arranged for the villagers to visit a Gurukul school and see the facilities. Enrolment in the coaching centre increased manifold; every tanda now wanted its own centre. Girls started coming for tuitions too - what a shift in mindset!

That year, five students got admission and there has been no looking back since.

However, the work of the trust did not end with admission. They continued to monitor the students' performance at the Gurukul school, and provide counselling and hand-holding. This ensured that there were no dropouts due to academic or adjustment issues. Meanwhile, after being exposed to the outside world, the kids brought winds of change to their villages.

SHG leader Mangamma came to Swathi with a complaint during one of her field visits.

"Akka, our children don't want to come home for vacation."

The reason was simple - they were now used to proper toilets. 'We are not willing to use the open fields now', the kids said. So, with 50% contribution from the trust and 50% from the tribals, 85 individual toilets were constructed.

The Gurukul scheme had a ripple effect, not only improving prospects for the children, but the village as a whole.

HEALTH IS WEALTH

Laxmi* visited the mobile health clinic complaining of stomach pain and weight loss. Her condition did not improve with medication. Suspecting a more serious condition, the doctor advised Laxmi's husband to take her to the city and get a battery of tests done.

These are the kind of cases which pour in to government hospitals in Hyderabad. Many patients - poor and illiterate - have no idea how to navigate the system. This is where Natco Trust's counsellors step in. Where to go, what to do – they scan medical papers and gently guide over 1000 patients a day.

"The patients come in tension, we talk to them and help with all the paperwork," says Sudha, a counsellor since 2006.

This sounds like a 'small thing' but it makes a big difference to patients. Apart from being the first point of contact, the counsellors also make sure that patients understand the doctor's prescription and return for follow-up visits. The program covers 6 government hospitals across Hyderabad, with a total of 12 counsellors who are on the trust payroll.

But the connection with health goes deeper. In 2003, Natco launched the first product in its cancer portfolio, a generic version of a drug for a condition called 'chronic myeloid leukaemia'. At the time, the MNC formulation was available for Rs 1,20,000. Today, the same drug costs just Rs 3000.

Affordable cancer care became a cornerstone of Natco's corporate philosophy, and an interest area for its philanthropy. It started with building a cancer block for MNJ Cancer Hospital in Hyderabad, and at KEM Hospital in Mumbai. Then, in 2018, Natco trust decided to do 'something bigger'.

The trust built a state-of-the-art cancer centre in the Government General Hospital in Guntur, at a cost of Rs 30 crore. While Natco created the infrastructure and provided cancer drugs, the government continued to run the hospital. It is now the go-to place for patients from Telangana in search of affordable, high quality cancer care.

Is this all part of the mandatory CSR that Natco must do, as a listed entity? Yes and no. A large project like the cancer care centre far exceeded the annual CSR budget.

"What we do is a combination of Natco as a company, and private philanthropy."

CSR allocation may fluctuate but the commitment to serve cannot. This approach ensures the continuity of ongoing programs, the ability to go beyond, and take up more projects.

In 2018, Swathi met with government teachers and aanganwadi workers, who had one and only one heartfelt request.

"Akka, so many problems we have. No proper toilets, poor buildings... Can you help us?"

Although budgets were stretched, Swathi could not refuse.

That year, Natco Trust took up the task of fixing infrastructure issues in government school buildings. Many anganwadis were operating from temporary structures. So, wherever villagers were willing to donate land, the trust constructed a building, using eco-friendly bricks moulded from red soil prevalent in the area.

IN CONCLUSION

Today, if you walk into the Natco Zilla Parishad High School in Kothur, you will see children in brightly coloured uniforms, walking with a spring in their step.

"I like coming to school every day," says 12 year old Ravi*, a student of class 6.

The spacious, airy building with clean toilets no longer looks like a neglected government school. The kids – mostly the offspring of migrant workers – now have a sense of pride and belonging.

In fact, both enrolment and attendance have increased manifold. The impact of Natco Trust is clearly visible.

With its growing footprint, Natco Trust's budget has increased exponentially.

When Swathi joined the trust in 2008, the annual budget was Rs 3 crore. In 2024, that figure was Rs 30 crore, of which 50% came from CSR and the rest from the promoter family's private wealth. This has resulted in enormous goodwill and support from the community.

Swathi and Rajeev's kids are still in school and will choose their own paths. There is no pressure to join the family business, or the family trust.

Meanwhile, Swathi and her team are experimenting with new programs. The goal is to drive sustainable, root-cause solutions within the public system.

For example, government schools undertake remedial measures in higher classes. But this often fails, because the kids lack a strong foundation. So why not nip the problem at the bud? Swathi's vision is to transform aanganwadis into 'Early Learning Centres' (ECE). To execute this ambitious plan, it was important to have knowledge partners.

In 2023, Rishi Valley School's child-friendly curriculum and pedagogy was introduced in the 34 aanganwadis supported by Natco Trust. A trained preschool educator was assigned to assist teachers in each centre. Central Square Foundation (CSF), Centre for Effective Governance of States (CEGIS) and Rocket Learning are also partners in the ECE effort.

"We have moved from charity to philanthropy to 'development' in its true essence," says Swathi.

Because 'kuch kiya' is not enough.
Kuch aisa kiya which truly makes a difference.

For more on Natco Trust scan:

ADVICE TO YOUNG PHILANTHROPISTS

I would say, take some time to understand the landscape, just as in any other profession, any other passion.

This requires you to know, to be passionate about and to be able to sustain in it. So do a good amount of legwork, visit the places that you would like to work in and get an understanding of what is going on.

The second thing is, find expertise that you may not have. Be mindful of it and be honest about the fact that you don't know it all.

I think most importantly and a huge learning for me has been data. So make sure your data practices are in place. You have to have a baseline - know where you started, what your intervention has done and why it has been of importance so that anyone else coming in after you doesn't have to start at zero.

I don't think you can pre-decide how long you run a program, it's not a budgetary or a fund allocation decision. I think when the issue no longer exists, or the government program has fully plugged the loophole you were trying to fill, that's when you can think of exiting.

"You don't need to have a foundation to start doing philanthropy."

All In A Day's Play

DR. SUNITA MAHESHWARI

Telerad Foundation

In 2007, this doctor set up a playground in a government school in Bangalore. What started as a small act of generosity has now become a movement.

B. L. Maheshwari grew up in the tiny village of Gugrah, near Ajmer. Through sheer brilliance and hard work, he reached America on a Fulbright scholarship in the 1960s. At UPenn, he fell in love with a fellow student - an American of Syrian descent. When he proposed to Sandra, there was one caveat.

"I want to return to India," he said. "Will you come with me?"

It was a big ask but Sandra agreed. The couple moved back to Hyderabad with their one-year-old infant, Sunita. It wasn't easy for a free-spirited hippie to adjust to India, especially her sasural, where women still wore the ghunghat. But, as they say, love conquers all and they made it work.

Sunita grew up in this eclectic household, where knowledge was prized but money was scarce. Her father turned down offers from the Tatas and Birlas, instead choosing to work at the Administrative Staff College of India. Young Sunita attended the local school, acutely aware that she was more privileged than her classmates.

She began volunteering at Mother Teresa's home, and at an orphanage down the street. When she was 13, Sunita had an epiphany – 'I want to become a doctor and work in a village'.

That became a burning desire, and a lifelong goal. After her MBBS from Osmania University, Sunita started her PG in OB-GYN at AIIMS in New Delhi.

Realising that her real interest lay in treating children, she decided to pursue a second PG in paediatrics, this time in America. As a US passport holder it was relatively easy: she took the USMLE, found a paediatric residency and eventually made her way to Yale Medical School, where she met and married her husband, Arjun Kalyanpur.

However, the promise she had made to herself – to work in India – was not forgotten. Sunita and Arjun packed their bags and returned in 1999. Today, the couple jointly run Teleradiology Solutions, a pioneering teleradiology company providing services to hospitals, globally.

Given Sunita's idealistic bent of mind, she constantly asked herself - how do we give back? There was no grand plan to set up a foundation, give grants and so on. It all happened organically, and simply grew. Starting with just one playground – using money raised in a carnival - Sunita has gone on to set up 700 playgrounds. Bringing joy to thousands of children in government schools.

Meanwhile, even as a business entity, Telerad has adopted a model where 10% of its time and resources are allocated, free of cost, to rural hospitals in remote locations.

"I did not work in a village," says Sunita. "But in my own way, I have made a difference!"

Cardiologists open hearts;
philanthropists open their hearts.

Sunita Maheshwari does both. That's rare. That's special.

Sunita Maheshwari was being roasted by her medical school classmates, and she had it coming. All through her MBBS, even at the dissection table, she would talk passionately about her dream – working in a village.

So, now you're in the big village of New York, they teased her: 'Greenwich Village!'

"I'm an eternal optimist," she said. "Now that I'm here, let me make the most of it."

Working in the boondocks of America – Chattanooga, Tennessee – was not enough. Sunita worked hard, and aspired for the Ivy League. When she shared this dream with a faculty member at Chattanooga, he said, 'You are good, you deserve to go'.

He gave Sunita a fantastic reference letter, which helped her to get into Yale.

It was her first big learning in America – as you grow, support the growth of other people. The second was learning how to communicate. As a child, Sunita was so shy that when there were visitors, she would hide inside her mother's pallu. America forced her to 'come out of her skin', go beyond her comfort zone.

In class, when she mumbled answers, her professor Dr. Norm Siegel would say – Maheshwari, speak up! So that's how she learned to come out of her shell. Empathy had always been her strong point. But learning to talk to patients, making them comfortable, explaining – 'this is what I am going to do' – was a newly acquired skill which soon became a part of her.

Yale Medical School had an excellent paediatric cardiology program. Sunita recalled, from her AIIMS days, that even the most prestigious hospitals in India were lacking in paediatric cardiology. That's when she decided to become a heart specialist for children. What's more, she got into the Harvard program, at Boston Children's Hospital.

However, Arjun was at Yale, and living apart at the start of their marriage didn't feel right. One night, while on duty in the ICU, Sunita mentioned her dilemma to Dr. George Lister, head of the paediatric cardiac ICU at Yale. That was on Friday night.

On Monday morning, she got a call from Dr. Charlie Kleinman, the head of paediatric cardiology at Yale.

"George called me - he says you're very good. We've opened a position for you."

Sunita was astounded. Recognising merit and opening doors for people in their professional journeys was what America was all about. And this, she would carry back with her, to India.

For, despite all the glamour, and the big bucks they could earn in the US, Sunita had been clear that one day, she would return.

Like her father, she had asked her would-be spouse, "Are you willing to return to India?"

Luckily, he'd said 'yes'. And before joining Yale, Sunita told Dr. Kleinman, as well. Once she was done with the program, she would be moving back.

He said, "That's fine, we train for the world."

The young medical graduate knew that in India, many facilities routinely enjoyed in America, would be luxuries.

In the US, doctors were super-specialised; in India, she would need to be a jack of all trades. So, Sunita decided to stay on for a year and get hands-on experience, from device closures to balloon valvuloplasties.

Meanwhile, Arjun appeared for his radiology board certification. A half-a-million dollar salary waited on the other side of it. Could they, would they, should they? For now, the decision was on hold...

THE ROUGH ROAD

The year Sunita spent as an interventionist was eye-opening. At Yale Hospital, the young doctor observed that expensive medical equipment was being discarded after just one use. That was the standard practice in America. But in India, a catheter was sterilised and reused at least four to five times. So, Sunita went to Dr. Kleinman and made an unusual request.

"Would you mind if I took all the stuff you're throwing out? I will collect and take it back."

Word got around. Soon, there was a small network of hospitals sending her once-used cardiac catheters. By the end of the year, Dr. Maheshwari had amassed Rs 10 crore worth of life-saving medical equipment. Yale offered both Sunita and Arjun faculty positions. It was indeed tempting to stay back but returning was a promise Sunita had to keep, to herself.

In July 1999, the young couple backed up their boriya-bistar and boarded a plane to India, with their three-year-old daughter Alisha. Arjun's parents were in Mysore, Sunita's in Hyderabad, so they chose to live in Bangalore. A city which was booming, bustling, and bursting with opportunity. Or, so people said.

Six months later, the couple sat in their modest apartment in Richmond Town and wondered – did we make a mistake? Despite best efforts, neither Sunita nor Arjun had landed a job.

Hospitals turned Arjun away, saying he was 'overqualified'. Paediatric cardiology? They didn't have a department for that.

Arjun was ready to throw in the towel but Sunita was adamant. One morning, she cold-called Dr. Devi Shetty, who was then at Manipal Hospital.

"Dr Shetty," she said. "I'm a US-trained paediatric cardiologist. I want to work with you."

"When can you start?" was Dr. Shetty's reply.

Having a job was great. But functioning on the job? Not easy. There was hierarchy, ego tussles. Sunita would often come home in tears and vent. To which Arjun would reply, well, we can always go back. And Sunita would shake her head and say, no, I'm going to make this work.

"As a doctor, I was always giving back but I felt, okay, what can I do outside of medicine?"

Things were even tougher for Arjun. For three years, he was mostly at home with Alisha. A man 'sitting at home' was a big deal in India. But Arjun's sense of humour got him through it.

When people asked, he would simply say, "What to do, no one wants me here. So, I'm a full-time babysitter."

Technically, he still held a faculty position at Yale. Just in case 'that crazy wife of yours' changes her mind, they'd said. So, he had the option of taking 'locums' - teaching at Yale for a month, then being in India for three months. This unusual arrangement would, in fact, open up a new phase in their lives.

Meanwhile, one fine morning, the container with medical equipment landed in India. It was opened at the customs office in Whitefield and Sunita was informed that 'goods cannot be released'.

"Yeh to aap bech rahe hain, duty padegi," said the customs department.

The good doctor was up against a wall, so, finally, she met the senior-most officer.

"Sir," she said. "I will be using this equipment to conduct free procedures for children."

The officer was not convinced.

"Well," she said. "If you allow, I will take the consignment and use it. If you want to keep it, you keep it."

He stared at her for a long time, and finally said, "Release maadi."

So finally, those painstakingly collected catheters would be put to use...

PAYING IT FORWARD

When Dr. Devi Shetty set up Narayana Hrudalaya, he asked Sunita to join him. She agreed, on the condition that she would run the paediatric cardiology department independently, and have the freedom to build her own team.

Dr. Shetty agreed, and finally, all the things Dr. Maheshwari had learnt at Yale were put into practice.

Those were heady days, full of passion and the desire to serve. When a poor patient walked in, Dr. Maheshwari had the ability to say – 'free ballooning' – without a second thought. Because she had so much free equipment at hand. The patient was happy, Dr. Shetty was happy, a win-win for all.

Meanwhile, it was becoming clear that one Sunita was not enough. She could see 25 patients a day, and there were just 10 other paediatric cardiologists like her, in all of India.

If only I can train the next generation, imagine the number of kids with heart disease who can get treated.

Following this train of thought, Sunita instituted a two-year fellowship program at Narayana Hrudalaya which would upskill a young cardiologist into a paediatric cardiologist. She taught the program exactly the way she had learnt it at Yale, from first principles. Her first fellow was Dr. Amit Misri, from Delhi.

18 months into the fellowship, there was a case with a hole in the heart. Sunita was to operate it, Amit to observe. But as she went to scrub in, a confident, young voice called out.

"Ma'am," said the understudy to his senior. "I got this."

Dr. Amit Misri did the case on his own, from start to finish. In the end, he took off his gloves and touched his mentor's feet.

Sunita had tears in her eyes. She had created another human being who could go out and treat the children of India. It was paying forward all that she had received, from her mentors and well-wishers in America.

The program would grow and prosper, creating an entire cadre of paediatric cardiologists who now run world-class departments in hospitals across the country. With demand from PGs all over India, Sunita started an e-teaching program. This was in 2010, much before Covid. The same lectures were now available to any student, anywhere.

As a doctor Sunita saved lives. But hey - wasn't that her job? There are so many other ways of 'giving back', she would think. And those ways would soon become clearer.

OPPORTUNITY KNOCKS

It was a casual remark that set off an entire chain of events that changed the trajectory of their lives. When her son Adil was born, Sunita decided to accompany Arjun to the US, while she was on maternity leave. The Chairman of Yale, Jim Brink, generously offered the use of his six-bedroom mansion to the young family, as he was going to be away for six weeks.

As he was giving the keys, Jim remarked, "You know, Arjun, I can't get anyone to do the night shift here at Yale."

Arjun and Sunita exchanged a look – the solution was obvious.

"Jim, he's not doing anything in India," Sunita said. "He can do your night shift."

Today teleradiology is widely practiced; in the early 2000s it was a revolutionary idea. When he returned to India, Arjun set up a computer, figured out how to get the images, report and send them back. Drawing on this experience, Arjun and Jim Brink published the first in-depth article on the feasibility of international teleradiology.

Their study showed that a doctor reporting scans from India was 15% more accurate than the doctor on night shift in America. The American was tired, the Indian was fully alert. After the article was published in 2002, Yale gave Arjun the position. It was an excellent arrangement, but six months later there was a hue and cry about outsourcing jobs to India.

Luckily, at the same time, Arjun got an offer from Sathya Sai Baba Hospital, to set up their radiology unit.

They shifted to Whitefield, a far-flung and little-developed area of the city back then. But being close to his place of work, Arjun could drop in and be with the kids during the day. That allowed Sunita to put her heart and soul into her work.

Things were going well, they had moved back to practice medicine in India, and that goal had been achieved. And yet... Something was brewing in Sunita's mind.

"Too bad the Yale project ended," she said. "Can't we do this work for other hospitals?"

The idea had merit but how would they find customers? Arjun's nephew, Vikarna, was an engineering student in Mysore at the time. Can you build a website for us, they asked him.

'Teleradiology for the World', proclaimed the homepage, built for a thousand rupees. To their surprise, they soon got a client – the Albert Einstein Hospital in Philadelphia.

That's how Telerad began in 2003, in the guest room of their house. At first, Arjun hired a couple of transcriptionists. Then, Dr. Anjali Agrawal from Baylor got in touch. She wanted to move back to India and work with Telerad. At that point there wasn't enough work for two US-trained radiologists. Nevertheless, they hired her.

Anjali and her husband Anurag stayed with Sunita and Arjun for an entire month. She then started working from Delhi. A third doctor, Sanjay Kamath from UMass, reached out. He wanted to return to India, as his parents were getting old. There wasn't enough work, at that point. But once again, Arjun embraced the risk.

Software was an issue; it wasn't available off the shelf. So, engineers were hired and, guided by doctors, a jugaadu solution was found. As the work increased, an accountant came on board, along with support staff. So they rented the apartment next door, and then a second apartment in the same building.

One day their neighbour said, this is a residential building - it's time for you guys to move to an office!

That's when they bought a piece of land in Whitefield, with whatever little money they had. This was in 2006, luckily it was still cheap. Initially, the plan was to build a single floor.

But then, a client said to them – think big!

Adding on floors later is difficult, said the contractor. So, even though Telerad had just 20 employees at the time, they went ahead and built five floors. There was a global shortage of radiologists, the business was bound to grow. So, they placed a bet on the future, and it paid off handsomely.

MONEY MATTERS

While Arjun was at Telerad, hands-on, growing the company, Sunita was working full-time, running Narayana's paediatric cardiology department. Working as a doctor gave her immense satisfaction. It was seva. A businessman, on the other hand, was only interested in making money. It was greed. She struggled with this polarity in her mind.

"What drives you?" she would ask her entrepreneur friends.

"You won't understand," they would reply.

Arjun was more pragmatic. He would give the example of Nandan Nilekani, a fellow Konkani. See, he built Infosys, created jobs for thousands of people. And slowly, Sunita's mindset changed. As the company grew, it employed more and more people, radiologists, as well as support staff. And that, too, gave a sense of santushti.

As the work with American hospitals grew, the question remained, what are we doing for India? So, very early on, Sunita and Arjun decided to set up the Telerad Foundation, whose mission was to use the company's domain knowledge, staff and infrastructure, to provide diagnosis in remote parts of India.

"One of the things that keeps us young and that keeps us happy is gratitude."

They went to Ramakrishna Mission hospitals with a simple proposition. If you don't charge the patient, we won't charge you. Similarly, if it was a charitable hospital charging lower fees, Telerad would charge lower fees. The company was making good money from its international clients, so it could afford to subsidise hospitals catering to the poor.

"It's a little bit of Robin Hood model," said Arjun.

So, all this was happening but somewhere Sunita had this urge, to do more. She became part of a group formed by a Canadian lady who was very passionate about giving back. Once a month, the group would meet at her home and have intense discussions. Then, they would have a nice meal and go back home.

So, as a group, they didn't actually do anything but the discussions helped crystallise 'what I want to do'. One member, Sumir, who was a businessman went on to set up creches in his factories, which employed 10,000 workers. The Canadian lady, Maureen Berlin tried to set up a health centre at St John's. And Sunita went on to set up playgrounds.

It happened like this. There was a carnival in the community they lived in, which raised 15,000 rupees. Nobody knew what to do with the money. So, Sunita said - the school across the road doesn't have a playground. Why don't we give one to them? 'Great idea', said the community. Little did Sunita know what she was getting into!

A set of slides, swings and monkey bars were installed; they were yet to be painted. Kids were already jumping up and down on them. Their gleeful smiles made Sunita realise, something her kids took for granted was a 'luxury' for these kids. Every government school had lots of land, but no play equipment.

That day in 2007, she decided, let me be the one who puts up playgrounds. The modus operandi was simple – after the Thubarhalli government school, she located the next school down the road. Met the principal, who was more than happy. And then, found a vendor who could supply, and install, the equipment.

"There was no foundation, it was just me and my driver, Raghu!"

And before she knew it, they had put up a hundred playgrounds. That's when Sunita realised she needed a structure. A trust fund was set up, so that Telerad could become a donor. Friends came forward, as well. So, now, they could put up 75 playgrounds a year. There was no need to visit schools anymore, principals were calling them.

"Madam, my children didn't get playground, why you don't like my school?"

And just like that, a small act of generosity acquired its own momentum. And became a movement.

TRIAL AND ERROR

Rome wasn't built in a day, nor were 660 playgrounds. It took 17 years to reach this number, and there were many learnings along the way. Initially a playground was put in the middle of the field, where it was unbearably hot. Now, installation is done in a shaded area, wherever possible.

"It's small things, which you never think of, which make a big difference," says Sunita.

As an independent director on the boards of GlaxoSmithKline, and HDFC Bank, Sunita saw how CSR money was deployed, with various checks and balances. More thought and structure was needed, she realised. The issue of child safety had to be taken into consideration, when setting up a playground. A checklist would ensure that all necessary norms were followed.

In February 2025, a partial sale to private equity led to a substantial inflow of money for the founders. Now, Sunita has hired a chief impact officer and support staff. The goal is to set up 700 playgrounds every year, at a cost of Rs 70,000 per playground. There is already a long waiting list, with calls coming in from Tumkur, Shimoga, and as far as Uttar Pradesh.

Sunita wants to take the idea further, incorporating some facilities for older kids. For example, a basketball court, to keep them active. There is also a plan to introduce rainwater harvesting in the existing schools. The water thus collected can be used to plant trees and improve the environment, as well as make children eco-conscious.

Since 2010, Sunita has been working full-time with the Telerad group. The group has over 1000 staff members and serves emergency rooms of 150 US hospitals during their night shift. Telerad also works with the Ministry of Health of Singapore and the Ministry of Health of Qatar. While 90% of the company's bandwidth is allocated to paying clients, 10% is for charitable hospitals in India.

Alongside Telerad, Sunita and Arjun had started another venture called RxDx, which runs multi-specialty healthcare centres across Bangalore. When an RxDx doctor has an empty slot, that time is used to provide telemedicine in rural centres. Telerad works with 50 centres in Karnataka and Maharashtra, in partnership with the local government and CSR efforts.

"So, in a convoluted way, without actually going there, I am able to impact rural India!"

AI has also made a huge impact in the world of diagnostics.

Telerad's in-house engineering team has been developing AI algorithms which the company is keen to share with the medical fraternity. Currently, Telerad has tied up with NIMHANS to deploy its AI algorithm for stroke, free of charge, to the hospital and patients.

"If this works well, we will take it to government hospitals across the country," says Arjun.

Once again, in an indirect way, impacting the grassroots.

THE POWER OF GRATITUDE

Success and accolades made Sunita and Arjun acutely aware of the debt they owed to their alma mater – Yale Medical School. The university had welcomed two foreigners with funny Indian accents, taught them, even created positions for them.

So, when Yale reached out to Sunita and asked for help with mentoring students, it was an instant yes.

"It started with giving my time, then we instituted a corpus to give grants."

Students were coming up with innovative ideas in the area of public health. With this grant the idea could be fleshed out, and made a reality. The selection for the grant is held twice a year, with Sunita and Arjun as part of the jury.

This connection with Yale is a wonderful continuing source of energy and yet another way of giving back.

> *"Start small, plant those seeds. When you have more, you can accelerate."*

Growing up with parents with such a strong bent towards serving society has impacted the couple's two kids. One value that Sunita inculcated in her children from a young age was – be nice. Talk to maids with respect, smile at the drivers. If a kid at school is getting bullied, stand with that person, not the bullies.

When Alisha joined medical school, Sunita encouraged her daughter to help out her classmates, even share her notes. Inspired by the idea that 'giving back' is not just about money, Alisha painted all the walls in the children's ward at JIPMER with vibrant colours, bringing a smile to many a sick child.

After completing her MBBS, Alisha took the unusual step of working in a tribal hospital in Gudalur. What's more, she helped set up Rural Hospital Network (ruralhospitalnetwork.org), a portal which helps these hospitals attract specialised doctors and nurses. Currently, Alisha is pursuing her PG in Surgery but continues to be involved with RHN.

Sunita's son Adil Kalyanpur was an ace tennis player and former junior India number one, until he was hit by a spate of injuries. During Covid, he composed a rap song titled 'Captivity of Negativity', about feeling depressed. It touched a chord with listeners and thus began Adil's journey into 'impact rap'.

Since then, he's rapped about masking up, breakups, anxiety, terrorism, and even Pahalgam.

As Sunita and Arjun expand their philanthropic footprint, they remain deeply inspired by the work of the Nilekanis. As a fellow 'amchi' (Konkani), Nandan was always supportive of Arjun's entrepreneurial efforts. It was a joy to observe the thought and energy that Rohini put into each philanthropic project.

"It made me realise that 'giving well' takes passion, as well as commitment."

And in this journey of life, one must never forget the people who stood by you, through thick and thin.

When the private equity deal happened, Sunita and Arjun decided to distribute Rs 10 crore among all their employees, including housekeeping staff. Recently, a member of the staff, Sarasamma, shyly came up to Sunita and said 'thank you'.

"For what?" asked Sunita in Kannada.

"The two lakh rupees I got from you, madam," Sarasamma replied. "I paid off my loans."

There are so many ways to open your heart; to share and to care, to do your part.

So pay it forward with love and with grace,
and bring a smile to someone's face.

For more on Telerad Foundation scan:

ADVICE TO YOUNG PHILANTHROPISTS

Philanthropy is a very fulfilling journey to embark on. Figuring out what you are passionate about is important because when you bring passion to a project, it keeps going.

Also think - do I want to do it myself? Or am I happy collaborating with an NGO partner?

If you have a thousand rupees, you don't have to spend it all. Spend one rupee. See how you feel about it; then spend two. The journey will evolve, the path gets clearer as you do it.

And even if you don't have big money today, start small. Plant those seeds. When you have more, you can accelerate.

Gyaan

Philanthropy as problem-solving,
with a burning desire to achieve scale.
Driven strongly by the mind.

"I am driven
to maximize the
impact of every
rupee I give."

The Multiplier Effect

VIKRANT BHARGAVA

Veddis Foundation

He became a multi-millionaire at 32. That entrepreneurial instinct is now being put to use, to find stand-out solutions for societal problems.

Vikrant is your typical boy next door. He grew up in cement factory colonies, playing tennis ball cricket in the corridor. Vikrant's father worked for ACC, which had 17 factories across India. The job was transferable, which meant the family moved every couple of years.

"I've lived in a lot of different places... I consider myself a true Indian in that sense."

The Bhargavas lived decently but had very little savings, partly because Vikrant's father was generous to a fault. If a friend or relative was in need, he would help them out. Often, more than he could afford to.

When Vikrant asked aap aisa kyun karte hain, papa would say, "Beta their need is greater than ours..."

Like most middle class Indians, Vikrant grew up mentally insulated from poverty. However, as a teenager, he recalls eating an ice-cream and throwing the cup away. An urchin plunged his hand into the garbage bin, fished out the cup and licked it. Vikrant looked away, horrified.

Living in a colony full of engineers, B.Tech. was the logical career choice. Taking things apart was his passion but when he got a high rank, Vikrant opted for electrical engineering instead of mechanical, and never quite enjoyed it.

A resident of Jwalamukhi hostel, Vikrant was part of the Rendezvous organising committee in 1992. That's where he met his wife, Surbhi Virmani, then a student at Lady Hardinge Medical College.

When he graduated from IIM Calcutta, Vikrant had two ambitions; 1. explore the world 2. make lots of money. And that's exactly what he did – in record time.

He joined Partygaming.com, a dotcom that launched online poker and had a mega-IPO in 2005. At age 32, Vikrant Bhargava had $450 million in the bank and no idea what to do with it.

But he had time, he had money, and the urge to do something for the greater good.

In 2009, Vikrant formulated a three-page note outlining his thoughts on philanthropy, with an amorphous idea of helping NGOs do their job better.

Since then, his foundation has set up India's first peer-to-peer fundraising platform, experimented with running a 'livelihood lab', and worked with the Rural Livelihood Mission in various states.

In 2021, Vikrant Bhargava committed Rs 100 crore to evangelise evidence-based development, and work with the government on effective public service delivery.

Because an entrepreneur must solve problems at scale
And therein lies, a fascinating tale.

Vikrant Bhargava sat in his plush office at Barakhamba Road, stared out of the window and sighed. He had joined British Gas hoping that it would be more exciting than his campus placement at Bank of America.

But it was a 'baby elephant' compared to the cool startups his IIT batchmates were working for in the US.

"I was desperate to dabble in tech, or at least go abroad."

Using the slow-motion VSNL dial-up connection, Vikrant applied to dozens of jobs and he got one – with L N Mittal's steel plant in Mexico. In December 1999, at age 27, he reached Lazaro Cardenas to be greeted with 'hablas espanol'?

No, he did not speak Spanish and could not pick it up in four weeks flat. Desperate to move out, Vikrant reached out to his IIT Delhi network. He was willing to take up any offer that came his way.

Fast forward three months, Vikrant was in the Dominican Republic, working for a tiny startup looking at three nascent verticals – e-commerce, online payment processing, and online gambling. It was the gambling bit that took off.

One fine day, a customer exploited a bug and cashed out a million dollars. Looking at ways to 'derisk' the business, Vikrant came across poker. The game had an element of skill, and a clean business model. You could drive traffic to the site and let people play, then take a small commission to settle transactions.

"The funny thing is, none of us even knew how to play poker!"

In 2001, Partygaming.com launched online poker and business took off like a rocket. By 2004, the company was rolling in cash; the founders paid themselves substantial dividends.

At this point, Vikrant knew that he was financially secure for the rest of his life.

In 2005, the company went for IPO, with an $8 billion dollar valuation. And things went crazy. Unicorns had not yet been sighted, so a multi-million-dollar IPO was big news. Paparazzi lay in wait outside Vikrant's apartment building, eager to show the world who these newly rich dudes were.

Even as he was adjusting to this new reality, there was a change of leadership at Partygaming.com. Vikrant did not see eye to eye with the new CEO. So, one fine morning, he simply quit.

At age 33, Vikrant Bhargava went from being super-busy to having nothing to do.

"I was miserable. I felt like my child was snatched from me."

Wealth is liberating, but it can also be tiresome. Vikrant's only 'job' now was to oversee his money and to grow it. Sitting in his pyjamas at home, he bought real estate, invested in a few startups, and had discussions with bankers who came with 'opportunities'.

Living in Gibraltar – in the middle of nowhere – he felt very alone, and very bored. So, in 2008, Vikrant moved to London. That same year, the financial crisis hit the world. Vikrant watched his portfolio shrink and felt a sense of panic.

"After this, for years, I just kept cash in the bank. I was nervous putting money to work."

The one thing Vikrant did which gave him a lot of satisfaction was gifting a substantial sum of money to his father.

"Aap jisko dena chaho, de dijiye," he said.

In this way, the Bhargava family started supporting multiple NGOs with small cheques. This gave Vikrant a chance to meet non-profits and philanthropists, whenever he visited India.

KYA KARNA HAI

Looking for someone to bounce ideas with, Vikrant reached out to his IIT Delhi hostel mate, Sanjay Agarwal, who had joined the civil service. On Skype calls and emails, they went back and forth.

If I want to do something, which sector should I give to?

Where will it have the maximum impact?

What about so many people who are doing great work?

Vikrant's cousin, Dr Anurag, was a doctor from AIIMS, who had teamed up with his colleagues and started a hospital in Bastar. They were doing a fantastic job of treating patients but always struggling to raise funds.

"What if I hire a small team which can be a shared resource for multiple NGOs?" was one of the many ideas discussed.

Vikrant and Sanjay then co-authored a three-page document, putting down these thoughts. They put a name to the foundation – Letzdream – with the logic that it could be expanded to multiple sectors. For example, Letzeducate, Letzcare, Letzshare, and so on.

The process started in 2009, but it took a couple of years to turn intention to action. Instead of helping NGOs with their numerous operational problems, Vikrant eventually decided to focus on just one area: fundraising. And clearly, the future lay online.

In the UK, Vikrant came across a platform called JustGiving, which had pioneered social fundraising. Let's say you strongly support a particular NGO. You reach out to your friends and say, "I am running a marathon in support of a particular cause. Please will you make a small donation?"

There's a high likelihood they will cut a cheque because they know you, and don't wish to be embarrassed.

It was the early days of e-commerce, but Vikrant's gut said India is ready for the 'social giving' model. He decided to set up Letzchange, a platform for credible NGOs to fundraise efficiently. He hired a development team in India, to start coding the website.

A year into the project it was clear that it needed a dedicated, full time CEO.

Rahul Chovva, a 2011 IIT Kanpur graduate, had failed to clear the civil service exam in his first attempt and was at a bit of a crossroads. A batchmate passed on a lead : 'Someone called Vikrant Bhargava is searching for a CEO for his startup'.

Rahul had no idea who, except that he was a fellow IITian. That was enough for him to reach out and explore the opportunity.

"From the start, I was impressed by Vikrant's ideas and his clarity of vision," says Rahul.

*"I'm not an expert in any sector,
I use common sense to solve problems."*

Rahul had no exposure to philanthropy, or tech, but that didn't seem to matter to his future boss. In fact, Vikrant was looking for a young person with high energy and enthusiasm. Someone who could be guided and moulded to execute his vision, and lead it hands-on in India. Rahul fit the bill perfectly.

When Rahul joined in 2014, Version 1.0 of the Letzchange was ready. The site had videos and profiles of various NGOs and one could donate using CCAvenue. But there was no 'social giving' functionality. Back then, the idea of P2P (peer to peer) was very new and a small team working across time zones was not ideal.

Even NGOs were skeptical – who will give us money online?

A CULTURAL SHIFT

If you are stuck with a website that doesn't do the job, do you wait for it to get fixed? Well, Rahul decided to make the best of it until version 2.0 came along. The team created project pages for each NGO to circulate, with a 'donate now' link.

The ultimate goal remained that Rahul Chovva, or Rashmi Bansal, or anyone out there, could create a page for an NGO of their choice, share it in their network, and raise money.

To test the viability of this idea, Letzchange reached out to Bhumi, a Chennai-based NGO. The founder, Dr Prahalathan, was tech-savvy and keen to participate. He had volunteers who raised money going door-to-door. Now, a page was made for each of these volunteers, and they were delighted.

In its first year of operations, ending March 2015, Letzchange raised Rs 1.5 crore, of which Bhumi raised around Rs 25 lakh.

"We were thrilled that our MVP is done, it works!"

Convincing NGOs to embrace the idea remained a challenge. Vinayak Lohani is a founder who has leveraged his IIT KGP and IIM Calcutta alumni network extremely well. Every year, he would approach Vikrant and say, "I'm falling short of, say, Rs 20 lakh... can you chip in?" And Vikrant would happily do it.

But in 2015, he said, "Vinayak, use Letzchange, raise funds, I will match each donation."

Match funding was Vikrant's idea, one more way to 'give back'. To that, Rahul added a competitive element. The NGO which raised the most funds on the platform would win prize money of Rs 25 lakh.

This further energised Vinayak and his volunteers to run with it and cross the 'finish line' to victory.

The Letzchange Online Fundraising Challenge went on to become its principal growth engine.

It was designed to take advantage of the phenomenon of 'year-end' giving. Companies would wake up in March, realise they had extra funds, and donate to an NGO to claim tax benefits.

This led to an important insight. If donations are event-driven, why not link donations to more events, such as, birthdays, weddings, anniversaries? People could say – no gifts please, here's the NGO I support, donate to them.

And yes, it worked. When a Bhumi volunteer was getting married, he asked guests to donate to Bhumi, instead of buying him gifts, and ended up raising Rs 5 lakh.

In 2016, the peer-to-peer fundraising product was ready to be launched. A Letzchange team member – Deeksha Goyal – was participating in the Airtel Delhi Marathon.

"I am running to raise money for an NGO," she said. "Everybody does that."

This opened Rahul's eyes to a whole new world of fundraising. Indeed, it was the practice in all major marathons across the world. However, people who ran for a cause did not have an online page to collect money – it was all done physically. So, here was an opportunity not to be missed!

Letzchange partnered with Isha Vidya for the Airtel Delhi Marathon. They had a large number of volunteers who understood the product, made their campaign pages and raised Rs 6.5 crores in just one and a half months.

Letzchange then partnered with the Airtel Hyderabad Marathon, Airtel Chennai Marathon, TCS Bangalore Marathon and several other marathons.

Each runner could create a page saying, 'I am running for XYZ cause, please support me'. In addition, there was a leaderboard so that everybody could see which NGO was raising how much.

In 2015, Airtel Hyderabad raised Rs 7 lakh; in 2016 that number shot up to Rs 45 lakh. The platform had found its sweet spot. By 2018, Letzchange was on a roll, raising more money that year than the preceding three years combined.

GIVING AWAY THE BRIDE

Indeed, Letzchange was a smashing success and poised to grow exponentially. While the team in Gurgaon had grown, Vikrant remained in London, but stayed in constant touch.

For the first two years, he had daily calls with his young CEO, at 7 a.m. UK time.

"I had crazy energy and ideas but I needed guidance," says Rahul.

Vikrant was a problem-solver, constantly asking questions. How do we get people to give? How do we increase the credibility of NGOs? How do we increase conversion rates? They tracked numbers, tech-startup style.

It's important to note that 100% of the money raised on Letzchange was given to NGOs. No admin fee, no processing fee – those expenses were borne by Vikrant himself. The annual cost of running Letzchange – Rs 3 crore a year – was also treated as his personal philanthropy. Apart from this, he also contributed match funding.

In 2018, Rahul Chovva expressed the desire to move on. He wanted to move beyond the non-profit sector, and Vikrant understood his desire for personal growth.

"I won't be selfish and ask you to stay," he said to his CEO.

"He was almost like a brother counselling me," recalls Rahul.

It was a special relationship, hence, Rahul promised to help find a CEO to replace himself. The criteria was 'someone who is as passionate, or more passionate than me', who will not see the role merely as a job.

They did locate such a candidate, she was ready to join. And then, there was a twist in the tale.

Venkat Krishnan, founder of Give India, had just stepped down. Rahul was surprised to hear this news. He had read about Venkat in the book 'Stay Hungry Stay Foolish'. A line from the Give India's first annual report was etched in Rahul's mind.

"Give India will close by 2020," Venkat had said.

His hope was that by then, the idea of giving would be so widespread, that Give India would not need to exist. Clearly, that had not happened. Instead, Venkat had handed over the reins of Give India to Atul Satija.

An outsider who had taken the plunge into the social sector.

In 2015, at age 38, Atul quit the unicorn InMobi to do something 'at scale' in the NGO world. He set up the Nudge Foundation, a social incubator. Additionally, he had the task of making a Give India ver 2.0.

"Let's find out what his vision for Give India is," said Rahul.

"We are not a traditional NGO... our mission is to find solutions and enable rapid scaling."

- Murugan V, CEO, Veddis Foundation

A meeting was set up between Vikrant and Atul; 45 minutes stretched into three hours. Letzchange had the tech, and a young, energetic team. Give India had the brand recall.

"Why should I look for a new CEO?" said Vikrant to Atul. "Let's merge my platform with yours."

The meeting ended with a handshake. Paperwork would follow but, in that moment, the two entities became one.

Essentially, Vikrant gifted Letzchange to Give India, and committed a certain amount of philanthropic capital to keep it going. He also joined the NGO's board. It was a rare, successful merger. With the exception of Rahul, the Letzchange team stayed on, eventually shifting to Bangalore.

With Give India adopting the Letzchange tech platform, fundraising from retail donors skyrocketed. At peak, during Covid, it touched Rs 1250 crores. Today, the March Fundraising Challenge is a marquee event for NGOs on the Give India platform. Vikrant could not have asked for more.

"I invested roughly Rs 15-20 crore to build and run Letzchange," he says.

Give India now raises Rs 600-1000 crores per annum using the Letzchange tech platform at the back end.

In 2019, Vikrant exited the board, satisfied that the platform was doing well. It was time to step away, like a father who has performed the kanyadaan of a beloved daughter.

LABORATORY OF CHANGE

That's the remarkable story of Letzchange. There's also the work of Letzdream, which was completely non-tech, and happening in parallel. In 2013, Vikrant decided that the foundation would work with a thousand rural households, identify their problems, and test out different solutions. Whatever worked could then be executed at scale.

"We looked at a map for a place close to Gurgaon and landed up in Alwar district."

The Sub-Divisional Magistrate was young and helpful, he suggested they meet an NGO called SPECTRA which was doing good work with women. This NGO offered to take Vikrant and his team to a village called Ratakhurd, where they ran Self Help Groups (SHGs).

It was a bumpy ride over non-existent roads, to reach a village with no pucca houses, no running water, and little employment. But the people were extremely warm. They invited the visitors into their homes for tea, and even offered a place to stay overnight.

"Aap dekhiye to sahi, hum yahan kaise rehte hain," they said.

That day, Vikrant decided, inke saath kuch to karna hai.

Letzdream took up a simple campaign – to increase milk production in each household. With one cow or buffalo, there was just enough for the family. But if you helped them acquire a second animal, there was surplus milk to sell. Saras Dairy set up a local collection centre, which meant the women got a better price for their mehnat.

Over a two and a half year period, the 1400 families of Ratakhurd saw a 70-75% increase in their household income. And this had been achieved with an outlay of just Rs 2.5 crore from Letzdream. What's more, the confidence level and thinking of the women had changed completely.

"Aap humein London kab bula rahe hain!" they joked.

The obvious thing to do was 'scale it up'. Letzdream spent two months exploring how to take the program national, until a team member asked a fundamental question: will this model work everywhere? In reality, India does not have a milk shortage.

So, the success of Ratakhurd may or may not be replicable all across India.

The main learning, however, was that a small intervention could significantly increase household income.

"We have a prototype, we should be working with the government," was Vikrant's view.

The Letzdream team met Mr C S Rajan, then Chief Secretary of Rajasthan. Vikrant had gone prepared to wait; to his surprise, the meeting began five minutes before time.

"Tell me, what can I do for you?" said Rajan.

Vikrant shared the work done on Ratakhurd and added, "I am more than happy to write a cheque, or help in any other way, so that the government can take it further."

Rajan stared at the earnest young man, and shook his head.

"Look, we, the government, don't need your money. But we'd love to have good people."

It was a highly productive meeting, which eventually led to Vikrant thinking in a completely new direction – shaping policy and governance.

Less than three months later, Letzdream signed an MOU with the government of Rajasthan, to work with rural households under an existing scheme called Rajeevika (Rajasthan Rural Livelihood Mission). The foundation employed 42 people to work in 42 clusters across 8 districts, to help with implementation and monitoring.

As word spread, the Haryana government approached Letzdream – aap hamare liye bhi kijiye. The foundation hired people to work in 20 clusters across the state. Vikrant worked from London, with a small supervisory team in India. And it was getting frustrating.

Running payroll for 70 people, monitoring their work in far-flung rural locations, dealing with government officials. Had they bitten off more than they could chew?

WINDS OF CHANGE

Murugan Vasudevan moved back to India in 2007 but was bored with his job at a global MNC. His closest friends, and his wife, were in the social sector. And that's where his heart longed to be. But before Murugan could put in his papers, V C Gopalratnam, head of Cisco India, asked if he would like to lead the Social Innovation Group in South Asia.

"There's a new CSR law. I need you to do something about it!"

Over the next 6 years, Murugan designed and implemented Cisco's CSR strategy, with an annual budget of 30 crores. He enjoyed working with young, entrepreneurial, non-profit founders – especially those who were willing to measure the effectiveness of their work and constantly make improvements.

In April 2020, quite by chance, Murugan got connected with Vikrant. One of the few joys during lockdown was running; a fellow enthusiast mentioned overhearing a conversation at his 25th reunion in IIT Delhi.

An introduction was made and, in the very first call, Vikrant and Murugan struck up a strong rapport. They had common ideas on the 'why' and 'how' of philanthropy. And enjoyed brainstorming on what more could be and should be done.

Murugan loved Vikrant's passion and authenticity. During one of their many Whatsapp video calls, Vikrant shared the complexities of the rural livelihood mission work.

"Sometimes I think, I should just shut this whole thing down and give up my FCRA!"

"No, no, no," said Murugan. "Let's find a way to make it better."

As an external observer, Murugan could see various issues more clearly. Not only was the foundation knee-deep into the rural mission, it was also writing cheques to support a number of small organisations.

There was no clear strategy and no answer to a crucial question – 'Am I a donor, or a doer?'

A key piece of advice from Murugan was: create a captive centre. This was a popular and proven model in the IT sector; why not apply it here? Then, instead of managing 70 relationships with direct employees, you manage only one – with the partner. This made a lot of sense to Vikrant.

In December 2020, Vikrant made an offer; Murugan made a counter-offer. The foundation's budget was Rs 3 to 5 crore a year, when Vikrant's capacity to give was many multiples more. So, Murugan went all-in and threw him a challenge.

"Make a commitment to give Rs 100 crore over the next three years," he said. "Announce it publicly, I will leave Cisco and join you."

Three weeks later, Vikrant called and said, "I'm ready to do it."

On January 12, 2021, Murugan put in his papers. By September, Letzdream had been rebranded as Veddis Foundation, and a public announcement was made.

"Our Foundation is committed to investing over Rs 100 crore in the next three years in organisations engaged in solving complex societal challenges in India."

GETTING GOOD GOVERNANCE

In a developing country, the surest way for philanthropic capital to make the largest impact is working with the government. What they needed was a smarter way to do it.

The first thing Murugan implemented was the captive centre model, which meant giving a third-party agency full responsibility and accountability for field work.

Having worked with SPECTRA for several years in Rajasthan, they were a logical choice. The foundation migrated its field workers to the NGO, and work continued smoothly.

"I never believe that we know the 'best way' of doing something."

Veddis Foundation only employs the analytical staff which sits in the state capital, working closely with the State Rural Livelihood Mission team (SRLM).

"SRLMs have a budget, and staff; we help make sure that the money is better spent."

For example, when the Veddis Project Management Unit began work in Himachal, it noticed that the credit cycle in the State Rural Livelihood Mission was broken. SHGs took loans from the Cluster Level Federations (CLFs) but did not repay them. Because the government had not even asked.

Once a ledger was maintained in the cluster office and a demand note was raised, money started coming in. 70% of the SHGs paid their loans to the CLFs and were then able to borrow a higher amount the next time, as the corpus had increased.

It's the kind of problem often created when the state works in 'mission mode'.

When a scheme is announced, officials scramble to meet targets, and disburse money. The government machinery moves on to the next scheme, and the next. Processes and systems to monitor and assess the impact of these initiatives are critical, but the 'mission mode' state just does not have the time to set it all up.

This is the gap filled by the Veddis Project Management Unit.

It starts with writing a comprehensive handbook, laying out the roles and responsibilities of the state mission, the district mission, the cluster, the villages, and the federations. Training is also given on practical aspects, such as how to run the weekly meetings.

In the non-profit world, this kind of work is known as 'technical assistance'.

The Veddis Foundation spends Rs 3 to 5 crore in each state that it works with, which covers the salaries of its project management unit and the cost of the captive unit run by SPECTRA.

In addition, there are four full-time employees based in Gurgaon who constantly travel to the various states.

While this model works well, Veddis is not expanding. Instead, the foundation is using this experience to develop tech tools, which will help the SRLMs work more efficiently.

Let's say a welfare scheme is started with good intentions. Does anyone ever sit down to evaluate how well it's working? Or, between scheme A and scheme B, do we ask, which one has more impact?

It's the kind of analysis every company does in pursuit of better results, but mostly absent in the government system.

This bothered Vikrant. The government has a huge, huge, huge budget, so even a marginal improvement in its efficiency would make a big difference. Why not help sarkari departments do their jobs better?

"Let's fund the people who can provide evidence and analysis to policymakers," said Vikrant.

J-PAL (Jamal Poverty Action Lab) run by Abhijit Banerjee and Esther Duflo at MIT is one such organisation. In 2019, the duo won the Nobel Prize in Economics for pioneering randomized controlled trials (RCTs) in development economics. However, an RCT is an expensive and time-consuming exercise.

"The government has enough money," says Murugan, "but there's too much red tape."

Every department must float an RFP (Request for Proposal) before hiring a vendor. But then, it's all about who can provide a service at the lowest cost, not the highest quality.

This is where philanthropic capital can make a difference.

E FOR EVIDENCE

In Oct 2021, Veddis Foundation announced a grant of Rs 46 crore to J-PAL, to be utilised over a three year period. This was used to co-found ASPIRE (Alliance for Scaling Policy Impact through Research and Evidence), enabling J-PAL to enter into long-term partnerships with the government.

"Our belief is that it's an utter waste of intellectual capital if someone finds a solution, it gets published in a paper, and that's the end of it."

One of JPAL's most successful Randomized Control Trials (RCTs) is the 'Graduation' approach. This was an experiment first conducted in Bangladesh to provide sustainable livelihood for the ultra-poor (those earning less than a dollar a day).

It was later replicated in West Bengal, with similar success.

Let's take Rani*, an ultra-poor village woman. The first thing you do is give her a productive asset, say, a buffalo. Then, you give her some training and hand-holding for six months In this period, Rani will also receive a small amount of sustenance income, to stay afloat.

"Think about solving large scale problems in a smart way, not just throwing money at it."

There is additional, low-touch maintenance for 12 months. At the end of 18 months, Rani would have 'graduated' from the ultra-poor category.

The Bihar government decided to implement this model at scale through its rural livelihood mission, Bihar Jeevika. The CM carved out some funds for both the asset and monthly income transfers, enabling more than 1.5 lakh women to 'graduate' from ultra-poverty.

Now, ASPIRE has developed a playbook which can be used by any state which wishes to implement the program at scale. The Ministry of Rural Development is working with multiple NGO partners to make this happen. ASPIRE remains the process monitoring partner which ensures the scale-up.

Veddis Foundation is also a key funder for CEGIS (Centre for Effective Governance of Indian States), which works in the area of strategic public finance, including the principle of 'outcome based budgeting'. For example, if the budget allocated money for a bridge, the auditor will ask – was the bridge built?

"No one asks, did the bridge serve any purpose," says Murugan.

A government hospital buys an MRI machine worth Rs 5 crore. However, it lies unused because they did not hire a technician. In outcome-based budgeting, the finance department will ask the hospital, iss MRI machine ka aap kya karoge?

The hospital may say, "I will diagnose 100 patients a month."

So, when the machine arrives, they are accountable for this outcome. The technician will be hired and patients will benefit. But the state needs help to shift to this new way of thinking.

In February 2024, Veddis foundation signed an MOU with the UP government, to fund professionals from IDinsight, a professional firm deputed to work with people in their finance and planning departments. Veddis Foundation has given a Rs 15 crore grant over 18 months to cover their salaries.

EYE FOR IMPACT

While analytics are certainly crucial for the government, Vikrant realised that donors need this information as well.

I want to give but am not sure where the impact will be the greatest.

This is the dilemma faced by many trusts and high-net-worth individuals. There are models available but they are formulated by global agencies, who do not understand the nitty-gritties, the nuances of working in India.

For example, the infant mortality rate in Kerala may be similar to Western Europe, while in a certain district of Jharkhand it is similar to sub-Saharan Africa. However, models are formulated on the basis of 'national average'. And that just did not sit right with Vikrant.

"We believe that philanthropy has to be able to address regional imbalances in India," he says.

To address this issue, Vikrant has co-founded a non-profit startup – Raising Impact – which will use national, state and hyperlocal data to provide high-quality analytics.

The startup has found its first client – a funder who wishes to deploy Rs 10 crore on solutions that will improve farmers' income. Raising Impact is currently studying the available solutions, the organisations who work in the area, and how cost-effective they are. The client will get recommendations, based on the best SROI (Social Return on Investment).

The goal is to provide a bespoke advisory service to help influence and channel at least Rs 100 crore into highly effective solutions over the next three years, and it looks achievable.

After a decade in philanthropy, Vikrant Bhargava has tried, failed, scaled; tried again, reflected, course-corrected; and remains determined as ever, to keep walking the path. His wife, Surbhi, and their three kids support his ambition but are not yet actively involved in the work of the foundation.

"Surbhi is a doctor, she's been doing public service much longer than I have!"

Yehi to zindagi ki asli kamaai hai
Is mein sukh hai, aur sachchai hai.

For more on Veddis Foundation scan:

ADVICE TO YOUNG PHILANTHROPISTS

When people want to do something good, they tend to follow their hearts as opposed to using their brains.

I would urge people to think deeply about what cause they are looking to support. Will you be solving a problem at scale? Is it going to have long lasting impact? Are you getting the maximum bang for their buck?

What you don't want to do is create one more school or one more hospital or one more 'something that already exists', when there are many structures sitting around, not being used properly.

The best thing you can do is give your brain power. Think about solving large scale problems in a smart way, as opposed to just throwing money at it.

It's a hugely rewarding journey if you are actively involved. But if you are busy with something else and you can only write a cheque, that's also good. There are smart people running organizations, identify them and allow them run with it!

*"I'm head-driven
but I wouldn't
be here if
my heart
wasn't in it too."*

Jai Hind

SUNIL WADHWANI

Wadhwani Initiative for Sustainable Healthcare & Wadhwani Institute for Artificial Intelligence

He believes that technology must improve the lives of the poorest. To make that happen, this philanthropist works with the central and state governments across India.

His family fled from Sindh in 1947, leaving everything behind. Paisa, property and a place in society built over generations. They were now known as refugees. Living hand to mouth - in makeshift tents – but with indomitable spirit, determined to make something of themselves in their new country.

"Not once did I hear my parents complain about all that they had lost," recalls Sunil.

Even when times were tough one thing was non-negotiable – a good education. At a time when there was no concept of bank loans, Sunil's father borrowed on his goodwill, to keep his kids in a reputed school. The young man went on to study at IIT Madras and Carnegie Mellon University.

In 1980, he founded his first company - a healthcare startup. When it failed miserably, it hurt like hell. But Sunil went on to set up a second company, in an 8 by 8 square foot room in the Carnegie Office Park. The company was still struggling when he got married to Nita in 1987. But she supported him all the way.

Mastech (later renamed as iGate) would defy death a few more times before joining the big league. But in the mid-90s Sunil found himself reflecting on his life and concluded.

"I've worked hard but, I've also been very, very lucky."

What if he'd been born in a slum a kilometre away, or in a rural area with no electricity, no roads, no hospitals? Could he really have achieved the same success? The obvious answer was no. This soul-searching led Sunil to start his giving journey in his early 40s.

It started with financial support to some well-meaning NGOs. Through them, Sunil Wadhwani got exposed to the 'real India' living on $2 a day. The NGOs were certainly doing their bit to bridge the gap but they had no serious ambitions to scale.

Hence, Sunil Wadhwani decided to set up his own foundation in 2014. Over the last decade WISH (Wadhwani Initiative for Sustainable Healthcare) has been working hands-on with the Government of India to fix the primary healthcare system in India.

The early years were spent in field work, understanding ground realities, in both rural and urban settings. Along the way, the hard-charging entrepreneur has had to take off his business suit and think for the aam aadmi.

"Innovation means nothing," he reflects. "Unless it reaches the people who need it most. And that, is challenging work!"

While Sunil Wadhwani has seen great success as an entrepreneur, the satisfaction he gets from social sector work is far greater.

Stock prices go up and down, companies go bust.
Only good deeds will live on, in Jhulelal we trust.

The principal of St. Columba's School raised his eyebrow and looked the expectant father straight in the eye. "Your son cannot walk, Mr Wadhwani. We cannot admit him to our school."

The little boy slumped in his seat and stared at the floor. He had passed the entrance test with flying colours. Didn't his brain matter more than his stunted legs? His father certainly thought so and addressed the principal in a brusque but firm manner.

"I take responsibility. I will ensure Romesh is able to attend all classes."

It was a huge commitment. Three times a day, Tekchand Wadhwani left work and came to the school to carry his son from class to class. Why was he willing to make this sacrifice? Because, for this family, education truly mattered.

This story is about Romesh Wadhwani, Sunil's older brother, who was born in Karachi 10 days after India's independence. Romesh bore the brunt of those chaotic times when the family fled to India, even contracting polio as an infant.

By the time Sunil came along in 1952, the family was once again well settled. Tekchand Wadhwani had joined a British bank and was doing extremely well. When he was transferred to Bombay, Romesh and Sunil joined the prestigious Campion School. The family lived comfortably in a 3000 square foot company flat near Churchgate. Then, all of a sudden, things changed.

The British Bank got acquired by HSBC and overnight, the top management – including Tekchand – were sacked. At that time, he had invested in a flat in Bombay which was stuck in legal troubles. Hence, there was no liquid cash. In the space of 30 days, the Wadhwani family had to shift from a palatial house to a dingy one-room kitchen.

"Let's shift the boys to a government school," said their mother Shanta, who was now managing the household on a tight budget.

"Absolutely not!" said Tekchand. "I will arrange for the money..."

These are the pivotal moments in life that make you – or break you.

Both Romesh and Sunil went on to study at IITs, pursue their masters in the US and set up extremely successful companies. But are we truly exceptional, Sunil often wondered. Over time, he became acutely aware that he was standing on the shoulders of giants.

Eventually, he would hire a researcher to interview family members, scour archives and check vahis (genealogical records) maintained by pandits at the ghats in Haridwar. The Wadhwani family tree was traced as far back as 16 generations. Over the last 300 years, they had been respected educators and principled administrators.

"We have a huge sense of gratitude for the family we were born into."

In the 1940s, their paternal grandfather, Hiranand, was headmaster of one of the largest schools in Sindh; their maternal grandfather, Dr. Gianchand Hingorani, held the highly respected position of Surgeon General of Sindh. And yet, when times changed, they accepted the call of destiny and rebuilt their lives from scratch. What courage, what resilience, what sacrifices were made by multiple ancestors!

I can't pay them back but maybe I can pay it forward?

PHILANTHROPIC JOURNEY

Logically, a man first steadies his ship and then sails into new waters. When Sunil Wadhwani started supporting NGOs in India, the boat was still leaky. His second startup wasn't wildly profitable; it required hands-on, full-time attention. Nevertheless, he took the plunge into 'giving'.

Given his reverence for education, you'd think that's what Sunil Wadhwani would focus on. But he surveyed the landscape and chose healthcare – because it was neglected.

"Even in the 90s, I could see innovative stuff happening in the education space," he says. "Healthcare – not so much."

Sunil identified a few NGOs doing good work and began funding them. What's more, he took time out to go with them to remote villages and 'see what is happening' for himself. Sitting on the mud floor of a farmer's hut, smoke from the chulha stinging his eyes, Sunil Wadhwani got an unforgettable lesson on the 'cycle of poverty'.

Speaking in chaste Hindi, ghunghat covering her gaunt face, Parvati Devi narrated her tale of woe. When she started getting pain in her lower back and legs, she went to the gorment dawakhana. Doctor saab was not on duty. Two weeks later she went again. This time, the doctor did a quick check-up and prescribed some medicine.

However, Parvati's condition did not improve. In fact, it got so bad that she had to stop working, effectively cutting the family's income in half. Now, two years later, she'd been diagnosed with diabetes.

What a tragedy – and a completely avoidable one. If only she had been administered a simple blood test.

"This should not be happening 50 years after independence!" thought Sunil on the ride back to Jaipur.

One of the NGOs he was involved with operated a 'hospital on a train'. This train would go to remote parts of the country and remain there for three weeks. Volunteer doctors treated around 5000 patients at each location. At the NGO's board meeting, Sunil exhorted, "Why don't we roll out 5 trains, then 10, then 20? I am ready to provide the funding."

"NGOs say we can't scale due to lack of money. But it's really lack of thinking at scale."

Oh, that's a fantastic idea, everyone said. But kuch hua nahin. Well, you might say, it's easy for an entrepreneur who's created a large business to say 'let's think at scale'. For a resource-constrained NGO, the idea is daunting. But there is another, deeper reason for the hesitation.

As an angel investor, Sunil works closely with dozens of startups. Even the ones who survive initial challenges often get stuck at 80-100 employees. Because the founder is unwilling to give up control. The same malaise exists in the social sector. Unless you empower your team and let them take decisions, you cannot grow.

Eventually, Sunil Wadhwani realised there was only one way to make things happen his way. With a bigger vision. At scale.

I'll have to do it myself.

WALKING THE PATH

In 2014, Sunil Wadhwani set up WISH (Wadhwani Initiative for Sustainable Health) Foundation with a focus on primary healthcare. Ideally, Primary Health Centres (PHCs) take care of

80 to 90% of issues in a community. However, this basic facility functioned poorly in low-income areas of low-income states in northern, eastern, and central India.

The journey started with a small team of 4-5 people who started asking questions:

If the goal is to transform rural primary healthcare, how will we do it?

What's the model to apply?

What forms of innovation do we use?

"Looking back, my initial thinking was fairly naïve," admits Sunil.

Having built companies at scale, Sunil was all gung-ho about applying some of those lessons to the social sector. His first (failed) startup was in the area of medical devices. Incorporating healthtech at the first point of contact was thus an integral part of the foundation's overall plan.

The devices had to be hardy – capable of working despite power outages, low internet connectivity, and dust. The WISH team undertook a survey of the most disruptive healthcare innovators in India. After shortlisting 200, they narrowed it down to about 25. Ten were chosen and procured.

But the basic problem in the PHC was absenteeism. Instead of treating 50 patients a day, a doctor would see 10. The rest would be told to go to a private clinic next door and pay for consultation. So how does one fix this faulty system? By replacing handwritten ledgers with a simple electronic medical record (EMR).

What if a PHC did not have a doctor at all, or the case was complicated? In that case, a tele-health solution would be used. Data like BP, blood glucose and so on, taken by portable devices, would be transmitted to a physician in Jaipur to make a diagnosis.

"It sounds pretty routine now ,but remember, this is 2014 – years before COVID!"

So far so good. But the WISH team soon realised the hard truth; you solve one problem, and another emerges. Diagnosis ho gaya, ab patient ko dawaai bhi to chahiye. Medicines were rarely in stock at PHCs – they were largely pilfered. A more robust delivery mechanism was the need of the hour.

"When you tackle one problem, you have to also take care of two, three side problems."

The WISH team worked with a local innovator to develop a 'medicine vending machine', similar to a Coke or Pepsi. This machine would stock 95% of commonly prescribed medicines. Thus, when a doctor in Jaipur wrote a prescription, it could be dispensed by the vending machine in a village 200 km away.

Armed with a concept note, WISH was ready to start working. Somewhere. Anywhere. But who would give this NGO with no track record a fighting chance?

IN THE TRENCHES

In May 2014, Vasundhara Raje was re-elected as Chief Minister of Rajasthan. Perhaps she would be open to new ideas? A gentleman in the state health ministry liked the concept note and took it to the health secretary. A meeting was then arranged with Vasundhara Raje herself.

"Give us the worst-performing clinics in your most backward districts – we'll turn them around," said the WISH team. "And we will spend our own money to do it."

It was an offer that the CM could not refuse.

"Good news!" said Sunil Wadhwani. "We've got the green signal!"

The bad news was that WISH would not be taking over just 10 clinics. The government was giving them TWO HUNDRED clinics. And the work had to start.... in 90 days.

One of the hallmarks of being an entrepreneur is that you never say 'no'. A client wants something impossible? You figure out a way to deliver it. 90 days later, the tiny team of 5 people had expanded to 400, including 30 doctors, a sizable number of nurses and medical technicians – mostly recruited by word of mouth.

Dinesh Songara, an MSW graduate working in rural healthcare, heard about this unusual initiative from a friend at UNICEF. A casual meeting with Soumitra Ghosh, WISH CEO at the time, convinced him it was a project with a difference. There was an energy and ambition rarely seen in the sector.

"In the very first meeting, my CEO told me, we will be innovative."

Dinesh was impressed by a demo of internet-enabled smart devices which could monitor blood sugar and haemoglobin remotely. However, a field visit revealed that there were far more basic things to tackle – hygiene being one of them. Each and every PHC was thoroughly sanitised, cleaned and painted. Then came the issue of staff.

One PHC that Dinesh recalls vividly is Reenchha in Dungarpur district. Located in a remote, tribal, and hilly area, the OPD in this clinic opened for only two hours a day. In the last 20 years, there had not been a single assisted delivery. Maternal and child mortality rates were far higher than the state average.

How do you turn around a situation like this? By doing something so out of the ordinary that the villagers simply had to sit up and take notice.

"We declared that this PHC will run 24x7. Any emergency or delivery, you walk in and care will be available."

On the very day it opened, the Reenchha PHC created history. Instead of delivering at home or travelling 50 kms away, a child was born under the expert supervision of a General Nurse Midwife (GNM). It was a celebratory day for a village that had been promised all kinds of things in every election, but never received the benefits.

Aakhir, kuch to badal riya hai.

Behind-the-scenes the story was more complicated. Although it was called a PHC, the Reenchha centre had the infrastructure of a sub-centre. Since putting up a new building takes time, the team functioned from two small rooms for a few months. Eventually, they did construct – not just a building but even a much-needed tubewell. Any other non-profit would have gone back to the government and said, please sanction some funds.

WISH had the money – it simply got the work done.

WORKING AT SCALE

6 months after taking over, WISH was running 200 well-staffed, well-run clinics. Patient volumes had gone up from 20,000 a month to over 70,000 a month. Metrics such as immunisation levels, ante-natal checkups and infant mortality had also improved significantly.

Generally, a PHC has a staff of 11, including a female medical officer, 2 or 3 nurse-midwives, 1 lab technician, 1 pharmacist, 1 ASHA worker, and so on. The overall budget for a PHC when run by the government was between Rs 8 and 10 lakh, as staff were employed as per sarkaari pay scales and perks.

However, WISH ran a much tighter ship.

"We recruited staff through NGO partners, so we managed a PHC in Rs 4 lakh p.m."

Following the success of the pilot, the state cabinet issued a note allowing PPP (Public-Private Partnership) in PHCs across the state. When the RFP was announced, WISH won the contract for 24 PHCs. The government of Rajasthan would now share 50% of the cost incurred per PHC (Rs 2 lakh per month).

However, there was one new clause: staff could not be outsourced. The existing people were therefore taken on the WISH payroll. Despite that, shortage of personnel was a constant problem.

It was clear by then that a doctor's presence in the PHC is crucial. Technology came second – whether blood pressure was checked manually or with a fancy machine hardly mattered. This was an aha moment for Sunil Wadhwani.

"I went in thinking that devices would be game-changing," he admits. "I was wrong."

That's not to say out-of-the-box thinking was not required. The key issue with doctors was their unwillingness to work in remote areas.

How could they be incentivised?

WISH made two suggestions to the Government of Rajasthan:

1. Allow retired doctors to work in PHCs, without losing their pensions

2. Give preference in MD admissions to MBBS graduates who work in rural areas

The government accepted these suggestions and it made a dramatic impact. The same thinking was applied to attracting nurses and midwives to backward districts. Anyone who worked in a PHC received 10 bonus points per year. These points gave them an edge during interviews for government jobs.

Running clinics in rural Rajasthan with dedication and efficiency is no mean feat. The bureaucratic grapevine was buzzing with interest – kaun hai yeh NGO? It was around this time that the Aam Aadmi Party (AAP) won the assembly elections in Delhi. One of the flagship programs in their manifesto was the community health clinic.

"We like your model – can you adapt it for urban health?"

That's how WISH became the knowledge and implementation partner for the program which came to be known as the 'Mohalla' clinic. In this model, the Delhi government provided the infrastructure and paid for the doctor and medicines. Lekin clinic banana aur clinic chalana are two different things.

When Dr Yogesh Kumar Singh joined the Pankha Road Mohalla Clinic in September 2016, it was in a rented shed, and he had one phlebotomist as support staff. He was instructed to enter all details about each patient in a tablet, a completely new protocol for him. In the first few weeks, there were hardly any patients.

And then, as word spread, the trickle became a flood.

"I would reach at 7:55 a.m., and already there was a line of patients outside the clinic," he recalls.

Examining patients was not a problem. It was entering data into the tablet that flummoxed the good doctor. He simply could not keep up. Something had to be done.

TESTING AND TWEAKING

Taking feedback from doctors into account, the original model was quickly adapted. Each clinic would now have a pharmacist and a clinical assistant, also equipped with tablets. Vitals and prescriptions would be entered by staff, allowing the doctor to examine more patients in the same time.

"So from 1 TAB we switched to 3 TAB model, ie 3 tablets per clinic," says Akhil Chaudhary, field supervisor at WISH.

However, adding staff in a sarkari setup comes with its own problems. Monitoring attendance became the new headache. Technology to the rescue – real-time biometrics were made compulsory. But the game-changer was linking each staff member's pay to their punctuality.

There is no fixed salary at a mohalla clinic. Starting from the doctor, down to the assistant, you are paid a fixed sum based on the number of citizens who are treated. For example, the doctor is paid Rs 40 per patient. This may seem like a small sum but on average, a mohalla clinic gets 125-150 walk-ins per day.

"Electronic Medical Records (EMRs) is one innovation which really made a difference."

Let's say the doctor arrives at 8 a.m. each day but the assistant strolls in at 9 a.m.. The assistant will only get paid for the patients who come to the clinic after 9 a.m. This simple tweak boosted on-time attendance significantly.

Jeb se paise kat rahe hain... Uff, ab to time par jaana hi padega!

"When we started we didn't know what problems will come," says Akhil. "Every day was a new learning."

WISH bore the cost of software development, servers, and project monitoring; the government provided space, paid doctors and staff, and subsidised medicines. Based on this experience with Mohalla Clinics, WISH decided to pivot its model. Instead of working hands-on in individual clinics, it would operate as a back-end support partner.

Thus, when the five-year MOU with the Rajasthan government ended in 2021, the clinics were handed back to the state health department. But WISH provided a Technical Support Unit (TSU), the goal being to scale the model they had implemented in 200 clinics, to 10,000 clinics across the state.

"TSU means 10-12 WISH staff embedded with the health ministry in Jaipur, It is a win-win arrangement for both."

Today, WISH is working in TSU mode with multiple states, including MP, UP, Assam, Uttarakhand and Meghalaya. The Mohalla Clinic model has been replicated with BMC in Mumbai (Aapla Dawakhana) and urban areas of MP (Sanjeevani clinics).

Soon, it may travel to countries like South Africa, Kenya and Bangladesh.

Anyone would say, shabaash, your job here is done. For Sunil Wadhwani, it is just the beginning. Operating clinics was the need of the hour, but take a step back and you realise – this is treatment.

What about prevention?

Striking at the root cause of illness?

An admirable goal, but then comes the question...

How the hell do you change human behaviour?

BACK TO THE FUTURE

As a long-time board member of Carnegie Mellon University, Sunil Wadhwani was fascinated by the research happening on campus. By 2017, he sensed that Artificial Intelligence (AI) was reaching a tipping point. There was just one problem. Everyone wanted to use AI to make more money.

"You know where the real opportunity in AI lies?" he said to his brother Romesh, when they were chatting one evening. "Using it for social good!"

Romesh agreed wholeheartedly. The two brothers are extremely close but have always had independent business ventures. Romesh ran his own foundation focussed on skills and entrepreneurship, whereas Sunil's non-profit worked in public health. But this cause appealed to both of them, so why not join hands?

In 2018, the Wadhwani brothers set up the Wadhwani Institute for Artificial Intelligence (WIAI), a nonprofit foundation. Its goal is to harness AI to solve problems which affect the bottom 3-4 billion people on the planet. The principle is simple: develop for India, share with the world.

However, a road paved by good intentions is never free of potholes. First of all, attracting high-quality talent in AI/ML is a challenge. Wadhwani AI competes with giants like Google and Microsoft, who can and do pay more. But working for the greater good is a powerful motivator.

Wouldn't you rather build an AI solution to save babies than one that ranks cat videos?

Makarand Tapaswi, senior ML Scientist at Wadhwani AI certainly thought so. Over the last 3 years, he has been part of the Anthropometry solution. In plain English, that means, measuring the birth-weight of babies in remote areas using a smartphone.

"Estimating the weight of a baby from a short video is a challenging and stimulating computer vision problem," says Makarand.

At ground zero, it reduces infant mortality. The system automatically tags low-birth-weight babies and guides frontline health workers (ASHAs) to make interventions. However, developing an app which ASHAs can use easily is no mean feat. Varied in age and background, the women are not completely at ease with smartphones.

This is why the tech teams work closely with domain experts and conduct extensive user research before developing a solution. Design researcher Shivi Kapil was part of one such interdisciplinary team that travelled across Maharashtra, Gujarat, and Jharkhand to understand the mindset of ASHA workers.

Initially, the ASHAs spoke in monosyllables, but, over tea and snacks, they warmed up and spoke more freely.

"Madam, mere paas to keypadwala phone hai," one of them said.

She had started working as an ASHA long before phones were in vogue and found it difficult to operate one. But at such times, she took help from an ASHA sister or her kids. Clearly, the lady had found a method to 'get things done'. But the team could not help thinking – can our solution itself be designed to be more inclusive?

70% of Wadhwani AI's work is currently in the area of healthcare, the rest in education and agriculture. The leadership team works closely with the relevant ministries to identify problems that are high priority. One such is tuberculosis, the biggest infectious disease killer in India, with over half a million deaths every year.

Today, Wadhwani AI has developed five different solutions in TB alone, each addressing a specific area of concern. One solution is dramatically speeding up sputum analysis – one of the two methods used to diagnose TB. Results that used to take weeks are now possible in a day in all 64 accredited laboratories in the country.

Another AI model predicts who is likely to fall off the medication and develop multi-drug-resistant (MDR) TB. This allows case workers can focus on this narrow subset of patients and make sure they stay with the program.

However, the icing on the cake is an app which will be able to detect TB from the sound of a cough, recorded in a smartphone. This app currently has an accuracy of 85% and will be rolled out as soon as it hits 95%.

"WHO has told us this can be a game-changer," says Sunil, beaming proudly.

DO AUR DO PAANCH

At the end of the day, a good partnership achieves more than a well-meaning solo effort. Working with the government as technical support, WISH ensures that our tax money is spent thoughtfully, without the leakage that plagues sarkari schemes. Technology plays a crucial role in implementation.

"What most governments want from us is a dashboard," says Sunil. "So that officials from top to bottom know what is working."

The 'partnership effect' is also clearly visible in the collaboration between Sunil Wadhwani's non-profit siblings. WISH knows how India works, which helps Wadhwani AI develop realistic, user-centric solutions, as well as run pilots to test them before a national rollout.

While Wadhwani AI has 250 full-time people and an annual budget of Rs 80 crore, WISH has 80 employees, and an outlay of

Rs 40 crore. But even as non-profit work consumes a significant amount of his time and bandwidth, Sunil Wadhwani remains an active investor, with a focus on healthcare.

LEAVING A LEGACY

At the height of Covid, he set up a personal VC fund in India, to invest in digital health companies building solutions in mental health, diabetes management, among others. In addition, Sunil recently seeded India's first 'Venture Studio' to launch companies in areas of unmet healthcare needs.

The goal is set up 25 companies in 5 years, in areas such as pain management, oncology and kidney dialysis, where an innovative approach is lacking. According to one estimate, the companies set up so far have impacted over 20 million people.

"To me, these are all different ways of addressing the core challenge, which is improving healthcare in India at scale."

> *"Many can give money but few have this kind of passion and clarity of vision."*
>
> *- Dr Rakesh Kumar, CEO, WISH*

Yes, it takes a lot of time, a lot of energy, trips back and forth. That's commitment for you.

While his friends 'take it easy', Sunil Wadhwani continues to put in 16-hour days.

He is lucky to have the unwavering support of wife Nita. She 'holds the fort' while her husband fights the good fight.

80% of Sunil Wadhwani's wealth has been pledged to his non-profits. What's more, both his children – in their early 30s – are taking an active interest in this work. When they visit India, they spend time in the field, and with the AI team, to stay updated. Sooner or later, they will take up a leadership role.

"It's a journey," says Sunil, with a contented sigh. "I know that they will keep it going."

Being in the field, satisfaction it does yield
Challenging for sure but ready for more.

For more on WISH scan:

ADVICE TO YOUNG PHILANTHROPISTS

Start small but start early. The best way is to work with one or two NGOs. It could be nutrition, or hygiene, or women's empowerment – whatever feels right for you.

Don't just give money but get engaged with the NGO, go out to the field and learn about what's actually happening.

You can't go in saying – I have all the answers. You will create much greater impact if you approach the problem with humility. When you speak with people, observe them, listen to them, ask open-ended questions. What challenges do you have? What can we do to help you?

A key strategy for any philanthropist who wants to scale in India – partner with the government. They have the knowledge of how to design and run programs at scale.

And from my experience I can tell you, being part of the solution and its implementation is much more satisfying than just giving money.

"My aim
is to create
winners
on the field,
and in life."

The Early Bird

ANKIT NAGORI

Simply Sport Foundation

At 39, he runs a fast-growing startup, and a foundation which supports grassroots sports. Proving that youth and philanthropy can go hand in hand.

Ankit Nagori grew up in Delhi, a typical 90s kid who was crazy about Nirula's pizza and cricket. Watching Sachin Tendulkar's batting was the ultimate, playing cricket was the next best thing. At age 10, Ankit graduated from gully cricket to cricket as a serious sport, played with a hard ball.

"For me, it was not just a game but a very important part of my character building!"

Much as he loved the game, Ankit knew cricket wasn't a career option. In class 11, his parents said, enough, ab padhaai par dhyaan do. So, he prepared for the IIT JEE and got into IIT Guwahati. On a campus where every student was smart, Ankit built his identity around sports, becoming captain of the IIT Guwahati cricket team.

A design major, Ankit was intrigued by the eBays and Yahoos of the world. By the end of his Bachelor's, he knew that the internet was his calling. So, regular placements had no appeal, he wanted to learn how to build companies. After six months with a tiny startup, Ankit launched a social media platform – Youthpad.

When that didn't take off, he joined Flipkart in late 2009, as an assistant manager. Six years later, Ankit was the Chief Business Officer of an ecommerce giant, with significant ESOPs. When the Walmart deal happened, there was significant wealth generation, setting the foundation for future endeavours.

He teamed up with Mukesh Bansal (ex-Myntra) to launch Cult.fit, which went on to become India's largest fitness chain. Post-pandemic, the health food subscription business was hived off into a separate company.

But even as Ankit poured himself into this new business, the desire to do something above and beyond it grew.

It started with giving back in small, random ways, followed by a larger donation to his alma mater. But when he took the Giving Pledge in 2022, things became more concrete. Ankit and his wife Kanika put aside close to 15% of their wealth into a separate account, which was used to set up an endowment fund.

In 2020, they set up a foundation, to work in the area dearest to Ankit's heart – sport. But Simply Sport is not another Olympic Gold Quest, it has a unique vision and mission of its own.

The foundation supports academies which nurture grassroots athletes, who struggle against all odds to train for sports.

"We also want to equip players to have life skills, become more employable," says Ankit.

Because creating winners in sport
Creates winners in life.

It was a cold email to Binny Bansal that changed the course of Ankit Nagori's life. After struggling for two long years to gain traction, he had taken the difficult decision to shut down his startup. It was time to learn some hard skills, and what better place to do that than at the young and gung-ho Flipkart.

"I feel what Binny and Sachin brought to the company was audacity," says Ankit.

Binny was 27, Sachin was 28. But how confidently they declared – we will be India's largest ecommerce platform! In late 2009, when Ankit joined, Flipkart only sold books. In the next six years, they would do exactly what they had promised, selling everything from shoes to mobile phones.

It was the best of times, and the busiest of times but somehow, in the midst of it all, love blossomed. Ankit and Kanika were classmates from Delhi Public School in class 11 and 12. He went on to IIT Guwahati, she studied at Sri Venkateswara College, followed by an MBA at Narsee Monjee. But through it all, they stayed in touch.

In 2011, their parents were in matchmaking mode. Kanika would crib to Ankit about the kind of boys her family was introducing her to; Ankit had his own share of woes. That's when they thought, hey, maybe we should start dating. One year later, Ankit and Kanika had a big fat Marwari wedding.

Coming from a hardcore business family, Kanika had a fair idea what she was signing up for. Flipkart was growing at a crazy pace; it was all hands on deck. Yet, the one thing Ankit never missed was waking up early on a Sunday, to play cricket. The sport was that dear to his heart.

While he was at Flipkart, Ankit came to know about a junior colleague who was a footballer, wanting to compete in a tournament in Europe. However, he didn't have the money for his air tickets. Ankit stepped forward to sponsor the trip — a quiet gesture that meant the world to a fellow athlete.

Kanika was not at all surprised. Over the years, Ankit had often talked about 'giving back to society'. Although he didn't know how, when or in what form. In another instance, a girl who had cracked the JEE but could not pay the fees emailed him. What's more she was on a wheelchair.

"Bhaiyya, can you help me in some way?" she asked.

Ankit supported her by paying her fees, and buying her a laptop. Then, in 2015, he felt the urge to go back to IIT Guwahati, and 'do something'. So, Ankit met the Dean Dr. Ravi Mokashi and committed a 'smallish amount' towards the institute's infrastructure. The exact way in which the money would be used was left to IIT.

Meanwhile, like Ankit, many Flipkart employees exited and launched their own ventures. This group came to be known as the 'Flipkart mafia'. Investing in these companies became a matter of pride, and solidarity. Ankit was an active angel investor and for him, at some level, this was 'paying it forward'.

Yet late at night, just before he fell asleep, a question nagged him. Am I giving enough?

A SOLID STRUCTURE

When you have a singular passion in life, choosing a cause becomes easy. For Ankit, that passion was sports. He could have done a little bit here, a little bit there. Instead, in October 2020, he took the bold step of setting up his own foundation.

At that time, he was just 35.

"Abhi yeh sab karne ki tumhari umar thode hi hai," said his father-in-law.

Implying, this is the time to 'make money', not give it away. And if you do want to donate, give to the blind school, or to some hospital. Sports mein paise kyun waste kar rahe ho?

Luckily, Kanika understood where Ankit was coming from and was fully supportive. That's how Simply Sport Foundation came into being.

The first professional hired to run the operations was Darshan NK, a sports management graduate from Coventry University. Darshan had worked with the World Sport Group and XLR8 Indoor Sports, before joining Cult.Fit, where he was responsible for partnerships and scouting. This was a whole new ballgame.

For the first one year, Simply Sport was yet another organisation supporting elite athletes. But very soon, Ankit realised that there was no point in being a me-too. There was enough and more support for sports at the highest level, from organisations like Olympic Gold Quest (OGQ) as well as the government.

"Finding the right athletes to support takes a lot of hard work."

It was athletes at the grassroots who had no sponsors, no access to training. The question was, where does one find them? As Scouting Head for Cult.fit, Darshan was plugged into the ecosystem – that's how he had recruited trainers. One organisation he'd worked closely with was the Jungle Crows Foundation, based in Kolkata.

At the end of his diplomatic career, Paul Walsh settled in India and set up a foundation which trains slum kids in the quintessential British game – rugby. Over the last two decades, Jungle Crows has trained over 4000 children, some of whom play for local clubs, the state, and even for India.

"In fact the older boys and girls took the game into their bustees, and trained younger kids, as a way of giving back," Paul says.

But rugby is not cricket – tournaments are few and far between. They needed to find a steady source of income. Paul thought long and hard about this, where could these boys and girls add value?

Finally, he found a good fit – working at Decathlon. That's where Cult.Fit discovered this talent pool and quickly employed them as trainers.

There must be dozens of Jungle Crows across India and to reach them, Simply Sport started a program called 'Simply Grants'. Every year, they would pick foundations/ academies/ clubs which were training boys and girls from underprivileged backgrounds. The idea was to help them in every way possible.

Another early connect was with Mrida Foundation, situated in Mandla, a remote, rural area of Madhya Pradesh. Set up by ISB graduate Priya Nadkarni, the foundation runs a residential school for tribal kids, where football was introduced to make learning fun. The kids embraced the game wholeheartedly and excelled in it.

"What was surprising was the impact football had on our girls," says Priya.

Wearing shorts and 'playing like boys' boosted their confidence; travelling for tournaments opened up a whole new world. While travelling, players need accommodation, and that's where Simply Sport stepped in. They connected Mrida with Oyo, who agreed to provide free stay to the girls.

"What I appreciate is that Simply Sport does not have its own agenda," says Priya.

When Mrida asked for a strength and conditioning coach, they arranged for one. Whether it was equipment, physiotherapy or advanced training, Simply Sport was willing to go the distance. A single club actually meant supporting the 50-100 kids under them, making it a pretty large exercise. But a deeply satisfying one.

PAIN POINT

The journey of a startup is about product-market fit. And sometimes you stumble upon it, when least expected.

In Feb 2021, Aditi Mutatkar joined Simply Sport. Aditi began playing badminton at age 9 and went on to become India #2 and a Commonwealth Games silver medallist. After leaving the sport, she studied public policy in the US and returned to India. She joined Simply Sport in February 2021.

"Aditi had lived experience as a female athlete, which led us down a whole new path," says Ankit.

One of the things that had always bothered Aditi as a sportswoman was the silence around periods. It was a completely taboo subject, despite being a natural part of a woman's life. At best, a female athlete might say 'I have a stomach ache' and the coach would not push her on that day.

But there was no deeper understanding of a woman's body, or the effect of the monthly cycle on her performance. This is not surprising, as 97% of coaches in federation-approved academies in India are male. A sportswoman on her period had just two options – power through it, or take a pill.

As she delved deeper, Aditi realised that even the Indian Olympic Association (IOA) had no framework or protocol for a menstruating athlete. In the 2024 Paris Olympics, this may have made all the difference between a medal and 4th position for Indian weightlifter Mirabai Chanu.

In mid-2021, Simply Sport launched an awareness program for coaches, to dispel myths and misinformation around menstruation.

"Only two people logged in to our first online seminar," says Aditi. "It was a disaster!"

But slowly and steadily, the word spread. The program caught the eye of the Sports Authority of India and was made a part of their coaching program.

To reach the grassroots, Simply Sport created handbooks and animated books in multiple languages. Moving to offline mode, the foundation has conducted over 600 workshops, in partnership with Reliance Foundation and Capri, a finance company which owns the women's cricket team UP Warriors.

Although it started small, and faced many obstacles, 'Simply Periods' quietly became the foundation's most successful program. Real, practical, impactful.

STRIVING FOR EXCELLENCE

The third piece in the foundation's mission is the 'Excellence in Sports' program. While the government and Olympic Gold Quest do a great job, Ankit knew that 1-2% of deserving athletes still fall through the cracks. The idea was to give them a fighting chance to make it to the top.

"The program consists of scholarship, leadership and monetary support," says Ankit.

First of all, Simply Sport bears the athlete's education expense, so that they are not tempted to drop out. This may be anywhere from Rs 5-10,000 per month. When it comes to leadership, the mentees receive classroom training in communication, PowerPoint, Excel and finance for beginners.

Lastly, there's financing. The biggest expense for athletes is travelling for tournaments, more so if you are an individual athlete playing badminton, tennis etc. It's important to play these tournaments to improve your game, as well as your ranking. Simply Sport provides the funding, to make this possible.

In addition to all of the above, the foundation has undertaken a fourth initiative to nurture sporting talent : a Badminton Excellence

Academy. The academy is being set up in Bangalore in partnership with Arvind Bhat, who was world number 20 and among India's top three players during his playing days.

The program started in 2023, at a leased facility. However, Simply Sport's own state-of-the-art infrastructure is in the last stages of construction. It is a significant physical investment, with 8 badminton courts, a gym, yoga and recovery room, as well accommodation for 50 kids.

Ankit was inspired by the Centre for Sports Excellence in Bangalore, a massive project which houses Prakash Padukone's academy, among others. With existing training facilities for badminton doing a fine job, would yet another academy make a difference? You have to see the proteges of Simply Sport to get your answer.

Saneeth D.S., India's no 1 singles player is one such name. A Kannada boy, the foundation has been supporting him since 2021, even before its own academy came into existence. Additionally, two girls are in the world's top 50 and two boys in the top 150.

"At least one of them can make it to the Olympics in 2028 or 2032," says Ankit.

The dream is to expand, to repeat the formula with one or two other sports in the near future. For who knows, what is truly possible?

INCREDIBLE IMPACT

In five short years of existence, Simply Sport has defined a unique mission, and delivered on its promises. 'Simply Periods' is an outstanding success, it has educated over 7000 coaches and is even the official partner for various sports leagues. Female athletes now aim for peak performance, no matter what time of the month it may be.

"At the grassroots, our goal is that girls should not give up playing sports when they reach puberty," says Aditi.

To this end, the foundation constantly runs workshops in the hinterland, through its network of volunteers. The Bihar government, in particular, has been very receptive.

The grassroots program is now called 'Simply Grants'. Over 100 sporting foundations and clubs applied in 2024-25, of which 12 were selected. 6 people from this ecosystem played at the annual Khelo India Games, 5 represented India at the last Asian Games. And the numbers are only growing.

Tejaswini, a class 10 tribal girl nurtured by Mrida Foundation has become a star whom football clubs are vying for. Sandhya, from Siliguri, became the national captain for women's rugby and is now the national coach. Suraj from Jungle Crows went to the UK for his Master's and is now CEO of Paddle Park, a global brand setting up operations in India.

No matter what the level of achievement, sports brings tangible benefits.

"Had I not been playing, I would have been married off at 16," said one regional athlete.

Sports also builds character – discipline, focus and performance become second nature. The trouble is that many athletes do not complete their formal education, which makes it difficult for them to find employment once they quit sports. What's more, they lack fluency in English, which is a must in almost any career.

Hence Simply Sport embarked on a very large English-speaking program for athletes across the country. When it began online, there was good traction. However, over time, it did not scale. Now, the foundation runs localised classes with a physical teacher, based on demand.

Initially, job placements were ad-hoc, now Simply Sport approaches companies to understand their requirements and creates a funnel accordingly.

For example, Godrej has signed up to hire field sales staff, in particular women. The USP of hiring sportswomen is simple.

"They are physically fit, and have no problem travelling to remote places!" says Aditi.

As for Simply Periods, it has been a runaway success and may even be spun off into an independent NGO, dealing with all kinds of women-specific health issues eg PCOS.

All good but working the world of sports comes with its own challenges. Identifying athletes and supporting them is not enough, you have to keep them motivated. Three bad tournaments and an athlete may say - I give up. And with that, years of effort goes down the drain.

Another learning is that you have to take the coach into the loop, assure them that you won't be replaced. This is time-consuming and requires tact but can't be escaped.

MANAGING IT ALL

Simply Sport is run by a small core team of 12 people, with about 30 paid volunteers conducting period training. The badminton academy is managed by a 12-person team.

Ankit spends three hours every Saturday to review progress while Kanika devotes an entire day of her week to the work of the foundation.

"So, she is the port of call when the team needs anything," says Ankit.

While Kanika always supported Ankit's vision, initially, she did not have the same passion for sports that he did. However, as she travelled with him across the country, meeting boys and girls who'd given it their all, Kanika developed awe and admiration for the sporting life.

The majority of grassroots athletes cannot afford to have milk, let alone badaam, or chicken. They spend 8-10 hours a day playing rugby, or cricket, or football, with no guarantee of success in their field and, no education to fall back on. Yet, at home they are told - beta, pursue your dream, we are with you.

"As a mother, I am amazed by how parents allow it!" says Kanika.

Apart from guiding the Simply Sport team as and when required, Kanika has taken up the issue of mental health. Athletes face enormous levels of stress and anxiety, which affects their performance and can even lead to depression. This is something the sporting ecosystem needs to be mindful of.

With the help of 'Live, Love, Laugh' foundation, Kanika conceptualised a program called 'Simply Smiles' to educate coaches. What are the warning signs, when should one intervene, and what should be the course of action – these are the core concerns. There is also a helpline number the coach can reach out to.

"If you don't make it in sports we want you to be ready for the world."

As a mom, Kanika is conscious of the fact that their son Kiaan is growing up in a bubble. As a budding badminton player, Kiaan knows that sports requires grit, guts, and gumption. But Kanika also makes sure he is aware of the other challenges that Simply Sport's grassroots athletes face.

"Always be grateful, we tell him. You've got so much, make the most of it."

At the very start, Ankit and Kanika set aside a significant portion of their personal wealth to create an endowment fund that covered the foundation's annual costs (approximately Rs 4 crore). There was no external funding. In year three, Ankit organised a dinner for friends and well-wishers where he showcased the work of Simply Sport.

"Yaar, when did you start? We had no idea you've been doing all this!" was the reaction.

Some of them wanted to contribute, either in their personal capacity or as a CSR activity.

In 2024, Simply Sport raised a crore of rupees from 'friends of Ankit'. Apart from the money itself, that meant more people talking about sports at the grassroots, giving the cause visibility and connects.

In 2025-26, Simply Sport will spend Rs 5 crore on program cost, and Rs 5 crore on building infrastructure for the badminton academy. Ankit is also in talks with IIT Guwahati to upgrade their sports infrastructure and his former hostel Kapili. And he's willing to put his money where his heart is.

Having signed the Giving Pledge at age 37, Ankit truly espouses the idea of starting early.

"The way I see it, by the time I'm old, I should have given away 25% of my wealth."

With Curefoods also scaling, Ankit Nagori will soon have a happy problem on his hands – how to increase his philanthropy manifold. He believes that India can learn much from countries where sports is the primary culture. Citizens are more resilient, more tough - ready to face anything they encounter in life.

"Our mid-term mission is to enable 100,000 people," says Ankit. "And then a million."

Kyunki khel ke maidan mein jo awwal aayega
Jeevan ke maidan mein bhi safalta payega.

For more on Simply Sport Foundation scan:

ADVICE TO YOUNG PHILANTHROPISTS

Most people think, I will do it later. But it's never too early to set up a foundation. Put a sum of money aside, so that you can't use it. Once you do that, you will need to find a cause that you're really passionate about. Then it is not an obligation, it becomes fun. Like, when I meet athletes, I feel so proud.

Had I started later in life I would have had more money but more money doesn't equate to more impact. Thousands of girls and boys are benefitting from our work in the here and now and not in the distant future.

Be smart about how you give and remember, spending time is much tougher than giving money.

"Money without a purpose is just a piece of paper."

Skill Pill

PRAMOD BHASIN

Founder, Genpact and Chairman, ICRIER

His first philanthropic venture may have failed but it helped Pramod Bhasin understand the 'aam aadmi of India'. He's now working with J-PAL to make public spaces safer.

Pramod Bhasin was born in Sindri, Bihar in a middle class family. At the time, his father worked with the Fertilizer Corporation of India. Later, Satya Dev Bhasin moved to the multinational ICI, and the family lived comfortably, in a large house, with a car and driver, and club membership.

"But the truth is, we never had much money – back then salary was in the form of perks."

Growing up, Pramod watched his father not only do justice to his corporate job but actively work for society. As a devout Arya Samaji, Satya Dev volunteered for various activities, from seva in the mandir to dispensing medicine to the poor.

In his late teens, Pramod went to London to do Chartered Accountancy with two pounds in his pocket. But the lad survived, and thrived. Pramod went on to work with GE in America, where he got exposed to the idea of giving. Not when you become rich and have 'retired' but right here, right now.

In 1994, CEO Jack Welch sent Pramod Bhasin to India to set up GE Capital. RBI put a spanner in the works but it proved to be a blessing in disguise. What started as an experimental pilot project went on to pioneer the BPO industry in India, and globally. This business would split from GE to become Genpact. In August 2007, Genpact was listed on the NYSE, creating significant wealth for shareholders. That's when it hit Pramod.

"I have more money than I will ever need, what do I do with it?"

Pramod knew that he did not want to start another business for the sake of making money – it had to have a higher purpose.

In 2013, Pramod exited Genpact. He teamed up with Pia Singh from DLF, to launch an ambitious non-profit in a space he knew well. With a small, handpicked team 'Skills Academy' set a target of skilling five million people over the next 10 years.

The plan looked great on paper. But corporate India and 'real India' are very different. What works in Gurgaon does not work in Ganjam. This may seem obvious in hindsight but it's an important lesson for anyone entering the world of philanthropy.

"Skill India was a complete failure," admits Pramod. "It basically turned everything I knew on its head."

So why is a non-profit that does not exist today included in this book? Because, we all learn from our mistakes. Thank you, Pramod, for being brutally honest and reflective.

A little poorer and lot wiser, Pramod Bhasin remains as committed as ever. To use his time and money to make this world a little kinder. A little happier.

To be remembered as someone who cared
Who tried and failed but dreamed and dared.

Sacred fire crackled in the havankund, as his parents chanted Vedic mantras. A six-year-old boy sat mesmerised, with samagri in his palms.

"Om svaha, svaha, svaha," they all chanted.

A plume of smoke arose, as all gathered around the fire poured their offerings. This was a weekly Arya Samaj havan at home, which Pramod looked forward to. Like many Punjabi families, the Bhasins had embraced the popular reformist movement led by Swami Dayanand Saraswati. Established in 1875, 'Arya Samaj', quite literally, means a community of people with high moral character.

Pramod's father certainly lived upto that description. He spent his free time doing seva, which included running a charitable pharmacy at the local Arya Samaj mandir. Satya Dev Bhasin derived as much or even more joy from this work, as he did from the job that paid him money. And that left a lasting impression on young Pramod.

Growing up, he was always conscious that 'I am lucky to be born where I was'. Being from a well-to-do family did not mean you showed off your wealth, you still lived frugally. So when Pramod was paid a pittance in London as an article clerk, it was okay. He lived on 10 pounds a week and loved it.

"I was impressed not by money but by those who had achieved a lot in their profession."

Pramod's mamaji was the famous Supreme Court Judge Hans Raj Khanna, who gave a judgement against Indira Gandhi during the Emergency. The Bhasins had friends from all walks of life – artists, authors and civil services. So the aspiration was not to pursue a career which was highly paid.

Having joined the world of business, Pramod Bhasin was not very ambitious initially. That changed when he moved from London to the US to work with GE, a company led by the brutally performance-driven Jack Welch. Ironically, it was here that Pramod also discovered a softer side of corporate America. The side that believes in 'giving back'.

United Way had pioneered a simple fundraising program in companies across America – salary deduction. An employee could pick a charity to donate a fixed sum, say $100, each month. The employer would match this amount. Easy to implement and effective in raising large sums, the effort also galvanised the entire organisation.

There was competition amongst various divisions of GE – 'let's see who can raise the most'! Everyone was strongly encouraged to participate. A little too strongly, thought Pramod. He observed the enthusiasm of his colleagues but remained unmoved. Until one fine day, the boss noticed one name was missing from the list.

He came to Pramod's desk and asked, "Why won't you give?"

When confronted like that, there was no good answer. So, Pramod did start contributing. Some of his all-American God-fearing colleagues gave away 10% of their salary.

"I wasn't giving that much, to be honest..."

But it made Pramod conscious of the 'spirit of giving' which seemed to permeate America. An undercurrent of goodness he'd never seen anywhere. Not in India. Not in the UK. It wasn't just the rich but ordinary people giving freely. The wealthy and not-so-wealthy leaving their savings to charity.

Meanwhile, the young and ambitious Pramod was handpicked by Jack Welch to return to India and set up operations for GE.

Little did he know what he was signing up for...

BEYOND THE BOTTOMLINE

It was a circular by the Reserve Bank of India which changed the trajectory of Pramod Bhasin's life: 'Banks will not lend to non-banking financial companies (NBFCs)', it said.

The decree was like a death sentence for a fledgling GE Capital. Now what, go back to the head office with a sorry face? Nah. There must be some alternative.

Necessity is the mother of invention. Back then GE Capital India had its back office in Chennai. While visiting the city, Pramod had a lightbulb moment. If GE Capital can be headquartered in Delhi but run its operations from Chennai, why can't a GE company anywhere in the world do the same?

Today, outsourcing is a widely accepted business practice. Back in 1997, it was a bewildering proposition. Nevertheless, Pramod convinced GE Capital to sanction two million dollars for this one-of-a-kind experiment. And GECIS (GE Capital International Services) was born.

Anju Talwar was the third employee of GECIS and an integral part of the founding team. She recalls going to 'sell' the idea to GE business units in small town America.

"Oh, you're from India," they said. "Do you use PCs there?"

It took time but once GE units warmed up to outsourcing their back office operations, there was no looking back. By 2005, GECIS was an unqualified success story and was spun off into an independent entity which would also serve non-GE customers. At this time GECIS was renamed as Genpact (Generating Business Impact).

On August 2, 2007, Genpact got listed on the New York Stock Exchange. At that time it had 26,500 employees in 9 countries.

Standing at the very top of the summit you feel the euphoria of achievement. It is also a moment of truth. On the floor of the NYSE, a reporter from NDTV asked Pramod a question.

"What are you going to do with this money?"

"That was an inflection point for me... I reflected on how valueless money is, just sitting in my bank account."

Pramod would continue as CEO of Genpact for another 4 years. But something inside him had changed. He would one day move on... but to do what? Starting another business did not excite Pramod in the least.

Whatever he chose to do, it had to have some purpose.

On reflection, Pramod realised that his greatest achievement at Genpact was not its valuation, but the value it had added to the lives of others. The thousands of people from small town India who had been skilled, whose lives had dramatically changed. In particular, young women who got their first taste of freedom.

What if such skills could be made available to young people across India?

KUCH KARTE HAIN

It was Christmas 2011, a slow time of year, when Anju Talwar asked Pramod, "What will you do, after Genpact?"

Pramod had just put in his papers, he shared his plan of setting up 'Skill Academy', in partnership with Pia Singh from the DLF family. Anju was intrigued. She had just lost her mother-in-law after a long battle with cancer while her son had gone off to college.

"I was at a stage where a corporate job didn't excite me anymore... I wanted to give back to the community."

Anju Talwar joined Skill Academy as its CEO on April 1, 2012. There were 3 other team members – all of them Young India fellows in their early 20s - along with Saipriya Sarangan, who had worked for McKinsey.

On Day 1, they sat in a tiny office inside Genpact, and talked about 'mission' and 'vision'.

To skill youth – age 18-25 – and place them in jobs. How many? Five million in five years.

"We had good intentions but no understanding of 'real India'."

"Whatever I do, I must do it at scale. There's no point doing little things."

15 days later, Anju found herself in the chaotic bylanes of Kurla, getting her first exposure to that reality. Rows of tiny windowless houses, with life spilling onto the gullies and gutters, brought them to the doorstep of Vandana Foundation. An NGO set up by former Mumbai Police Commissioner Anami Roy. It was the team's first 'field visit'.

Back then, Vandana Foundation ran a microfinance program in Mumbai's slums. Through their network, Anju and her team invited low income youth to a round table. To 'understand the market'. Clearly, office jobs were the most in demand, so Skill Academy rented a space to conduct a pilot program in the BPO and banking space.

The pilot was extremely successful. One of the boys – Vinod* - even got placed with HDFC Bank at a salary of Rs 18,000 per month. But he refused to join. Anju was shocked. In Delhi, Genpact was hiring entry level employees at Rs 12,000 per month. Why wouldn't a young man who was just 12th pass jump at a job paying 1.5x?

Well, Vinod explained why the job made no sense to him. First of all, he would spend 2-3k a month on travelling to the office. The company would also deduct PF.

"Mereko nahin parwadega," he shrugged. As per back-of-the-envelope calculations, Vinod would make less than what he earned as an electrician, tax-free. Well, Vinod was probably an outlier. A bit rattled but nevertheless gung-ho, Skill Academy decided to expand its program to the hinterland.

But their troubles were just beginning...

WHAT YOUNG INDIA WANTS

It was a scorching summer day. Under a makeshift tent in a village in coastal Andhra Pradesh, Sudhir Marisetty addressed a group of boys and girls in their late teens.

"Do our course and you will get a good job in Hyderabad," he promised.

Coming from a small town called Tadepalli in West Godavari district, Sudhir knew a bit about aspiration. Few got the kind of opportunities he had – studying at BITS Pilani and with the Young India Fellowship at Ashoka University. Impressed by a guest lecture Pramod Bhasin had given during the fellowship, Sudhir had jumped at a chance to work with him.

"I knew that it would be a great learning opportunity."

In Andhra Pradesh, Pramod used his connect with the founders of SKS Microfinance, to help Skill India enter remote villages. By then, microfinance was in doldrums in AP, due to government regulation.

SKS still had a large number of people on their rolls with a valuable local network. So, the tie-up was a win-win for both.

After a good amount of chappal-ghissing, Sudhir launched a 3 month program to prepare 10th and 12th pass students for jobs in retail. Now came the crucial question – were they willing to pay? Because although Skill India was a Section 25 company, Pramod's long term vision was to make it self-sustaining.

Well, the initial batches did shell out Rs 7000 and 70% got the promised jobs. But that was not the end of the story. Within two to three weeks, the joinees started trickling back home.

One young man complained, "They asked me to fold clothes. Chhee – I won't do that!"

He went so far as to say that no one from his caste would take up such a job.

Others complained about having to stand all day, or travel long distances to work. They were simply not used to life in the big city, where they would have to fend for themselves. The dream of working in Hyderabad and the reality of working there were very different, and Skill Academy could not bridge that gap.

Pramod witnessed this disconnect for himself, when he visited an accounting class in Mumbai's Dharavi slum. A roomful of girls, all in burkhas, were diligently taking notes and studying for the upcoming exam. When asked if they were looking forward to taking up jobs, they answered in unison – yes!

Not one of them actually accepted an offer. Why? Because attending classes was 'allowed' by their families. Working was out of the question. So, they would take one course after one other to keep themselves occupied, until they got married. It was yet another bitter truth to swallow.

But the worst was yet to come.

GORMENT MAI BAAP

By 2013, 'skills' had become a buzzword for both the state and central governments. Skill Training Centres were being set up all over the country, promising rozgaar to unemployed youth. What's more, these programs were 'free of cost', making it nearly impossible for Skill Academy to charge a fee.

"Our programs were of much higher quality but no one seemed to care!" sighs Anju.

As the old saying goes, when you can't beat 'em, you join 'em.

Skill Academy decided to start working with the government to deliver programs.

These ranged from English training to analytics, retail and healthcare. At one time, Skill Academy had 300 full-time employees, including teachers in remote areas, with close to 40 physical centres, from Srinagar to Srisailam.

The annual outlay was Rs 5-7 crore, with some payment expected from the government as part of the partnership. However, collecting this money was next to impossible. Send this file, send that file, send proof that they attended class, go and track down where they are working now – the demands were never ending.

"We were spending more time chasing all this than teaching!"

As per rules, a provider got paid only if the student got employed, and stayed employed, for three months. That was always a struggle. On top of that there were unwritten rules. Anju recalls going to a sarkari office where she was told – apne kisi aadmi ko bhejiye.

"Main hi boss hoon, bataiye, kya baat hai," she replied.

The peon shook his head, "Madam aapko nahin bataa sakte. "

The jugaad needed to make files move faster was beyond the bounds of her integrity. But many service providers had no such qualms. In fact, they were hand-in-glove with students. In Bihar, it was common for students to register and not attend a single class. All they wanted was a 'stamp of attendance'.

The 'trainer' simply gave the student a % of the sarkari paisa he received.Such practices drove Skill Academy to despair. In meeting after meeting, the issues were discussed but no solution could be found.

"The entire ecosystem was taking advantage of the money the government was pumping into skilling," says Anju, who was getting increasingly disenchanted.

However, she continued to try and make it work. As any management textbook will tell you, an organisation must focus on its core competence. Hence Skill Academy doubled down on training in BPO and financial services, a domain where the team had the experience and connects for placement.

However, not all employers were favourably inclined. Anju recalls waiting for hours to meet the CEO of a well-known Indian company. She had gone with a reference and an appointment, yet the CEO did not show up. This happened not once but on two separate occasions. Leaving Anju wondering what she had signed up for...

Pramod had a similar experience. When he proposed that the industry pay a little extra to jobseekers who came with a training certificate, there were no takers.

"I realised that small and midsize business owners are not good employers," rues Pramod.

In India, it is okay to employ workers on contract, deduct the cost of uniform from salaries, and wash your hands off anyone who may fall ill. The aam aadmi has little faith in the private sector.

This was validated by a study commissioned by Skill Academy, conducted by J-PAL, the Jamal Poverty Action Lab at MIT.

'Demand for a government jobs is 4X that of the private sector,' stated the JPAL report. So, you skilled someone and gave a job placement but, in their mind, it was a temporary position.

They would keep appearing for various exams on the side.

The quest for a sarkaari naukri continued as long as they were eligible (upto age 28). Only after that, did the candidate view a job in the private sector seriously.

NEW FRONTIERS

After three years of valiant effort, Anju Talwar put in her papers. She had joined thinking that this would be her second career. But things had just not played out that way.

There was also a fundamental difference of opinion. Having travelled to remote corners of Orissa, UP, Bihar and Maharashtra, Anju was convinced about one thing: people will not pay for skilling. Firstly, the majority lacked ability to pay. And secondly, the government was offering free schemes.

"I feel that if we had operated as a pure NGO our approach – and our outcome - would have been different," says Anju.

The parting was amicable and Skill Academy continued operations, even after the entire founding team exited. However, in 2017, Pramod Bhasin and Pia Singh finally bit the bullet. Together they had sunk over Rs 25 crore into the venture, which pretty much had to be written off.

And what of the psychological blow ? To be at the very top of your game and then stumble into that pit called 'failure'. It could not have been easy for Pramod.

But ever pragmatic, he says, "This was my re-education... it taught me to think about solutions far more deeply than what is obvious."

Pramod now directed more of his time and energy towards Asha Impact. Co-founded with Vikram Gandhi, Asha Impact helped pioneer a new kind of investing. The focus was on ventures solving issues unique to India and relevant to the masses. The criteria for investment centred on companies catering to the lower end of the pyramid.

For example, Vastu, a company in the business of affordable housing. Its founder, Sandeep Menon, had worked at GE Capital in a junior capacity. At a time when few believed it could be a viable business, Pramod Bhasin was willing to place a bet – that mortgages with a ticket size of Rs 10-50 lakh would find takers in small-town India.

"Pramod believed in me, and in our investment thesis!" says a grateful Sandeep Menon.

Similarly, there was Varthana, which gave small-ticket loans to parents who wished to send their kids to private schools. Another fruitful investment was in TruMeds, which sells generic drugs in tier 3 and 4 towns.

As they operate in nascent markets, these companies face unique challenges, as well.

"To be honest, it's a whole different game from a regular investment," says Pramod.

With Vastu, the entire supply chain had to be built from scratch. Who are the developers? How do you assess the customer?

It was indeed far more satisfying for Pramod to grapple with such issues, as a board member of a company like this. But it took effort to stay focused on the objective of Asha Impact – and not get swayed by more lucrative opportunities.

Today, Vastu is a leading player in affordable housing, with assets of Rs 6000 crore. As far as Pramod is concerned, the returns are not just financial – because of Vastu, thousands of families now have a roof over their heads.

KEEPING COMMITMENTS

After shutting down Skill India, Pramod continued to be involved with the social sector, supporting a number of organisations in both donor and advisory roles. Among them were Village Ways, in the area of telehealth, and Vishwas, which works with special needs children.

However, the non-profit he has devoted the most time and energy to is HelpAge, an old and established charity which needed to embrace new ideas. Pramod reached out to Kiran Karnik – whom he knew from NASSCOM – to chair the HelpAge board. Kiran was hesitant, at first.

"I saw that Pramod was deeply committed... that's what persuaded me," he says.

Like most NGOs, HelpAge was dedicated to the cause, but was not very mindful of metrics such as cost, efficiency or impact. For example, in the digital age, they still used only direct mail for fundraising. What's more, HelpAge spent 50% of its funds on administrative costs, which was increasingly becoming an issue for donors.

A small task force headed by Pramod was assigned the task of creating a five year vision.

"One of his major contributions was challenging the team and the board," says Kiran Karnik.

Pramod would make passionate appeals to drop incremental thinking and aim for a 10x difference – in the number of people Helpage reached, as well as the funds it was raising.

"Tell me what you need to make it happen!" he would add.

Things did not change overnight, but over the last five years, HelpAge funding has scaled up its operations significantly. Pramod is happy to have played a role in that. 'American Friends of HelpAge India', the fundraising arm in the US that he helped set up, is also yielding results.

Pramod is also a founder-trustee of Ashoka University, and more recently, Plaksha, which was conceived as a university which would rival any IIT. Built with philanthropic money and time contributed by the eminent people who back it, Plaksha is now in its fifth year, with 500 students, and growing steadily.

Pramod is deeply engaged with the building and landscaping of this campus, which has been consciously designed as a space for mingling and co-creation. Open air classrooms, herb gardens and fruit trees are all part of this plan. In addition, there are art installations spread across the campus, funded by Pramod.

"I want engineering students to be exposed to beauty and aesthetics!" he says.

Despite all these commitments, Pramod continues to harbour a dream. To take up the cause of gender harassment.

"That's going to be, I hope, my single-minded focus for the next five-ten years," he says

At present, he is working with J-PAL to understand 'where the problem starts', and what may be the best way to make an intervention. After extensive surveys in multiple cities, Pramod has decided to focus on gender-based violence. He has set up an NGO called Aparajita, which will provide legal aid to women and make public spaces safer.

Pramod's daughter Sonali and partner Malavika fully support this vision. Before signing 'Living My Promise, a commitment to donate 50% of his wealth, he had a discussion with his daughter. It lasted all of two minutes.

She said, "It's your money. Do what you want with it."

One summer evening, they were standing in a store in New York and Sonali liked something. Pramod offered to buy it.

"Dad, I like it," she said ."I don't need to own everything I like".

Me and mine is an illusion. A grand material delusion.

So, open your heart, open your mind.
Sharing and caring for humankind.

ADVICE TO YOUNG PHILANTHROPISTS

The first thing is, don't assume that what you've learned in the corporate world is what will apply to the social sector. In fact, in most cases, it will be the opposite. You will have to learn, relearn, rethink, because the economics that work in rural India are vastly different from urban India, and I think that learning should happen first.

I recommend that everyone read the book 'Poor Economics' by Abhijit Banerjee and Esther Duflo. It will change your view of India dramatically.

Two, I hope they can find what they love to do, because unless you are willing to devote your time and energy to the cause, it's not going to happen.

Three, think about scale. Too many people do small work, superb work, impacting far too few people. If you create a big company, if you run things, then at least you know scale.

And lastly, I would say, give most of your money away. Your lifestyle isn't about to change. So don't give money in the bank greater value than it deserves.

"If you have earned wealth, it is your duty to use it to uplift others."

A Life of Purpose

HARSH MARIWALA

Mariwala Health Initiative, ASCENT and Marico Innovation Foundation

He believes in active giving in the areas he is passionate about – innovation, entrepreneurship and mental health.

Harsh Mariwala was born into a thriving business family which made its fortune trading spices. Looking at his birth chart, an astrologer predicted 'great success' for the child. This expectation, however, was a great burden. He grew up to be shy, underconfident and unsure of himself.

"Then, after graduation I wanted to go to the US for an MBA... my father said 'no'."

However, this turned out to be a blessing in disguise. At age 20, Harsh joined the family business and began learning 'by the seat of his pants'. He absorbed how things were done, and aspired for more.

In April 1990, the consumer products business was demerged from the parent company, leading to formation of Marico, an FMCG business run by professionals.

Influenced by the work of Raj Sisodia and Prof Jagdish Sheth, Harsh Mariwala embraced a new journey. The purpose of Marico was more than making profit, it was to make a difference. Thus, in 2003, he set up the Marico Innovation Foundation, to identify and help scale up innovative organizations.

This was a radical departure from the tried and tested model of establishing a charitable trust or a school or hospital - which was how business families 'gave back to society'. The Mariwala Trust, for example, gave interest-free loans to deserving students. But this was not enough, as far as Harsh was concerned.

He wanted to be an active giver, in an area he was passionate about. And what could be closer to his heart, than innovation and entrepreneurship? This journey began in 2004 with the Marico Innovation Foundation and continued with ASCENT Foundation, whose goal is to help small and medium entrepreneurs learn from each other and scale up.

Over the years, ASCENT has become a community of 1200 entrepreneurs, representing businesses with a combined turnover of over Rs. 1 lakh+ crore. This initiative goes beyond money, it involves a significant amount of personal time and active advisory by Harsh Mariwala himself.

In 2015, when he stepped down as Managing Director, Harsh also took up a completely new cause – mental health. The Mariwala Health Initiative (MHI) was set up, with the goal of making mental health accessible to everyone.

For Harsh Mariwala, Corporate Social Responsibility is fine. But Personal Social Responsibility matters, as well. The astrologer was right when he predicted 'great success' for the new born baby of the Mariwala family.

"Success is just a means, not an end," believes Harsh.

Multiply your profits manifold.
Let the giving story unfold.
Ambitious, audacious, bold.

Once upon a time, coconut oil was sold in tin cans. A young man who had just joined his family business wondered, is a more aesthetic, user-friendly packaging not possible?

"No, no, don't launch plastic bottles," said the kiranawalas.

Another company had tried it and rats had chewed off the edges, resulting in a leaky mess. Now any other entrepreneur might have taken this well-meaning advice and stuck to tin. Not Harsh Mariwala. The team studied the problem in minute detail until there was a 'eureka' moment.

For two nights, they tested the new design. Bottles of oil were kept inside a cage, and observed by a closed circuit camera. The rats came, they tried and they failed. What had changed? The first set of bottles were square, the new ones were round. It was a simple innovation but one which altered the packaging landscape of FMCG back in the '70s.

Harsh Mariwala firmly believed in questioning conventional wisdom. Marico was built on the back of product innovation, as well as business model innovation. But very few Indian companies were willing to take a leap of faith and bet on new ideas. Could this mindset be changed?

That was the ambition with which Harsh Mariwala started his first non-profit, the Marico Innovation Foundation (MIF). Set up in 2003, the foundation was helmed by the eminent Dr R A Mashelkar, who at that time was heading the Council for Scientific and Industrial Research (CSIR).

"Innovation was not on the agenda of CEOs," recalls Harsh.

Indeed, even the press did not show up to cover the launch of the foundation. For the next 3 years, MIF conducted workshops and undertook research. However, in 2006, the foundation launched the Marico Innovation Awards, given once in two years, to recognise business, social and public service gamechangers.

In the year 2012, the foundation received 437 entries and selected 8 winners. Among them, Red Bus (in the business category), Akshaya Patra (social sector) and UIDAI (global gamechanger). The entries were judged on the magnitude of impact the innovation had made.

There were also several 'out of the box' ideas - from an ingenious way to recharge depleted bore wells, to a nano-technology model to provide clean water to the poor. However, they had not been able to make real world impact. This is when Harsh Mariwala had a realisation: innovators need help to scale.

This led to the launch of a Social Innovation Acceleration Program, which provided strategic support over an 18-24 month period to organisations with innovative social enterprise models.

For example, Akshaya Patra shifted from a centralised kitchen model to a 'hub and spoke' model. Increasing its ability to serve mid-day meals to schools.

However, the journey had just begun...

DON'T GIVE UP

If innovation is hard, so is entrepreneurship. A long and lonely journey, which Harsh Mariwala had experienced himself.

"The journey from small to medium, and medium to large is where most stumble!"

By 2012, there was a lot of buzz around startups. But Harsh decided to focus on small and medium enterprises (SMBs) with a proven business model. A segment which had no support from the ecosystem. The aim of this initiative - called ASCENT – was to help SMBs grow through the power of peer networks.

Every small business owner is caught up in deliverables and targets, with little opportunity for learning or reflection. So, ASCENT was designed around the novel idea of 'trust groups'. 10 non-competing business owners would meet on a regular basis, share their pain, their problems. And give each other support, strength and advice.

"You come into this world with nothing, you leave with nothing."

In the initial phase, ASCENT had only a Mumbai chapter with three trust groups for product companies and three for those in the service business. The groups were also based on the size of the companies eg those under 1 crore, 10 crore and 20 crore annual turnover. As they would be facing similar sets of issues.

In addition, ASCENT would provide mentoring and coaching through workshops, as well as an annual conclave with eminent speakers. While there would be a dedicated team to run the program, that cost was borne by Harsh Mariwala.

An early iteration of ASCENT was focussed on women entrepreneurs. However, the pool of applicants was too small and the program was widened to include men as well. A majority of these entrepreneurs had no IIT-IIM or business family pedigree. But the hunger to succeed was high, and that's what ASCENT was looking for.

Take the case of Prateek Kumar from Ranchi, who came to Mumbai to study at IHM, Dadar but got disillusioned by the hotel industry and joined an event management firm. Seeing the future of marketing in the digital space, he started his own firm in 2011. Like any small business, it went through its shares of trials and tribulations.

When he joined ASCENT, he was a bit skeptical — could this trust group thing really work? His group met on the first Saturday of every month and the process was facilitated by guiding principles. It proved to be invaluable.

As members opened up and shared freely, each one realised 'I am not alone in this journey'.

From the art of negotiation, to the importance of training, Prateek Kumar's eyes were opened to a whole new world. ASCENT members also got opportunities to directly interact with Harsh Mariwala but those had to be earned, by being an active member of the community.

"I was amazed by his simplicity. Ask for an honest opinion, he will give it," says Prateek.

Harsh Mariwala dedicated 20% of his time to ASCENT, much of it in one-on-one mentoring sessions. Helping others grow was his new mission, and it was immensely satisfying.

MENTAL HEALTH MATTERS

In 2014, Harsh Mariwala stepped down as Managing Director, handing over the reins of Marico to professionals. His focus now would now be on philanthropic activity. Mental health was an area that the next generation in the family was passionate about. It was clearly a large problem, but mostly ignored.

"I was drawn to do something in this area because it could have a large impact," says Harsh.

The societal and financial stress of poor mental health devastated families, employers and the health system as a whole. Here was a chance to do pioneering work.

The starting point was exploration – meeting various stakeholders, understanding the ground realities and existing challenges. Were there significant gaps, was there potential for innovation? This insight exercise revealed that the greatest need was in the most vulnerable communities. That became MHI's starting point.

Now, if the goal is to improve the availability and quality of mental health services to marginalised communities, what needs to be done? Harsh decided that it would be best to give grants to existing organisations who were doing good work.

"I don't believe in passive donations. I believe in active giving."

The first such grant was given to Initiating Concern for All (iCALL) in 2015 — a helpline staffed by trained psychologists housed at Tata Institute of Social Sciences, Mumbai. Anyone in distress could phone in and speak to a skilled counsellor, free of cost. Callers could remain anonymous, and could count on confidentiality and consistent support.

The demand for this service was so high that iCALL had to recruit staff who could speak in multiple languages. With calls coming from all over India. In a country where going to a psychiatrist is seen as a sign of 'paagalpan', this service addressed a crucial need gap. The empathetic ear of iCALL counsellors was a turning point for many in distress.

"When I hear that I feel wow, we have done something which is substantial!" says Harsh.

In 2016, Mariwala Health Initiative (MHI) was formally launched, with the mandate of funding innovative mental health initiatives. With diversity and inclusion at the forefront, MHI grew its grant-making portfolio. Among the NGOs that MHI supported was Anubhuti, set up in 2016 to work in rural, peri-urban and urban areas.

Founder Deepa Pawar belongs to the Ghisadi Gadiya Lohar community, one of the many Nomadic/ Denotified Tribes that her organisation works with. Growing up in a tent on the outskirts of a Mumbai slum, Deepa had experienced the struggle of being a nomadic girl, young woman, young mother and mental health survivor.

"Our priority has been to scale further into the grassroot – rather than scale-up only in numbers," says Deepa.

Working with fledgling organisations brought with it an important learning – the need to build their capacity. And this was something that went beyond funding. For example MHI, along with Marico's IT team, helped iCALL scale up their technology. In addition, Harsh Mariwala used his personal network to promote their work.

With an empathetic approach MHI was indeed able to establish its credentials, as a thoughtful, mindful and heartful leader.

TAKING IT FURTHER

In 2018, Priti Sridhar heard that MHI was looking for a CEO and applied for the job. A career banker, she had volunteered with several NGOs. Although Priti's CV lacked the necessary experience, the selection process did not discriminate. She was given a case study, followed up by a preliminary interview.

"What is marginalisation?"

"I don't know," responded Priti.

"What is intersectionality?"

"I don't know...!"

"What is feminism?"

Priti did answer that, but coming from a corporate background, it was – she later realised - an incomplete and elitist view. Nevertheless, she was invited for a second interview, this time with Harsh Mariwala. His questions were more about Priti's own aspirations. What would she like to do at MHI?

"I want to work in the area of tribal health," she responded.

Although there were more qualified candidates, Harsh Mariwala chose Priti Sridhar for the job. She was practical, and willing to absorb new ideas. On her very first day at MHI, Priti learnt the difference between equity and equality. It challenged the idea of merit which had been so crucial during her corporate career.

Priti's first field visit was to an urban basti, where she observed 'street corner conversations' conducted by a community worker. The NGO was Bapu Trust, who believe that mental health is not a stand-alone condition. It is also connected with nutrition, physical health, and economic deprivation.

So, for example, if water is an issue, a Bapu worker will initiate a conversation around that and try to help the community find a solution. This connect ensures that cases of schizophrenia, depression, bipolar disorder and so on, get reported and treated. The community worker will also support and counsel the caregivers.

"Talking to partners helped me understand their challenges. And that enabled us to fund the next level of work," says Priti.

"Respect, making a difference, and helping others- that's what truly matters in life."

Over time, MHI learnt that the same problem could be tackled in multiple ways, and it also depended on external factors. For example, DLR Prerna in Darjeeling and Burans in Uttarakhand work in the hills, where there is significant outward migration. Hence, their approach is different from that of an NGO in the plains.

Unlike many grant-making organisations, which rely on personal and social connects to attract fundees, MHI created a website inviting applications. There was no strict format, so organizations did not need to spend large amounts of time and energy on proposals and reporting.

Instead, the ask was a concept note. It could be in the form of an email, an attachment, or a brochure. MHI would speak to the founder, understand their model and if it appealed, there would be a field visit. In this manner, between 2018-2020, the number of grantees expanded from 6 to 15.

However during Covid, MHI decided to do away with field visits. If the vision and mission resonated, the NGO would be asked to submit a detailed proposal and budget number. After that, money would be disbursed. Although Covid ended, this is the process that MHI still follows.

BEYOND NUMBERS

Ratnaboli Ray vividly recalls her first meeting with Harsh Mariwala. She was ushered into a room with a huge conference table which had bowls of cashews, almonds and raisins. A tall gentleman in a green shirt entered, said hello and offered a glass of kokum juice. Ratnaboli was so nervous that she didn't have the heart to drink it.

"I made a presentation to the best of my ability but I knew it had not gone well."

As founder of the NGO Anjali, Ratnaboli had been working in the field of mental health since 2001. But she had never made a formal pitch, or been asked about 'unit cost'. Despite poor performance, Ratnaboli was asked to rework her proposal and pitch again.

The revised presentation was satisfactory and the NGO got funded. In subsequent meetings, 'unit costs' were never brought up. Over time, MHI had learnt that in the social sector, numbers can be interpreted in multiple ways.

For example, Anjali operates in six geographical areas in Bengal, each municipality has 35 wards, each ward has 7-15,000 people. One way to show impact is to say, our jan manas karmis (community mental health workers) did 100 awareness camps which reached 50,000 people. Another metric may be – 'we transformed 10 lives'.

Which one has more and deeper impact? MHI looks at these questions but doesn't claim to have all the answers. Incidentally, if any NGO that it supports is keen to do a formal impact assessment, MHI will fund it. But it is not some holy grail that every grant receiver must chase.

"Even when exiting, it is all planned, they don't leave you in the lurch," adds Ratnaboli.

Indeed, two years before MHI ceases supporting an organisation, it builds a runway. Introductions are made to other grant-giving philanthropists, with the assurance that this NGO has been vetted. This referral is worth its weight in gold. In fact, just MHI's presence has made it easier for mental health NGOs to be heard, and taken seriously.

In its annual report, MHI shares its findings, in the context of working with marginalised communities and its ongoing studies in the area of suicide prevention. Advocacy is an ongoing activity. From writing in journals to sending briefs for policymakers, MHI is constantly challenging the dominant narrative.

Day to day operations, however, are left to the CEO, who is given a completely free hand. You can try something, and fail. Harsh Mariwala will only ask – 'what did you learn from this'? When you present a budget he will discuss, he will pose questions but after that, the subject is closed.

"We don't have a funding cycle. If I need more money, I simply have to ask," says Priti.

In fact, until FY '24, MHI never managed to spend its annual allocation. Harsh always pushed them 'to do more'.

"If there was no limit at all, how much work would you fund?" he asked, in a meeting.

Because you have to dream it before you do it. So, dream big!

THE TRINITY

Today, all three philanthropic entities are thriving. The Mariwala Health Initiative (MHI) is supporting more than 75 partners across India. The amount of funding to an organisation ranges from Rs 10 lakhs to Rs 3 crore per year, spread over multiple years. The work is managed by a 15 member team working full time.

> *"MHI looks at intersections with climate, caste, class, sexuality and gender."*
>
> *- Ratnaboli Ray, founder, Anjali*

ASCENT has completed a decade and is going great guns. A 96 member team supports over 1200 entrepreneurs with a collective turnover of Rs 1 lakh crore.

"We plan to go pan-India and support 10,000 entrepreneurs."

The ever-energetic Harsh Mariwala will personally mentor 30 of these founders, purely as philanthropy. The investment arm of the Mariwala family – Sharrp Ventures – is run by son Rishabh Mariwala and kept at arm's length from ASCENT, so that there is no vested interest.

The oldest initiative – Marico Innovation Foundation (MIF) – has awarded 70 innovations, and helped scale more than 30 of them. One of the MIF's other significant initiatives has been in the area of plastic recycling and replacement.

In partnership with the Indian Institute of Science (IISc), MIF identified 15 innovative organisations,

One of them has developed a high-speed AI-powered machine which can segregate six tonnes of plastic waste per hour. MIF is helping this company set up a prototype plant in one city, with the goal of creating a circular economy. If this experiment succeeds, it will be rolled out in 15 cities with the help of NITI Aayog.

While his daughter-in-law Priyanjali looks after the pan-India growth of ASCENT, the rest of Harsh Mariwala's family is not actively involved in decision-making. However, they support his philanthropic vision wholeheartedly, and are proud of all that these efforts have achieved.

"Nothing that I achieved in business has given me as much joy as philanthropy," says Harsh.

The art of living. The joy of giving.
Nourish it, cherish it, relish it.

For more on Mariwala Health Initiative scan:

ADVICE TO YOUNG PHILANTHROPISTS

The key thing is do you want to do active giving or do you want to do passive giving? If it's passive giving you have to identify the right organization and give them money.

If it's active giving that's a different story. My approach is - can I give something back in an area where I can be a pioneer, a thought leader.

It's different than corporate social responsibility, which is also good, but personal social responsibility is something that goes beyond that.

I am against putting in a lot of money on hardware. I am more a person who wants to do catalytic giving, by providing the right inputs. So be a catalyser rather than create a school or hospital eg if I can help people lead the right lifestyle, a lot of people will not need to go to hospital in the first place.

"Use your skills to direct systemic change."

Let's Get Digital

RIZWAN AND REKHA KOITA

Koita Foundation

This IIT Bombay couple believes in clear thinking and strong implementation. Digital healthcare and digital transformation of NGOs is their focus.

As a child, Rizwan Koita often spent after-school hours in a small clinic at Mohammed Ali Road bearing the name: 'Dr Safia, M.B.B.S., M.D.'. While he was completing his maths homework, his mother examined women in various stages of pregnancy.

Whether the patient could pay or not, didn't matter. No one was ever turned away.

"Looking back, I think, how selflessly my mother served the community," says Rizwan.

Eventually Rizwan chose to become an engineer – like his father. He joined IIT Bombay to pursue a B.Tech. in Electrical Engineering. On a rainy afternoon, at the ticket window of Vikhroli station, Rizwan met Rekha Vardya, a fellow IIT student. She was one of just 15 girls in the 1992 batch; this was their first face-to-face conversation.

Both went on to pursue their Master's in the US, and then returned to India, to be with their ageing parents. Unable to find jobs suited to their engineering qualifications, they entered the emerging field of management consulting. One month after their wedding, Rizwan left McKinsey & Company to start his own venture in 1999.

In 2003, Transworks was acquired by the Aditya Birla Group; Rizwan then started his second venture, CitiusTech, in 2005. This company went on to become a unicorn in 2019 and a global leader in the digital healthcare space. Meanwhile, Rekha opted to explore alternate careers which would make it easier to manage the home front.

By 2016, her kids had grown up, and Rekha felt the urge to do something more. With Rizwan's enthusiastic support, she embarked on a bold new path – enabling the digital transformation of NGOs. Six years later, Rizwan followed suit, stepping down from his leadership role at CitiusTech, to pursue philanthropic work full time.

Both Rekha and Rizwan sit in the same office and work under the common umbrella of Koita Foundation, but their areas of impact are completely different.

Rizwan is working with the government and national healthcare organisations to help drive a digital healthcare ecosystem in India. His rich experience helps in creating robust digital solutions while Rekha uses her consulting expertise to help NGOs become more efficient.

A win-win for all concerned.

"An inner voice guided me in this direction; it felt like God's will for me," says Rekha.

The brightest minds working for the nation

Is the highest form of wealth creation.

It was one of those days when Rekha Koita was feeling stretched in too many directions. A client deadline, an absent maid, a sick infant, an ailing in-law - why did all the problems in the world pile up at once? No matter how much planning one put in, a day had only 24 hours. The world as she knew it, was spinning out of control.

Determined to continue working after her son was born, Rekha had opted for reduced hours. In reality, a five-hour workday always ended up being eight hours – leaving her feeling frazzled.

"I was neither doing justice to my job, nor was I feeling fulfilled as a mother," recalls Rekha.

She could not help wondering – is this really worth it? On the other hand, Rekha had never imagined herself as a stay-at-home mom.

Her father, Dr M. S. Vardya, worked at the Tata Institute of Fundamental Research. A very academic environment, where both boys and girls were encouraged to excel. Getting into IIT Bombay was a goal few teenage girls had – more so, girls from Marwari families. But on the TIFR housing campus, it was the done thing.

So it was only natural for Rekha to appear for the JEE and enter the hallowed halls of IIT Bombay, where she was one of a handful of girls in her batch. Graduating at the top of her class in Metallurgical Engineering, she went on to Carnegie Mellon University for her Master's in Material Science.

"I was passionate about my research in the field of thin film semiconductors," she says.

When Rekha chose to return to India in the late '90s, there were no jobs in her field. The IIT engineer was thus 'recast' into a management consultant. But as a young mother, the role she had once thoroughly enjoyed felt all-consuming. Work-life balance? It was something CEOs talked about, but in practice, not possible.

So, in 2003, when she was expecting a second baby, Rekha bit the bullet and quit consulting. This time will never come back again, she thought. Let me not miss out on Sahil and Samad's childhood. Picking up the boys from school, taking them to the park, cooking the meals they liked – she did it all, and with no regrets.

"Lack of technology hampers an NGO's efficiency, program outcomes and ability to scale."

As they grew older, Rekha felt ready to go back to work but not in consulting. Curious about the social sector, she got associated with Give India, first as a volunteer, and then as a consultant. Working in a non-profit was not easy, given the scarcity of time, talent, and money. Technology? That was almost non-existent.

At Accenture, Rekha had implemented IT solutions for so many clients, increasing their efficiency. Surely an NGO has the need for similar solutions, she thought to herself. But which consultant or IT expert will work with an NGO – a client who cannot pay?

This question would remain at the back of her mind, unanswered.

Eventually, Rekha moved to a boutique training firm run by a former colleague, this time in a teaching role. It was both satisfying and flexible enough to suit her needs. But by 2016, Rekha Koita was feeling restless.

It was at this point that Rizwan opened a new door for her.

"Rekha," he said. "You don't need to think about earning money, or climbing any ladder."

Do what you really want to do, he advised her. Because if not now, then when?

APPLYING THE MIND

Even as Rekha was wondering 'what to do', the IIT Bombay Class of 1992 was planning its 25th reunion. Living in Mumbai, while most of the batch was abroad, she became one of the key organisers. From fundraising, to identifying what to do with the money, to executing the various projects – Rekha was at the forefront of it all.

"The work I did for the reunion rekindled some kind of spark inside of me," she says.

Among the many projects implemented at the Powai campus was a hangout for students (Café '92), a mental health program aimed at preventing suicide and RISE (Rural Immersion for Students in Engineering).

Parallel to this, Rekha was once again exploring the social sector, and got connected to an NGO called Antarang, which works with adolescents and youth. As she got to know them better and understood the workflow, she realised that the right technology could be a gamechanger.

"They were doing very good work but could not scale due to lack of technology."

Antarang worked in the space of livelihoods, guiding youth into careers of their choice. While the number of students they were working with was growing year on year, the only tool they used was Excel sheets. All data was entered manually, which had become tedious and time-consuming.

When she discussed this issue with Rizwan, he said – let's build a solution for them. He introduced Rekha to a software company called Designscape, which designed a simple IT system to track students. It worked so well that a second system for career planning was introduced soon after.

This intervention, funded by the Koitas and led by Rekha, created a huge impact. Within the next two years, Antarang was able to scale up from 3000 children a year, to 50,000 a year. Over time, they built a number of systems for Antarang and also built capacity of the team. The NGO now counsels 200,000 children annually.

Magic Bus was the next beneficiary. The sports non-profit was struggling to make sense of data from its programs, which ran across 22 states. An easy-to-use analytics system solved that problem and made operations far more effective. However, it was not as simple as an NGO saying – this is the tech I want, build it for me.

"We never take the NGO's problem statement for granted," says Rekha.

Whether it is a non-profit working in the slums of Mumbai or in a remote district of Madhya Pradesh, the Koita Foundation will spend time on-ground, observing and interacting with field workers and program officers.

A typical conversation with a field worker goes like this:

"Aap roz kya karte ho? Tell me in detail what you do."

The field worker will show her diary, explaining how she plans her visits each morning.

"Mere ko subah ek ghanta isich kaam mein lag jaata hai," the lady sighs.

And thus is born the idea of a scheduling system which saves hundreds of woman-hours.

If an NGO does not have an online payroll system, it may need to hire an extra person. But if its field workers become more productive, or the program officer's efficiency improves, the impact of said NGO's work multiplies.

The result can be transformational.

This was an important insight which guided Rekha in her work with diverse NGOs.

METRICS MATTER

There was scepticism, even resistance to change. But once NGOs got hooked to a new way of doing things, there was no looking back. With the use of tools and dashboards every rupee they spent had 30-40% more impact. This created a buzz with donors and boosted the morale of the organisation itself.

"The work was not easy but it was truly rewarding," says Rekha.

By the end of 2017, she knew that this was the niche she wanted to pursue. A niche where her professional skills and desire to give back came together to make a real difference.

At this point, the Koitas set up a foundation, to give form and structure to this effort.

Rizwan continued to be hands-on with CitiusTech, however, he contributed his expertise in system architecture during review meetings with the vendor, which were always held on weekends.

It was a conscious decision to keep personal philanthropy separate from CitiusTech, which had its own CSR program. However, some employees of CitiusTech did step forward, in their personal capacity, to help with design and implementation of projects. But there was no formal team, it was one person bringing it all together – Rekha.

To keep the work focussed, and manageable, the Koitas carved out three principles:

1. We will work in only three sectors – health, livelihood and education.
2. We will work with NGOs whose leaders are committed, and open to change.
3. We will work only in Mumbai, as field visits are integral to program design.

These principles made it possible for Rekha to choose a small but meaningful number of projects to work with, as a solopreneur in the social space.

"Very few donors fund technology, they see it as an overhead, not a program cost."

After close to five years working in this manner, she decided to hire a full-time team member. In July 2021, Drishti Trivedi came on board. An engineer with a passion for the social sector, Drishti found herself thrown into the deep end. Here was a boss who did not micro-manage or give a list of 'things to do'. Rekha's approach was – this is the goal, make your own plan. If you need help, I am there but I won't be breathing down your neck.

"I had to manage my own time, find ways to get things done," says Drishti.

She was also struck by the clarity that Koita foundation worked with. Whom we will engage with, what we want to achieve, how we will do it – everything was well-structured. A project had three phases. First of all came discovery i.e. selecting an NGO to work with, then going with them to the field to understand the problems they face.

The second phase – development – involved a lot of back and forth with the vendor, finding a solution which would not just be efficient but also easy to use. Thirdly, there was the adoption phase, which was often the most challenging part. When Drishti joined, Vipla Foundation was struggling to get balwadi teachers to use its app.

Most of these women were middle-aged and not tech-savvy. In fact, most of them did not even have their own smartphone. So, first of all, Drishti decided to run a campaign asking friends and well-wishers to donate their old phones for a good cause. But even with smartphones in hand, they were not keen to use the app.

"Arey, it is so easy to fill the attendance in register, no," was the standard response.

When they finally started using the app, the teachers would not enter data in real time. With saam, daam and dand, the app was finally accepted, and using it became routine. This behaviour change took one full year. A felicitation ceremony was held for the teachers who used the app diligently, and were a role model for others.

At the ceremony, one of the felicitated women became emotional. Dressed in a silk sari, with flowers in her hair, she declared – this is the proudest moment of my life. Not only did the app boost the teachers' and mentors' self-esteem, they were able to spend their time more efficiently, and create greater impact.

When BMC saw their application, they said - humko bhi chahiye. The app is now used in 800 BMC balwadis!

FRAMEWORK FOR LIFE

NGO transformation was Rekha's baby, where Rizwan played the role of technical advisor, sounding board and cheerleader. At the same time, he had a plan of his own. Over the years, he had thought deeply about having all this – mostly unexpected – wealth.

"I have a personal framework – the three-box framework," says Rizwan.

Think of a box, with two smaller boxes inside of it. The innermost box is the amount of wealth Rekha and Rizwan need to lead a comfortable life. The middle box includes the money their two sons will inherit. Then there's the largest box, which represents all the money the Koitas have.

"I am in a very privileged position to have a third box, which is much larger than the first two boxes."

In 2019, Baring Private Equity acquired a majority stake in

CitiusTech, leaving Rizwan with the question – what next? The prospect of starting one more company did not excite him. It would only make the third box bigger, giving very little joy. Ever the logical thinker, the question now was - what's the most value-added way in which I can spend my time?

Can I align my philanthropy work with what I've learnt over the last 20 years?

During Covid, it became clear that while one could book a movie ticket with two clicks, there was no easy way to get a hospital bed. Digital healthcare was the need of the hour. However, Rizwan was acutely conscious that global software solutions and approaches were not the answer. India needs tools and strategies built for Indian conditions, Indian users.

"Dashboards, metrics, KPIs – the social sector had never used these words."

The journey began at the Koitas' alma mater – IIT Bombay. The couple had reconnected with the institute, thanks to the 'giving back' effort for their silver jubilee reunion, where Rekha had played a crucial leadership role. So when the thought of setting up a centre for digital health came to Rizwan, it was a no-brainer.

In July 2021, Koita Foundation signed an MOU with IIT Bombay to set up the Koita Centre for Digital Health (KCDH). The goal – to create the next generation of healthcare leaders and innovators by giving students a chance to work on healthcare problems in the real-world.

Within two short years, KCDH had built a strong application-oriented Healthcare Informatics curriculum with over 200 students signing up. Instead of modelling data from the internet, students worked on real-life problems in cancer, TB, malaria, making the course truly meaningful and exciting.

To connect with the clinical world, KCDH has partnerships with close to 20 leading hospitals across India. One of them being the Tata Memorial Hospital (TMH) in Parel. In fact, Rizwan reached out to Dr. C. S. Pramesh, director, TMH, to join the advisory board of the Koita Centre for Digital Health.

Dr Pramesh readily agreed, little knowing that a whole new journey was about to unfold...

TAMING THE BEAST

In 2013, Tata Memorial Hospital set up the National Cancer Grid (NCG), a platform to share knowledge and research with 360 cancer hospitals across India that serve 60% of patients. Rizwan got acquainted with the work NCG was doing, as he interacted with Dr Pramesh in his advisory role at KCDH.

"I think we had a meeting of minds, and then things just happened," says Dr Pramesh.

In its decade-long existence, the National Cancer Grid had had many donors and supporters. What made Koita Foundation different was Rizwan's hands-on involvement in the nuts and bolts of running the centre.

In 2023, Koita Foundation signed an MOU with the National Cancer Grid to set up the Koita Centre for Digital Oncology (KCDO) at Tata Memorial Hospital. Before that, NCG was a well-intentioned project run by doctors.

Rizwan brought an entrepreneurial mindset, domain knowledge and a 'quick and dirty' way of getting things done. Having quit CitiusTech in November 2021, he had the time, energy and the commitment to steer the initiative through weekly review meetings.

"For India to make a quantum leap, technology in healthcare is a fundamental requirement."

One of the aspirations of the National Cancer Grid was to create Electronic Medical Records (EMRs). NCG members were keen to adopt the technology but they didn't have the expertise to narrow down on a solution which did the job, and was cost-effective. Given this need, NCG decided – we will create our own EMR system.

"We discussed this with Rizwan and realised that developing an EMR solution from scratch was a huge, huge project."

Hence, NCG quickly switched gears. It made more sense for the nodal body to define the clinical features that an ideal, cancer-centric EMR should contain. In 2024, a 'wishlist' containing 210 criteria was handed over to multiple, existing EMR vendors so they could develop and refine their existing products.

An open tender was floated, to which 17 EMR vendors expressed interest. After a process of evaluation, 6 vendors were empanelled and their solutions were evangelised among the NCG member organisations. External CSR support helped to partly fund 20 cancer hospitals who were early adopters.

In this way, NCG-KCDO became an ecosystem enabler. And a strategy that worked for cancer could certainly be applied to another disease. This was the thought behind the establishment of the Koita Centre for Digital Diabetology (KCDD) in April 2024, in collaboration with Research Society for the Study of Diabetes in India (RSSDI).

Unlike Tata Memorial Hospital, which is a government organisation, RSSDI is a society of 12,000 diabetes clinicians. It has no central office, or physical location. In addition, diabetes is rarely treated in hospitals.

Hence, instead of EMR, Clinical Management Systems (CMS) need to be deployed in doctors' clinics for managing patients over long periods of time.

"We must digitise," say doctors, "but we don't know how to do it."

The average practitioner meets 30-35 patients a day and has time for little else. What's more, he or she has no tech background. Which software will serve my needs? What if I select the wrong one? Will I get support for installation? These are some of the friction points in the purchase process.

On the other hand, there are at least 50 CMS vendors, who have developed good products. But they are unable to market themselves or provide after-sales support outside metro cities.

A survey was conducted among RSSDI members to understand their digital priorities. An expert team then identified the key CMS features needed by diabetologists. The resultant document will help CMS vendors build better products which serve the needs of diabetes patients. Making it a win-win for all.

SETTING STANDARDS

In April 2022, Surabhi Goel joined Koita Foundation as COO - the first employee to join on the digital health side. A Chartered Accountant by training, she had worked in banking and consulting, before switching to education. Surabhi was seeking to move into public policy, when she stumbled upon the role at Koita Foundation.

"I took a leap of faith, because I believed in Rizwan, and his vision," says Surabhi.

There was no five year plan or roadmap, just a firm belief that digital has the potential to transform India's healthcare. And we will figure out a way to do it.

In 2022, Rizwan was invited to join the board of NABH (National Accreditation Board for Hospitals and Healthcare Providers). NABH is the body which certifies over 25,000 hospitals in India in the space of quality. The core clinical standards of NABH include over – 630 requirements from patient registration to clinical outcomes.

"We said to NABH, let's build a standard on digital health for hospitals," says Rizwan.

Digital Health standards for hospitals cover a vast set of operations. For example, can a hospital give an appointment online? Can it maintain clinical notes online? Can a doctor get an alert if there is an abnormal lab report? Can it provide patients access to their own records? Most Indian hospitals had never thought along these lines.

Koita Foundation supported NABH to develop India's first digital health standard for hospitals, which was launched in September 2023. In May 2024, NABH requested Rizwan to take the role of Chairperson, NABH.

"I cautioned them," Rizwan laughs. "Be ready for a very active and involved Chairperson!"

True to his word, Rizwan devotes 25% of his time to NABH – with the same passion that once drove him to build CitiusTech. Over the past year, NABH has introduced several new programs, expanded its coverage significantly and developed a robust partner program, in addition to driving a host of Digital Health initiatives.

Working with government organisations also comes with a huge advantage: the advantage of scale. For the last two years, Koita Foundation has been working with Maharashtra University of Health Sciences (MUHS), which governs the curriculum for 450 medical colleges, across 100,000 students.

Koita Foundation provided the overall Digital Health content and Digital Health expertise, while MUHS provided subject matter experts and access to its huge network. This curriculum was rolled out in the academic year 2024-25, making Maharashtra the first state in India to introduce Digital Health as part of its MBBS program.

The curriculum is now being adopted in other states, including Rajasthan and New Delhi.

Is working with the government easy? Well, it is a slow process but look at the bright side. First of all, there is no need for a senior bureaucrat to do something that is not part of their KRA. If you find a motivated official who wants to work with you, it's a huge opportunity. Grab it and make things happen.

"My biggest strength is that I don't have revenue pressures nor am I chasing any other targets," says Rizwan. "I can cherry-pick opportunities and work only with leaders I really want to work with."

FAST FORWARD

You can hand-hold an NGO, make it tech-savvy but eventually, it must build its own digital muscle. That is Koita Foundation's operating principle.

"The funding we provide helps partners hire and retain strong digital talent," says Rekha.

The foundation runs a tight ship, with just 20 full-time employees. However, it works closely with domain experts in technology, UI/UX design, content development, marketing and HR. These are not project-based relationships but true long-term partnerships, where both work together to accomplish a common goal.

"This collaboration model enables us to be agile and provide exceptionally strong support to our NGOs and Digital Health partners," says Surabhi.

One such partnership is with India Leaders for Social Sector (ILSS) to co-create the Koita Centre for Digital Transformation (KCDT). Anuradha Prasad, CEO, ILSS, says that it was serendipity that connected her with Rekha in late 2023. In the very first meeting, there was a meeting of minds.

While ILSS was working on a strategy to build the digital capacity of NGOs, Koita Foundation had been working with NGOs for several years, doing exactly that. Together, they have designed a course which is practical, rigorous and leads to visible transformation. 13 NGOs signed up for the first cohort, 25 for the second.

Among them is Seva Mandir, a 55-year old NGO based in Udaipur, whose CEO was a complete novice in the area of tech. With learnings from case studies and guidance from mentors assigned to each participant, Seva Mandir has adopted analytical tools and become a data-driven organisation.

"The Koitas are the best kind of philanthropists," says Anuradha Prasad. "We have a a great deal of trust and mutual respect!"

KCDT aims to directly impact 200-300 NGOs in the next few years and many more, through its portal dt4si.com (Digital Toolbook for Social Impact). This is a curated website with case studies, technology tools, training courses and trusted service providers. You could call it a Digital Public Good for the social sector.

> *"It's not how much we give but how much love we put into giving."*
>
> *– Mother Teresa's quote at the Koita Foundation office entrance*

The journey has been immensely satisfying for Rekha. Recasting herself time and again has worked.

Looking back, she realises whatever happened, it was the perfect thing for her at that stage of life. Taking it slow for a while gave her precious time to spend with both the older and younger generation. And now that she has fewer responsibilities, it is possible to devote more time and energy to this new path she has chosen to walk on.

As for Rizwan, he is 'happy busy', as always. The only difference is, he does not travel that much, or spend hours on late-night calls. But his aspirations remain the same.

"Even in working with the government I hold my team to the same benchmark that I held for client work at CitiusTech!" he says.

On the Digital Health side, there are eight key initiatives, with more to be rolled out soon. And although this keeps his hands full, Rizwan finds the time to conduct fortnightly reviews with all his teams, as well as a tight schedule of quarterly reviews!

Although their styles of working are quite different, Rekha and Rizwan share the same vision – that the NGOs they work with should 'graduate' and build in-house capacity. Thus, when Vipla Foundation said they would manage the next phase of their digital journey independently, it was indeed cause for cheer.

The same applies to the KCDH at IIT Bombay and KCDO at Tata Memorial. Both centres have been given significant funding, so that they can focus on research, advocacy and innovation. But in the long run, the hope is that each centre will attract its own funding, and be financially independent.

At the end of the day, the Koitas remain very real, very grounded. Rizwan insists on travelling with his team members in economy class, and stays in the same hotels. Their elder son Samad could have easily gone to the US to study but went through the slog of JEE and studied at IIT Bombay, like his parents.

Both Samad and younger son, Sahil, are keen to carve their own paths in life. And their parents believe that is the only way to thrive.

"We don't want to give all our wealth to the children," says Rekha. "It will not enrich their lives."

To find your purpose, to struggle and strive
'Tis the only way to be truly alive!

For more on Koita Foundation scan:

ADVICE TO YOUNG PHILANTHROPISTS

Like many things in life, it all starts with taking one step, then a second step. You don't need a grand plan of what and how on day one.

Point number two, you can donate money to educate 50 kids, or 500. But in a country like India, it doesn't move the needle. But if you have built a large company, and choose to direct your skills to create systemic change, then chances are that your contribution will be far more long lasting.

Because the amount of time we give and the value we can add, is far more than money.

You have to be very patient. In the best-case scenario results will be two years away, more likely scenario is four years away, and worst-case scenario, a few more years away. So, please be very comfortable with delayed gratification.

"Giving is more satisfying than taking."

People Engineering

FAIZAL AND SHABANA KOTTIKKOLON

Faizal Shabana Foundation

They made their fortune in Dubai but find their bliss in serving Mother India. The 'Nadakkavu model' shows that change is possible, and at scale.

Calicut is the city where Vasco De Gama set foot in India. It is one of the country's oldest trading hubs and home to many prosperous Malabar merchants. Faizal Kottikkolon belongs to one such clan, whose business extended as far as Burma. However, after World War II, the family shifted its base back to Calicut.

"As a child, I remember my father being very strict; we all woke up at five in the morning."

This discipline would stand him in good stead, later in life.

As members of a close-knit community, the Kottikkolon tharavad bustled with visitors, including people seeking small financial help. Faizal's father would always do what he could, and insisted that every visitor stay for a cup of tea. What's more, the children were asked to serve it. It was a lesson in generosity and humility that had a deep impact.

After completing his schooling in Calicut, Faizal went to Manipal Institute of Technology to study civil engineering, followed by an MBA at TAPMI. After a second master's in industrial engineering in the US, he began working for an MNC in New Jersey and had no desire to return. But everything changed when he was introduced to Shabana.

Shabana hailed from a wealthy family, which brought electricity and phone lines, as well as built schools and colleges in Thumbe, their native village in coastal Karnataka. Faizal fell for her simplicity; she liked his smile. After six months of long-distance telephonic courtship, they tied the knot in 1992. On Shabana's request, Faizal relocated to India.

Back in Calicut, Faizal's father invited his highly qualified son to join the family business. Together, they set up the first private steel plant in Kerala. An accident of fate resulted in the couple shifting to Dubai, where Faizal started a trading firm. After an intense period of struggle, the business blossomed into a leading global company with its own IP.

Through it all, Shabana was by Faizal's side. After the birth of their fourth child, she joined Emirates Techno Casting and played a crucial role in shaping the company's unusual HR policies, in particular, the vibrant community centre. In 2011, Emirates Techno Casting was acquired by Tyco, USA for $400 million.

Around this time, the sad state of education in their home state came to Faizal and Shabana's attention. They embarked upon an ambitious project to revitalise the 120-year-old Government Vocational Higher Secondary School for Girls' in Nadakkavu, which went on to become a model adopted by 1000 schools across Kerala.

Deeply inspired by the philosophy of Vedanta, Faizal and Shabana believe that giving, without any expectation of return, is a source of true joy.

"It brings stability in your thought process; it brings balance in your life," says Faizal.

Brahma satyam jagan mithya
Daanam mam nityapratigya

When Shabana married into the Kottikolon clan, she had no expectations about being a working woman. In such clans, and in the wider community, wives did not go to work.

On her husband's insistence, Shabana joined a computer course at NIIT. What's more, he encouraged her to do data entry work in the family business.

"Then, I got pregnant, and I had my first daughter, Sophiya," says Shabana.

But the baby had a whole joint family taking care of her, and Shabana didn't want to sit idle.

One of the things Shabana loved to pick up in Mangalore was greeting cards. Sadly, they were not available in Calicut. Well, this could be a business opportunity, said Faizal.

They travelled to Delhi to meet Anil Mulchandani, owner of Archies Gallery, and signed a franchise deal.

It was the first Archies Gallery in Kerala, the first store in Calicut with air conditioning, and it employed only women. And in no time, it became the coolest place for young boys and girls to hang out. Along with the regular 'I Love You' cards, the store also sold something unusual – pottery items made in a nearby village.

The 'potters' were local women in need of income - they were guided by a well-meaning social worker. When Shabana heard about this effort, she jumped in to help. Her little store would be happy to sell these pots and give the money back to those in need.

"That was the first time I tried to help the community, in my own small way," says Shabana.

As it happened, life suddenly took a completely new turn. In 1995, Faizal and Shabana went to Dubai to visit her brother, who had built a timber factory in Ajman. At that time, there were just 35,000 locals and 100,000 expats living in the region, with pristine beaches and sea-scented air adding to the charm.

While visiting his brother-in-law's factory, Faizal struck up a conversation with a visitor.

"What do you do," he asked the stranger.

"I am a scrap trader," came the reply.

Faizal's ears perked up. The steel plant in Kerala imported scrap from the United States. But where was scrap being generated in scantily industrialised Ajman? From the offshore oil fields. Out of curiosity, Faizal accompanied the man to the one very small steel plant which then existed in Dubai.

The plant procured scrap $10 cheaper than what they were importing from the US. This could be a significant saving for the family firm, which imported 3000 tonnes a month. Faizal sought permission from his father to set up a trading firm in Dubai. A whole new chapter in his was about to begin.

COMMUNITY IS KING

Early on, Faizal adopted a style of working which was inclusive. Even when he was dealing with scrap collectors, he did not exploit them. Instead, he taught them how to sort mixed metals into steel, copper, lead and so on. In that way, the scrap collectors got a better price. His generosity earned their loyalty and trust.

"Giving back is not something I thought about; it just came naturally," says Faizal.

In 1997, with the help of his family, Faizal Kottikolon set up his own steel foundry in Ajman. However, there were numerous challenges, from poor demand to a weak industrial ecosystem. One year passed, then two, then three – the company gasped for life. But Faizal did not give up.

"When you have a model which has scaled, people believe in it."

The turning point came in 2002, when Emirates Techno Casting (ETC) developed the technology to make superalloys in a vacuum furnace. These superalloys were in high demand in the oil and gas sector. What's more, by making steel in a vacuum furnace, pollution was eliminated. Thus, ETC became the world's first 'green foundry'.

From 2007 onwards, the company grew exponentially. The same year, the Kottikolons started what would become the jewel in the ETC crown – the Shabana and Faizal Community Centre. HR was Shabana's domain; along with Faizal, she often interacted with the foundry workers over breakfast.

A majority of the workers were from the Indian subcontinent – these informal meetings gave her a sense of the lives and their problems. They did manual jobs, which required little education and hence, could not even fill out customs and immigration forms on the journey home.

"We must do something for them," said Shabana, to which Faizal agreed wholeheartedly.

The couple decided to plough back $5 million of the company's profit into building a world-class centre. Spread over 60,000 square feet, the centre had gyms, yoga classes, coffee shops, sports facilities, community and movie screenings – the kind of perks IT companies provide but factory workers had never dreamt of.

Every day, workers were given 45 minutes of skills training, on company time. This could be in spoken English, computers, or hygiene. Inspirational stories and movies like 'Gandhi' were used to communicate lessons in human values. These efforts instilled a simple idea - you too can live a life of purpose.

The effect of the program was felt not just by the workers but their families back in India. Children were encouraged to go for higher education, they now aspired to become doctors and engineers. This change in mindset gave Shabana and Faizal a deep sense of satisfaction.

When you take care of your workers, they are happy and more productive. There is a common sense of purpose, of community. The company benefits. But for Shabana and Faizal, this initiative was not a strategic HR exercise. They truly believed in the idea that 'taking care of the other' is akin to 'taking care of oneself'.

Much later, when introduced to the teachings of Swami Parthasarathy, they learnt that there truly is no 'other'. This is the essence of Vedanta.

MOTHER INDIA CALLS

In 2007, the Ruler of Sharjah, His Highness Sheikh Dr Sultan bin Mohammad AlQasimi, visited the Hamriya Free Zone. He found Emirates Techno Casting to be the best factory, among the many he visited. The Sheikh was so impressed that, instead of fifteen minutes, he spent four and a half hours at ETC.

"It was a great honour for us," says Shabana.

Later that year, Dubai Holding, owned by the ruling family of Dubai, bought a stake in Emirates Techno Casting. The American corporation Tyco went on to acquire ETC for $400 million, giving Faizal and Shabana, as well as their investors, a lucrative exit.

Then, in 2012, Tyco sold its stake to another company – Pentair.

When the Pentair chairman visited the plant, he was blown away by the community centre. So, even though the Kottikolons were no longer owners, he decided to honour them by renaming the centre as 'Shabana and Faizal Community Centre'. This gesture touched the couple deeply.

Be that as it may, there was a sense of void. There was a company - KEF Holdings – but there was no business to run, just a lot of money in the bank. So now, what do we do? Travelling the world was a long-held dream, so that's what the couple embarked on. And then, a new purpose found its way to them.

In an interview with Rajeev Menon for Malayala Manorama, Faizal was asked to share his views on India. While optimistic, he expressed the view that there was a lot of work still to be done.

"The gap between the rich and the poor can be bridged only through education."

When the article was published, Pradeep Kumar, MLA, Kozhikode district called Faizal.

"You are interested in education," said the MLA. "Come and see a government school."

Faizal readily took up the offer. What he saw during the visit shocked him. Close to 1600 girls were studying in Government Vocational Higher Secondary School for Girls, Nadakkavu but there were only 8 toilets, dilapidated buildings and some structures which had only tin sheet roofs. Many questions buzzed in Faizal's head.

Does the government not have enough money?

Or is it just that they don't care?

And if a state like Kerala has such a school, what about schools in the rest of India?

In search of some answers, Faizal met Debashis Chatterjee, then director of IIM Kozhikode. They discussed the paradox of government-funded IIMs being top-class institutions while government-run schools were in a sorry state.

The director's explanation was that IIMs were autonomous while schools were a different cup of tea.

"The system is well-entrenched," he concluded. "It is difficult to change".

This remark only made Faizal more determined to 'do something'. Things can change, they must change... otherwise, how will India progress?

EDUCATION MATTERS

MLA Pradeep Kumar requested IIM Kozhikode to conduct a gap analysis, with funding from Faizal. The findings of the study were startling. The initial hypothesis was that government schools teachers were underpaid, underqualified. In reality they were more qualified and paid more than in private schools.

"However, the overall environment was so poor that they were lacking in motivation."

So the first task was clear – improve the infrastructure. When he met the CM, and the health minister, they gave the green signal. However, there was one condition.

"You will need to complete the entire construction during the school vacation."

Now that was certainly going to be a challenge. Faizal had read about Finnish schools being the 'best in the world'. So, Shabana, Faizal, and their architect Robert visited Finland. There, they discovered that schools were built with pre-fab technology, which was faster and more efficient than normal construction.

However, in 2012, pre-fab technology was unheard of in India. There was just one, very new company in Tirupur, venturing into the area. Faizal went to meet the owner and convinced him to lease the unit to him for 6 months. The architect proceeded with his design and in 6 months flat, the Nadakkavu school had a brand new building.

When the infrastructure was inaugurated on May 29, 2013, it created quite a stir. Two days later, A.R. Rahman visited the school and spent two and a half hours with the kids. At the end of it, the maestro announced that he would set up a music academy. The teachers and the students were delighted; it also caught the attention of the media.

"If one government school can be transformed, why not others?" was the question on everyone's lips. The political class was thus forced to sit up and take note.

"Give unconditionally and you will get more than you ever imagined in return."

The transformation of the Nadakkavu school did not stop at infrastructure. Training programs were introduced to boost both the skills, as well as the morale of teachers. Strong emphasis on sports and cultural activities ensured a more holistic, all-round development for the students.

All this was under the aegis of the Faizal Shabana Foundation. Upgrading one school within a moribund system is an achievement that anyone would be proud of; most would leave it at that. If anyone asks – what are you doing for society – here is the showpiece. But Shabana and Faizal were not easily satisfied. Their vision was to create a model which schools across the country could replicate.

MLA Pradeep Kumar had strongly supported the Nadakkavu school project. In fact, it made him a darling of the community. Soon, other MLAs approached the foundation.

"Please come to my district," they said. "We will also contribute from our MLA fund."

With a working model and a vision to scale the project, Shabana and Faizal met the Chief Minister of Kerala. They have a proposal to upgrade 100 more schools at a cost of Rs 10 crore each. Of this Rs 100 crore would come from the foundation, the remaining Rs 900 crore from the government.

Parallelly, Faizal started building the pre-fab construction company in Krishnagiri, Tamil Nadu. He believed that this technology could transform not just schools but infrastructure development across the country. Hospitals, factories, low-cost housing – any kind of building could be completed in quick time.

Alas, the path to progress is not straight, not easy and not timebound.

CHUGGING AHEAD

Kerala has the distinction of being India's most literate state, with a highly educated population. Yet, the government of the day did not approve the foundation's proposal. Nevertheless, Faizal and Shabana continued to champion the Nadakkavu school.

"We were disappointed but refused to give up," says Shabana.

Along with MLA Pradeep Kumar, the foundation created a concept called PRISM (Promoting Regional Schools to International Standards). PRISM was making an impact, however, they knew that the potential was much more...

In 2016, a new government came to power. This time, they proactively reached out.

"We want to take this model to 1000 schools," they said. "Will you help us?"

Shabana and Faizal were more than delighted. The budget allocated by the government was Rs 2500 crore, less than envisaged. However, it could still go a long way. Faizal had estimated that with pre-fab construction, the entire exercise could be completed in two short years.

Alas, the government did not share his enthusiasm. The established procedure is to issue a tender and attract bidders, with the project going to the company quoting the lowest cost. While pre-fab could promise higher durability and faster completion, it could not compete on price.

But 'rules are rules', so the schools were constructed the old-fashioned way. It took 9 years to upgrade 977 schools but today, Kerala is a state where private schools are unable to attract a large number of students. Parents from underprivileged backgrounds are proud to send their kids to government schools, and more so, in Kozhikode district.

While the foundation supports all schools in Kerala with training and soft skills, it gives mentoring to 11 schools with 13,000 students in Kozhikode district. These schools have a distinct aura. The students have been exposed to a wider variety of experiences outside academics from literature festivals to basketball coaching.

One such initiative was taking a chapter from the English textbook and converting it into a theatre production. 5 schools associated with the foundation participated, with the performances being held at one of the biggest halls in Kozhikode. This exercise had tremendous impact on the confidence and self-esteem of participating students.

Of course, this could happen because funding was available to hire a theatre person to train the children. But one foundation cannot support all schools in the state.

"It will indeed be wonderful if more foundations step forward to create similar opportunities," says Shabana.

RURAL RENAISSANCE

While pre-fab was not used to construct schools, the Kottikolons did demonstrate the power of the technology by building Meitra, a world class super-specialty hospital.

Assembled like Lego blocks, Meitra was completed in just 18 months and quickly established itself as one of the best hospitals in the country.

Even as they were evangelising pre-fab technology, Shabana and Faizal did not forget about the people working in and around their factory in Krishnagiri. They decided to work in eight villages, after commissioning a needs assessment study. Education, agriculture, toilets and literacy for women emerged as the areas which needed work.

"We started a school in the name of Dr A P J Abdul Kalam, who has been a great inspiration for us," says Shabana.

Initially, there were just 15 children. With patience and community efforts, attendance crossed 200, in just 60 days. The school was also used to educate women regarding various government schemes which they were not aware of. What's more, natural methods of farming were introduced, resulting in substantial rise in farmer incomes.

This sustainable development initiative has benefitted over 5000 families in the region.

In 2018, the Kottikolons sold the pre-fab construction factory to Softbank. However, they continued to support these activities with the help of a local NGO. A similar program was also initiated in Shabana's native village in Karnataka – Tumbe. The emphasis is on community-led development with women at the centre of it.

But there is one more area dear to Shabana's heart – art and culture. Along with AIACA (All India Artisans and Craftworkers Association), she is helping women involved in the painstaking craft of phulkari. These women embroiderers are now part of a co-operative and sell under a common brand name – Namo Phulkari.

This year, AIACA is incubating 5 women entrepreneurs working with craftspeople. The foundation is supporting their training in various aspects of production, finance and marketing. Lucknow-based Rolin Srivastava is an interior designer who recently started working with the craft of chikankari.

“I wanted to take chikan beyond apparel, so I introduced chikan lampshades,” she says.

Her brand – Inara Home – was struggling to standardise quality, and reach its audience. So when Rolin got a chance to join the first AIACA cohort, she jumped at it. In just four months, she has attended multiple online and in-person workshops and been able define Inara's vision, as well as nitty-gritties like correct pricing.

GOING BEYOND

Since 2012, Faizal Shabana Foundation has invested $30 million into philanthropic activities. This work is managed by 10 direct employees, along with several partners.

Of the various initiatives, the 'Nadakkavu model' has been the most impactful. It has been studied, as well as replicated, even outside Kerala.

“Once people see a working model, they believe that it is possible!” says Faizal.

Rizwan Ahmed, MLA from Shivajinagar, Bangalore, visited the school and requested the foundation to help him upgrade the school in his constituency. Similarly, on the request of the Jammu and Kashmir administration, Faizal Shabana Foundation is working with the Government Higher Secondary School for Girls at Kothibagh, Srinagar.

The foundation will spend close to Rs 20 crore on the Srinagar school project but the ultimate goal is much larger. The school will be a blueprint, to be adopted across J & K.

And if that happens, it will be a win-win for all. Impact assessment studies in Kerala indicate that gains have been substantial.

> *"We don't like the word 'CSR'. It is our responsibility to take care of the society."*

Government schools are producing state and national level athletes, musicians, artists, as well as academic performers. The average child is happier and more confident, while teachers have pride and a sense of ownership. Thus, the Nadakkavu model has impacted over 2 million students across Kerala.

In fact, the model has now reached Africa, with the foundation supporting three schools in Kenya and Uganda.

Shabana and Faizal's children are following in their footsteps. Sophiya and Sarah are both running their own companies, as well as a social initiative called 'Pause Café and Community' in Dubai. What started as an Instagram page for mental health during Covid has morphed into a physical space for community and conversation.

Like his dad, Zach is an engineer. He is pioneering a technology which repurposes petrol cars to electric ones. Zach loves running and has formed Runkwa, a run club whose members are encouraged to donate their old shoes. These shoes are sent to villages in Maharashtra and Africa.

The youngest, Czarina, has just finished her studies and is helping Shabana with a cultural platform in the UAE called Qissagoi.

"It is everything to do with South Asia – like dastangoi for music, arts, storytelling."

The children are not involved in day to day running of the Faizal Shabana Foundation but they are all on the same page, as a family. And see it as a legacy to be carried on.

Meanwhile, Faizal has embarked on his latest and most ambitious project - Tulah Clinical Wellness Sanctuary. Located near Calicut, Tulah is a compelling platform which combines modern science with the ancient wisdom of ayurveda, yoga, and Vedanta. This, he says, is India's gift to the world.

"I want to put Malabar back on the map, as a global hub."

They came for our spices, ivory and gold but left behind a form of wealth untold.

May knowledge, culture and ideas thrive.
Keeping our India truly alive.

For more on Faizal Shabana foundation scan:

ADVICE TO YOUNG PHILANTHROPISTS

Philanthropy is the most fulfilling thing a person can ever experience.

I think giving is more satisfying than taking and, in my experience, it brings stability in your thought process. It brings you balance in life. Your future generations will benefit out of it and it's a responsibility for every human being to give back, it is your duty.

So get into it as early as you can and you will enjoy the journey. We are enjoying the journey more than what we built in our professional careers. The foundation is the middle - every business is revolving around the foundation.

You don't have to start with a foundation, you can start by doing little things. In Vedanta we are taught that whatever you do, don't expect anything from it. When you don't have an expectation, there is no thing about looking for money, you are just doing selflessly.

The smallest thing you can do is smile or be kind - that's the simplest way of giving.

Daan

Carefully selecting and funding changemakers,
with a hands-off approach.
Driven strongly by trust.

"Charity is my fourth child."

A Mighty Heart

REKHA AND RAKESH JHUNJHUNWALA

He was known for making money;
few know how generously he gave it away.
A legacy that his wife and children vow to uphold.

At 23, she married a man of her father's choice. He had set up a bottling unit in Hyderabad, although what he really wanted to do was buy and sell stocks.

One fine day, he quit the bottling unit and sat at home for many months, 'doing nothing'. Did his wife not worry, ki mera husband yeh kya kar raha hai?

"No, not at all. I always believed in him", says Rekha Jhunjhunwala.

Her husband went on to become a legendary investor, known for his bold views and big bets. But even as RJ scaled new heights in the Indian stock market, his father remained unimpressed. A retired IRS officer, Jhunjhunwala senior spent most of his time and money on social work.

On his 75th birthday Mr Jhunjhunwala asked his son Rakesh for just one gift – Rs 75 lakh to use for charitable work. Eye camps, Jaipur foot camps, kavi sammelans – there were so many worthy causes needing support.

When he read articles about Rakesh's ever-increasing net worth he had only one thing to say.

"I don't care how much money you are making... Tell me how much you are giving."

It was this not-so-gentle prodding that made Rakesh Jhunjhunwala realise that money is not an end in itself. Slowly, he found himself drawn towards 'doing something for others'. As an investor, he was willing to bet on an unknown company with strong fundamentals.

And the same went for his philanthropy.

In 2002, he met an idealistic chap called Ramji Raghavan who'd quit a lucrative job with Citibank in London to pursue a wild dream. His mission - to make children fall in love with science. Ramji had no track record, yet, RJ bought into his vision and committed Rs 50 crore.

This was the RJ way. Once he believed in you, he went all in and pushed you to think really big.

All the non-profits Rakesh supported remember him with fondness and intense gratitude. Since Rakesh is no longer with us, you will see him and hear him through them.

RJ's brand of philanthropy was based on trust in good human beings and evangelising really big outcomes. He planned to accelerate his philanthropy from 2025.

"Nishtha, Aryavir, Aryaman and I will fulfil all his dreams," says Rekha Jhunjhunwala.

Here's raising a toast to a mighty heart
Which gave with sass, with spunk, with soul.

It was in the second meeting with Rakesh Jhunjhunwala, at his home, that Ramji heard the prophetic words which changed the trajectory of Agastya Foundation forever.

"Ramji, I can see it. I can see your mobile science vans all over India."

The Big Man added that it was a 'giant-sized project' which needed government support. Nevertheless, he committed around Rs 30 lakh to Agastya to buy and operate three such vans, in addition to the one he had already supported. In 2002, when Agastya Foundation was a fledgeling in the world of non-profits, this was a really big deal.

In their next meeting, Ramji showed Rakesh a map of the Agastya campus and he got a little irritated. Yaar, har baar, this guy shows up with something new. Such a big campus, huh, was his only comment. Ramji was deflated, nevertheless, he dropped in to Rakesh's office on his next visit to Mumbai.

The first thing Rakesh did was order mosambi juice for Ramji, from a roadside vendor near his office building. Because he remembered that his guest liked it, the last time.

Then he said straight off the bat, "Ramji, I'm not into charity, I've done enough".

Ramji felt like he was clean bowled but he refused to vacate the pitch. He looked Rakesh in the eye, summoned all the sincerity in his heart and these words tumbled out.

"Rakesh I'm not asking you to help, I'm begging you to help."

He didn't make much headway. They continued sipping juice from plastic straws, and then Ramji asked Rakesh another question.

"Who is the Chairman of General Motors?"

"Hoga yaar koi..."

"Well, even I don't know the answer but.... Who was John Harvard?"

"The benefactor of Harvard?" Rakesh deduced.

There were a few minutes of silence. Then, Rakesh looked at Ramji and asked, "How much did you say that building was?"

He committed the Rs 25 lakh Ramji asked for, with one condition - the building was to be named after his father. At this point, he asked Ramji to also start sending a report. Meanwhile, Ramji had a chance to visit the Exploratorium in San Francisco and was very impressed by it. Could something like that be built in India?

On the way back from SFO, Ramji stopped in Bombay and had dinner with a friend. As they stepped out of Trident hotel, a silver Mercedes pulled up and out stepped Rakesh.

"Hey, Ramji, you are in Bombay... You never called me?'

"You'll think I'm calling for money", said Ramji. "I felt that I should give you a break..."

Rakesh insisted it wasn't like that and the next day, he was, as usual, staring at the terminal, looking at stock prices. Even as Ramji talked about building an Exploratorium for rural India. Half an hour later, Ramji walked out with a commitment for Rs 75 lakh.

And, the next time, when showed him the model of phase one, Rakesh sighed.

"Do phase two also yaar", said Rakesh. "How much is that?"

Ramji was thrilled by this commitment for another crore of rupees.

Little did he know what lay in store ahead...

THINK BIG AND BIGGER

By 2005, Agastya was expanding its campus rapidly and Ramji was, as always, on the lookout for more donors. One evening, Rakesh broke the 'bad news' to him.

"Thoda thoda paisa maangne mein laga hua hai, tere vision ka kuch honey wala nahin!"

The good news was that Rakesh was willing to consider a long-term commitment.

"Can you come up with a 10-year plan?" was his ask.

Rakesh sent Manish Gupta, who was ex-BCG, to sit down with Ramji and formulate it.

"I go by the crusade and the crusader."

Over the next several months, they brainstormed and came up with a comprehensive plan. An ambitious but actionable roadmap — 90 crore rupees, to reach 6 million children.

A nervous but excited Ramji flew down to Mumbai, to make the presentation.

On slide three of the PPT, Ramji noticed that Rakesh had nodded off to sleep. He waited. Rakesh apologised and the presentation resumed. By slide six, there was gentle snoring.

Ramji waited. Rakesh woke up with a start and apologised. Then, he posed the crucial question – how much is the plan? On hearing the figure, he sat up straight.

"Ramji, this is India, not America... No one is going to give you 90 crores!"

At this point Ramji proposed to sell his ancestral property in Bangalore and give Rakesh the money to manage. Perhaps he could run Agastya on the returns thus generated? Rakesh snorted, simultaneously amused and insulted.

Manish Gupta piped in with a suggestion.

"Bhaiyya, let's start with a crore. Based on performance we'll gradually increase".

Rakesh then said something which captures his entire philosophy of investing.

"Arre Manish, if we buy into his vision, we must make sure he succeeds."

That day Rakesh Jhunjunwala committed Rs 50 crore to Agastya, over 10 years. His only ask was a seat on the board. Before taking the final call, he visited the campus in Koppal, three hours from Bangalore, along with his friend Bhaskar Bhat, CEO of Titan. To 'see for himself' what Agastya had built so far.

Ramji took them to a village school up a little hill where he saw a boy with snot running down his nose, untucked shirt, unkempt hair. Rakesh looked at Ramji, and smiled.

"I see curiosity in his eyes. You're really making a difference".

He would later admit that 'whatever I am' is because my father encouraged me to be curious. That Ramji was the first person who came to him and did not talk about educating children. But about 'sparking curiosity'.

So that was the 'heart' bit. The head did ask for a few metrics, to be defined by Ramji himself.

Manish would be monitoring the metrics but essentially, Rakesh assumed that Ramji would deliver. And as long as he was delivering, the money would always be there.

There was one final ask – to have the Jhunjhunwala name below the Agastya name. Because, 'this is going to become, a great NGO, possibly the greatest in Indian history'.

Ramji was a bit taken aback. With the Jhunjhunwala name on the masthead, would any other donors come forward? Nevertheless, he agreed, with a small caveat.

'Agastya Foundation, supported by Jhunjhunwala Family and others'.

Over the next 10 years, Rakesh kept his word. So high was the trust placed in Ramji that the money came with no strings attached. The freedom to use funds 'as needed' is rare in the donor world, and therefore immensely valuable. Neither did Rakesh send anyone to audit what 'Agastya is doing'. The only oversight was in board meetings.

In 2016, Agastya had far exceeded the goals it had set, in terms of numbers and on-ground impact. Ramji went back to Rakesh to make a presentation – the plan for the next 10 years. At the very beginning, he expressed his happiness, at how far they had come together. And once again, by slide 6, he had nodded off.

This time, Ramji continued, as if nothing had happened. Then Rakesh woke up.

"How big is the budget?" he asked.

"1600 crore", replied Ramji, with a straight face.

Rakesh agreed to fund 10% of it, 160 crores. And he apologised about nodding off.

"No problem", said Ramji. "Every time you nod off and wake up, good news follows!"

It started with Rakesh saying – be patient, your vision will be a reality one day. Over time it became 'our vision'.

When Rakesh Jhunjhunwala embraced a person, or a cause, he made it his own.

SHARING IS CARING

Nihal Kaviratne walked into Rakesh Jhunjhunwala's personal office in 2004 and saw him sitting in front of a multitude of screens, his eyes tracking the markets continuously.

"He was a very large man in all respects", recalls Kaviratne.

After a distinguished, four decade long career with Unilever Kaviratne was invited to the board of Titan and Agro Tech Foods. Rakesh was a significant investor in both companies and hence, Kaviratne had asked to meet him. Rakesh shared his investment philosophy, and a bit about his family.

In the midst of the meeting, a tiffin carrier arrived with piping hot khana. Rakesh insisted on sharing it with his guest, and offered a glass of whisky in the middle of the afternoon. The two kept in touch and when Kaviratne returned to India in 2006 and set up St Jude's, he talked about it with Rakesh.

It was an unfashionable cause that Kaviratne had chosen – the plight of children with cancer. They came from all parts of India seeking a miraculous cure at Tata Memorial Hospital. There were charities to fund the treatment but they had no place to stay. So they slept on the pavement outside the hospital.

"Use my money to leverage more money from others. I trust you to deliver."

Some would die of infection, rather than from cancer. Others got fed up and went back to their village. In fact, abandonment of treatment was the largest cause of mortality in childhood cancer. St Jude's was committed to solving this problem.

Providing physical, emotional, holistic support.

Kaviratne set up the first St Jude's centre out of his last year's salary from Unilever. After running a pilot with 8 rooms for 22 months, he felt it was time to replicate the model. And this was when he broached an idea with Rakesh. St Jude's had secured premises in the building of the Indian Cancer Society but needed around Rs 40 lakh to refurbish it.

By then, Rakesh Jhunjhunwala was a significant shareholder in around 40 companies.

"Could you ask each of them to donate one lakh rupees to St Jude's?" asked Kaviratne.

"No," was Rakesh's immediate reply.

"Why do you say no?" asked Kaviratne

"I'm not going to ask anyone else," said Rakesh. "I'll give it to you myself."

The reason, Rakesh revealed, was that his father was pushing him to start sharing his wealth with those in need. To find worthy causes and support them. Rakesh had only one request, that the centre be named after his father. He came to the inauguration on 26th November, 2008, with Rekha, Nishtha and Radheyshamji.

"There are many rich people who think only of becoming richer," said Radheysham Jhunjhunwala, in his inaugural speech.

"I am very happy that Rakesh is giving back."

Every quarter, Rakesh sent a personally signed cheque to St Jude's, to cover operating expenses. From time to time he would also drop by to meet the kids and play with them. For despite his size and stature, he remained a kid. With a big, bold, beautiful heart.

THE GOLDEN TOUCH

ISB grad Viren Rasquinha was all set to join a lucrative corporate job, when he met Prakash Padukone and Geet Sethi. And learnt about their dream - Olympic Gold Quest (OGQ).

"I couldn't say no to them when they asked me to join as CEO," he says.

As an Olympic hockey player, Viren had seen Team India narrowly miss out on a medal. He knew that much needed to be done, and who better for the job than a bunch of sportsmen? At the time he signed on, OGQ had no funds to pay Viren a salary. But, he had faith in the idea, and that somehow things will work out.

Thus Viren joined OGQ as 'employee # 1' and as it happened, he did get a modest salary. Which was largely funded by Rakesh Jhunjhunwala. In fact, when OGQ first met Rakesh, he loved the idea but refused to extend support. Until they agreed to hire a competent professional to run the organisation.

When Viren met Rakesh, he realised that he was not only passionate about the financial markets. But about India, and the country's performance in Olympic sports. At a time when OGQ was considered a pie in the sky, Rakesh made a large annual commitment and became a long-term donor.

One morning, in 2010, Rakesh summoned Viren, Geet and Prakash to his office, to make a presentation. He had also invited 10-12 of his close friends and associates, to listen to OGQ's unusual pitch. 5-6 of those present wrote cheques to the fledgeling organisation and continue to support OGQ, even today.

They were swayed not only by the idea of Olympic Gold Quest but the fact that Rakesh was a supporter. Usne paisa diya hai to kuch to hoga inme.

"Rakesh always encouraged us to use his name," says Viren. "He lit many candles for OGQ."

The 2012 London Olympics was the first Olympic cycle for OGQ. By day 7, India had not won a single medal, Viren was feeling a little down. Then, he met Rakesh.

“Look, whether you win a medal or not, don’t worry”, OGQ’s biggest donor assured the CEO. “I believe in you. I am here for the long run.”

During the course of the meeting, the 10 metre air rifle shooting final was going on. Viren and Rakesh watched the live telecast together, at the Bombay Gymkhana. Lusty cheers erupted when Gagan Narang won the bronze medal. Indeed, Gagan was the first athlete to be supported by OGQ to win an Olympic medal. Many more medals would follow.

What OGQ can never forget is that Rakesh Jhunjhunwala believed in them at a time when they needed it the most. The first seven years – 2009 to 2016 – funds did not come easy. At a felicitation for athletes after an Asian Games, Viren recalls making a presentation to an elite audience. During the Q & A, someone asked, what can we do to help OGQ?

From the back of the room, a voice piped up, “Just write a cheque!”

Put your money if you believe in it, and keep the faith. Quintessential Rakesh.

A CLEAR VISION

It was Bhaskar Bhat, CEO, Titan, who suggested to Rakesh that he look at the work of Sankara Eye Hospital (www.sankaraeye.com), founded by Dr. R. V. Ramani and Dr Radha Ramani in 1977. A meeting was arranged at RJ’s Nariman Point office where Dr. Ramani was received graciously.

But as the good doctor explained the Sankara model, he had a serious doubt.

“Rakesh’s eyes were on the five screens in front of him. I wondered, is he even listening?”

Finally, RJ turned his attention towards Dr. Ramani. He had

registered every bit of what had just been shared. After a few pointed questions, RJ made a declaration.

"I have a piece of land near Mumbai. I would like to donate it to build a hospital."

That was indeed wonderful but the hospital would also need a building and equipment. Done, said RJ. Additionally, in the Sankara model, 80% of the patients are treated free of cost. So there is an operational deficit for the first 5-7 years, until there are enough paying patients. I will take care of that too, said RJ.

In all, RJ committed upward of Rs 50 crore to Sankara Eye Hospital, Panvel. In 2018, he attended the Bhumi Pooja, with his family. When the hospital was completed in June 2021, RJ not only graced the inauguration but spent time in each and every department. By then, he had also made a sweeping commitment.

"Doc, now on, wherever you start, any number of places, I will make a 50% contribution."

"It's not the amount of money you give, but anybody giving, it matters."

For Dr. Ramani this meant no more headache of fundraising. He could focus on what he knew best – building and running hospitals. Over the last 7 years, Sankara has rapidly expanded its footprint, especially in north India, with an ambitious project in Varanasi that was very dear to RJ's heart.

In their last meeting, Rakesh Jhunjhunwala talked about the immense joy he got from the act of giving. He was positive and energetic, as always.

"With Rakesh, it was never the giver-taker feeling. More like, we are doing things together."

To build the nation. To heal the world.

THE SPIRIT LIVES ON

Rekha Jhunjhunwala was content to be a homemaker. She had only one deep desire – to become a mother. That wish was fulfilled when Nishtha was born in 2004, followed by twins Aryaman and Aryavir in 2009. Charity is my fourth child, Rakesh often said, in a light-hearted mood.

He is no more with us, so the unassuming Rekha has stepped up. For all his children.

"By God's grace Rekha ji has the same passion as her late husband", says Dr, Ramani.

In October 2024, PM Narendra Modi inaugurated the Sankara Eye Hospital in Varanasi. This is Sankara's 14th hospital and is committed to perform 30,000 free surgeries a year. The rush of patients has already exceeded expectations, meaning many more such hospitals are needed.

The family is committed to honour RJ's wish of being a part of every Sankara project. An MOU has been signed for the next Sankara Eye Hospital coming up in Patna. Rekha Jhunjhunwala has joined the Sankara Eye Hospital trust, as well as the board of Agastya.

"In fact, Rekha said Agastya was one of the closest to his heart," says Ramji.

In the midst of COVID, when the market had tanked, many corporates withdrew their CSR funding. A worried Ramji called Rakesh Jhunjhunwala.

"Ramji, 99.9%, you will continue to get my money", he said.

That spirit is being kept alive by the family. Nishtha is still very young, an undergraduate college student in the UK but she knows that this is a phase of preparation. When she has seen and experienced the world, she will be ready to return. And stand shoulder to shoulder with her mother. To uphold the legacy of Rakesh Jhunjhunwala.

There is an old saying in South India – in every village there is a temple cart. A huge cart. The entire village joins together to pull the cart. It's a collective effort but in spite of that, someone has to lead it. It's the same with philanthropic activity. Once Rakesh Jhunjhunwala was the head of your cart, you were at ease.

Even if the cart got a little heavier, he would help you pull through.

At a board meeting of Agastya, Ramji once related a story related to the Mahabharata.

Despite being on the wrong side, Karna had many great qualities, So, after death, he was sent to heaven. On the first day, at lunchtime, he was very hungry. The servers were ladling aromatic food into golden thalis, but when Karna's turn came, he got nothing. What could be the reason?

Indra comes up to him and comments, "Karna, you look worried, what's the problem?"

Karna replies, "I don't want to make an issue but the servers are avoiding me."

"Karna..." Indra admits. "I told them not to serve you".

"Oh, why is that?" asks a puzzled Karna.

Indra acknowledges that Daan Veer Karna was the most generous human being on earth. But there was one thing he didn't do.

"What is it that?", he asks.

"You never fed a hungry human. Am I right?"

Karna agreed, this was the truth. And hence, he must face the consequences, Indra said, by skipping his first meal.

When Ramji finished narrating the story, there was silence.

Then Rakesh said, "How much will it cost to feed the children on campus?"

On the spot, he committed another 50 lakh rupees.

The giver is often faced with a dilemma – dil ki sunoon ya dimaag ki.

From somewhere up there RJ is urging us all, 'Don't worry yaar, just do it'.

For more on RJ's philanthropic w[illegible]

ADVICE TO YOUNG PHILANTHROPISTS

RJ to Ramji Raghavan, Agastya

His first thing was, can I trust this guy's vision? Is it unique? Is it potentially transformative? Can I trust him to excel?

And then his concern was, are the economics compelling? What's the cost per exposure? He would keep quoting that line.

RJ to Dr. Ramani, Sankara Eye Hospital
Build a line of succession. Too many NGOs fail because the founders never let go.

RJ to Viren Rasquinha, Olympic Gold Quest
Believe in India, always stay positive.

"We have a responsibility to ensure that prosperity is inclusive."

Love Thy Human

AJIT ISAAC

Isaac Family Foundation

This family is systematically giving to various causes dear to their heart, with education and public health being at the forefront.

Ajit Isaac grew up in Anna Nagar, a middle class neighbourhood in the Madras of the '70s. His father was a first-generation immigrant from Kerala who worked at the tyre company Dunlop. Like many of his generation, Ambat Abraham Ithapiri was loyal to one company, one wife and one house all his life.

"There was a consistency and solidity about my father that shaped a lot of my thinking."

Ajit attended Don Bosco school in Egmore, which he considers to be his first 'lucky break' in life. After a B.A. from Loyola College, Ajit pursued his post-graduation from the Madras School of Social Work. This is when he finally became serious about his career.

The second big break was getting a job with Godrej & Boyce in Bombay. The city's relentless pace and ever-arching ambition rubbed off on Ajit. His next job with Shashi and Ravi Ruia of the Essar group gave him a glimpse of what it was to 'think big' and take calculated risks in a newly liberalized India.

In the year 2000, at age 33, Ajit Isaac quit corporate life to become an entrepreneur. His first business plan was for flower and grocery delivery but he quickly realised that human resources was his forte. Ajit then set up PeopleOne Consulting, a temp staffing company, which was bought out by Adecco in 2004.

His next company, Quess Corp, became a powerhouse employing over 600,000 people. And then, there was a realization. Life is transient, you are not an owner, only a trustee. It's time to start giving back.

In 2014, Quess Corp began its CSR journey, working to improve government schools in Bangalore. The family's personal philanthropic journey began in 2019, with big, bold choices, such as funding CMC Vellore's specialty paediatric hospital, as well as smaller but significant support to offbeat initiatives in prison reform and palliative care.

"I ascribe a large part of my success to luck and grace of God."

As a member of the Marthoma Syrian Church, Ajit has always believed in tithe – contributing 10% of his earnings to the church, regardless of how little or how much he earned. Philanthropy is taking that idea further, and wider.

As it says in the Bible, Corinthians 9:8:

"And God is able to make all grace abound toward you that you always having all sufficiency in all things, may have an abundance for every good work."

So take the lead. In kind thought, kind word, kind deed.

She was a Malayali girl who had grown up in north India, newly arrived in the city of dreams. He was a Malayali boy who grew up in Chennai, now a deputy manager at Essar.

She was living at the YWCA, he was at the YMCA next door. You could say, they were destined to meet.

"I could see even then, Ajit was the ambitious type," recalls Sarah Isaac.

She knew her parents would approve of this handsome boy, who was also a responsible family man. They got married in 1995, lived comfortably on two incomes but also gave generously – to Ajit's parents, his sister, to relatives in need. And also to their church, in the spirit of tithe laid out in the Bible.

Tanya was born in 1998, and shortly after, Ajit was bitten by the entrepreneurship bug. The family shifted to Bangalore, to start from scratch. A foolish move in the eyes of many but Sarah knew that once Ajit had set his mind on something, he made it happen. She stood by him like a rock.

It was a stressful time. Ajit worked long hours, while Sarah managed their daughter and two sets of ageing parents. When Ajit's first company got acquired, he plunged into building the second. The only thing he paid attention to, outside the business, was spending quality time with the family, especially young Tanya.

By 2013, Quess Corp was stable, and making a modest profit. The company had moved to its own headquarters in Bellandur, on the outskirts of Bangalore. One morning, Ajit noticed a dilapidated building on the road right opposite his office. A signboard with peeling paint read: Government Higher Primary School, Iblur.

Boys and girls with well-worn shoes and well-oiled hair marched in and out of the school. You could tell that the inside was as neglected as the outside. Ajit recalled his own formative years at Don Bosco, with its airy classrooms, expansive playground and caring teachers. A question flashed in his mind's eye...

"Would my life be a fraction of what it is today if I had gone to a government school?"

The answer was obvious, and Ajit felt compelled to 'do something'. Being in the temp staffing business where the average worker earns a mere 20,000 rupees a month, he knew that for many families, these schools were the only chance to receive any kind of education. Surely, they deserve better.

"I knew that if we could fix schools, we could change lives!"

In 2014, with the new CSR law coming into force, Quess set up Careworks Foundation. 2% of Quess Corp's annual profit was not a large amount, so, Ajit supplemented the CSR money with his own funds.

Smitha Sreenivas was hired to head the foundation and in her very first meeting with Ajit, she saw clarity, ambition and a long-term vision.

He talked about 14 goals for Careworks Foundation, which included better infrastructure, upgrading teachers, as well as making the model sustainable and replicable.

"When will we see the first doctors and engineers coming out of our schools?" asked Ajit.

Smitha shook her head in disbelief. Given the state of the schools, was that even possible!

ARCHITECTURE OF CHANGE

It started as a pilot project with that one school, across the road. But when Smitha approached the principal, she was not very enthusiastic.

"We already have 18 NGOs working with us," the principal said.

Akshara Foundation was teaching maths, Akshaya Patra providing mid-day meals. Teach for India sent its fellow, while Rotary club provided desks. But these individual efforts were like giving cough syrup to a patient with tuberculosis. The government school system needed much stronger medicine!

A cursory look at the school would tell you, it was in very bad shape. For example, there was no functioning toilet or handwash area. But hey, infrastructure was the government's responsibility, right? NGOs did not enter that space. Until Careworks decided that someone's gotta do the job. Let us do it.

It took 36 trips to the education department to get the necessary permission. Finally, when Ajit met with the architect, he pulled up a picture of his own school.

"Can we make these schools look just like that?" he asked.

It was a bit idealistic as goals go, but even small improvements such as clean toilets, bigger windows and a pakka courtyard began paying off. The foundation then conducted medical and dental check-ups for the kids, with several getting much-needed spectacles.

The morale of the teaching staff also shot up, thanks to training.

By year 2, attendance at the school had practically doubled. Indeed, the pilot was showing excellent results. Ajit often visited personally, to check the progress and his daughter Tanya – then a high school student – even volunteered to teach the kids art during her summer vacation.

The government saw the merits of private sector participation in education and started a 'school adoption program'. Given the large number of corporates in Bangalore, this looked like a good idea on paper. But as Careworks expanded and Smitha approached more schools, she often encountered principals who were indifferent.

Some companies had come to these schools with ill-thought out projects in the name of CSR. All they did was put up a plaque, take a photo, and disappear.

"Nobody asked us what we really need," was the common grouse of principals.

Careworks Foundation (CWF) structured its program differently. The foundation hired two civil engineers to go to each school, understand its issues and get a buy-in from the principal. Initially, when asked, they came up with fanciful ideas but with guidance from CWF they were able to participate constructively.

For example, at one school, students got meals from Akshaya Patra but ate in a dusty courtyard, under the midday sun. When the principal brought up this issue, CWF did the tiling and roofing, making it a space which also doubles up as an open air theatre and classroom.

In 2021, Careworks decided to introduce a life skills program. Initially, they approached a dozen NGOs doing similar programs but the costing was too high. So CWF devised its own curriculum. The entire process was carefully documented, along with pre and post testing of students to assess the impact.

"Ours is a result-based approach," says Smitha. "We also know that results take time."

For speed matters in business; patience bears fruit in philanthropy.

THE GREATEST WEALTH

Amidst the pulls and pressures of running a startup, there were challenges on the home front, as well. Ajit's father suffered a stroke, resulting in paralysis from the neck down. He needed constant care. Sarah stepped up and took responsibility. Subsequently, her parents were also diagnosed with cancer.

"The most outstanding thing about Sarah was, she never once complained," says Ajit.

Home was his happy space. Where, on an off day, Sarah would quietly arrange for a plate of piping hot banana fritters, and lift her husband's mood.

Even as their health worsened, Ajit's parents insisted on living in Chennai, close to their church community. In 2010, his mother developed multiple myeloma, a blood cancer which affects the bone marrow. At the end stage Thankamma was in great pain, which was alleviated with the help of medical morphine. She passed away in April 2016.

> *"Philanthropy is not cheque-signing for me. It's problem-solving."*

The various health issues of their parents sensitized Sarah and Ajit to the importance of quality healthcare. While they had access to it, what about ordinary people? Ajit decided to set up a Trust in his mother's memory, with a focus on uplifting hospitals in rural areas.

Starting with institutions set up by the British, now under CSI (Church of Southern India).

The Thankamma Ithapiri Memorial Trust (TIMT) began working with Christian Hospital Chattarpur, a remote area of Madhya Pradesh. Catering to the poorest of the poor, the hospital's infrastructure needed an upgrade. Critical medical equipment would also need to be procured.

The grant from TIMT supported the hospital to upgrade its ICU, purchase a CT machine and build a new doctors' accommodation. Similarly, the Thankamma Ithapiri Memorial Trust also took up the modernisation initiatives at the Marthoma Mission Hospital, Chungathara.

Then, in March 2020, the world came to a standstill. During Covid, there wasn't much you could do. So Ajit would often go for a walk in the park near their home in Koramangala. Nandan Nilekani also took a walk in the same park, and that's how the two struck up a friendship.

During these 'walk and talk' meetings, Ajit got insight into Nandan's philanthropic work. He learnt that the Nilekanis supported smaller NGOs, and provided large grants to public institutions. Nandan also put forth the idea that philanthropists could fund innovative solutions which have a high risk of failure.

"I admire the work Nandan has done; it's a source of inspiration!" says Ajit.

The takeaway was clear – like a business, philanthropy requires structure, and strategy. A little good work here, a little good work there is nice but it leaves no lasting legacy.

The work done so far was like dipping a toe into the water. Now, it was time to dive into the deep end...

LEGACY BUILDING

To do great work in life, you need great partners. Ajit Isaac found such a partnership with a man known as the 'Warren Buffett of Canada'. In the very first meeting, there was a meeting of minds. So, even though Prem Watsa's Fairfax Holdings offered a lower valuation than other investors, Ajit Isaac decided to go ahead with the deal. Fairfax – through Thomas Cook – acquired a 74% stake in Quess (formerly known as IKYA Human Capital Solutions).

"It was one of the best decisions I have taken," says Ajit.

Prem would go on to become an inspiration as well as a sort of father figure. In 2014, Prem had placed a huge bet on India, with a promise to invest a billion dollars. Four years later, when he called on Narendra Modi, they discussed a variety of topics. And at this meeting the Prime Minister had a suggestion.

"Why don't you do something in paediatric care?"

Prem exited the PMO, called Ajit and they decided to hire KPMG to do a study. After meeting multiple hospitals, KPMG recommended CMC Vellore as a partner. One of the busiest hospitals in India, with 10,000 OPD patients a day, CMC was actually in the process of building a new 1500 bed hospital, 10 kms from the original location.

The new hospital was a super-speciality facility but did not have paediatric care.

"If you can fund it, we are happy to set up a paediatric care hospital," they said.

CMC had explored the idea and dropped it, as it would cost approximately Rs 300 crore to set up a 340 bed hospital with 20 specialisations. Who would fund such a 'dream project'? It so happened that after initial discussions, the country went into lockdown. The project was put on the backburner and it seemed like maybe, it was not to be...

To CMC's joy and surprise, Ajit reached out again. He wished to visit Vellore, along with the Fairfax team, to understand how CMC worked and what it hoped to achieve.

“Ajit didn’t come with any agenda,” recalls Dr. Vikram Matthews, Director of CMC Vellore.

As a pioneering not-for-profit hospital, CMC was quite particular when it came to partnerships. Working only with those funders who fully aligned with their vision.

As it happened, Fairfax, Quess and CMC were all on the same page.

An MoU was signed in May 2022 with a shared vision - to create India’s finest research, teaching and practice centre for paediatrics. Fairfax committed Rs 270 crore, with Rs 15 crore put in by Quess Corp and Rs 15 crore from Ajit Isaac’s personal funds. Additionally, the Sick Kids Hospital, Toronto, was roped in as a technical partner.

Around this time, Ajit Isaac got a feeler from the Indian Institute of Science (IISc), which was setting up a medical college. Would he be interested in funding it? Ajit’s initial reaction was ‘no’, because the paediatric hospital project was already coming up. But it seemed a shame to give up a chance to do something with an institution of such eminence.

That’s when dinner table conversations that Ajit had been having with his daughter Tanya sparked an idea...

ONE VS THE MANY

From an early age, Tanya Isaac wanted to become a doctor. Watching her grandparents grapple with physical and neurological issues, sparked her interest in studying the human brain. But during her undergrad years at Tulane University, Tanya was required to take a course in public health. And that, changed everything.

“I realized that I didn’t want to go to medical school and treat individuals,” says Tanya.

She now wanted to pursue a career in public health. Tanya was passionate about the subject and when in India, on vacation, she loved to share all the new things she was learning with her dad. Discussions about ‘infectious disease’ and ‘chronic disease’ were par for the course dinner talk.

The importance of public health became all the more clear during Covid. It was an emergency that the country had no idea how to deal with in a systematic manner.

So Ajit said to IISc, “I have an interest in public health. Can we do something together?”

IISc came back with a proposal for a Centre for Public Health. As a science and engineering institution, IISc was happy to marry medical science with data science. There was clarity of vision on both sides, and a strong sense of purpose. With her background in public health, Tanya provided valuable inputs.

“If you can’t measure it, you can’t manage it.”

There are many factors, apart from biology, which determine health. The pricing of drugs, access to sanitation, air pollution – to name just a few. It was important to design the centre to look at health holistically. To not just study health problems after they occur but find ways to prevent them from happening in the first place.

An MOU to set up the Isaac Centre for Public Health (ICPH) at the IISc Medical School was signed in March 2022. Barely a month after the initial discussion.

“It’s rare for a donor to make a quick decision about such a large donation!” says IISc Director Govindan Rangarajan.

The Isaacs committed Rs 105 crore to the centre, which will be modelled around the Johns Hopkins School of Public Health. The centre will work in tandem with the medical and engineering schools to not only conduct research, but offer a master's degree in public health.

In addition, a programmatic component has been built in, with funds being disbursed to support visiting professors and international exchange programs. The Isaacs would be a part of the ICPH advisory committee meetings every quarter. So, it would be an ongoing relationship.

Because for Ajit Isaac, philanthropy means going beyond just signing a cheque.

EASING THE PASSAGE

When you hear about suffering, you offer sympathy. When you see it before your very eyes, you develop empathy. Thankamma's long and difficult illness made Ajit and Sarah acutely conscious of the challenges faced, when a loved one is diagnosed with terminal illness.

"We had 24-hour nursing for our parents, how many can afford that?" wondered Sarah.

A few patches of medical morphine which Thankamma had been prescribed remained, after her passing. The Isaacs thought it would be best to donate them to others who may be in need. So, they visited Karunashraya, one of the very few palliative care centres in the country.

While 10-14 million people require palliative care annually, less than 1% receive it. Mainstream hospitals do not provide it because it doesn't make enough money. The maximum that has been done is in Kerala, with a home care/community care model. The more Ajit reflected, the more he felt the need to 'do something'.

When working with rural hospitals, Ajit had reached out to Dr. Naresh Shetty, who was then heading the M.S. Ramaiah Medical College and Hospital. Dr. Shetty's team visited the mission hospitals at regular intervals and provided technical inputs. This time, Ajit reached out with a different request.

"I would like your help to set up a modern palliative care centre," he said.

Ajit envisioned a hub-and-spoke model – a facility with 100 beds which also provided home care within a 50 km radius. As they explored where, when and how to make this happen, they came across a remarkable lady called Mary Anchan. Along with her husband, she ran the Rural India Mission Hospital in Tumkur for over 30 years.

In July 2024, she lost her husband, and her son in October the same year. At age 91, Mary Anchan no longer had the energy to run the hospital herself.

"I am willing to donate this land to you for a good cause," she said.

With this beautiful gesture, the palliative centre now had a home spread over 2.5 acres. The Thankamma Ithapiri Memorial Trust would fund a modern, well-equipped building but the goal was to create a non-hospital environment. With ample open areas, greenery, a library, as well as yoga, music and meditation.

"In a hospital, everything is brick and mortar," says Dr. Shetty. "He wanted to build the centre around earth, water and air."

The centre plans to employ trained and compassionate staff, who desire to live in a community as well as serve others. Meanwhile, Ajit has also brought Johns Hopkins University (JHU) on board as a technical partner, to bring global best practices and research rigour to the project.

The foundation stone for the Tumkur Palliative Care centre was laid in 2023, with a two-year time frame to get the project up and running.

RISK CAPITAL

Entrepreneurs look at a problem and see an opportunity. That's a great mindset to have, even as a philanthropist. The trouble is, there are so many problems in society, where obvious solutions do not work. But who will dive headlong into a mess and innovate? Enter Gloria Benny, Sujith Varkey, Mekha T, and Navneeth Kumar, founders of 'Guardians of Dreams'.

It started in 2006. Gloria and Sujith were college students and walked into a Child Care Institution (CCI) for the first time. They expected to find children asking for treats; to their surprise, the kids asked for books. In fact, during their next visit, they even submitted book reviews.

That's when it struck Gloria - there is so much untapped potential.

Over the next 10 years, they immersed themselves in the sector, setting up volunteer chapters across 20 cities. But there were fundamental problems that remained unsolved. 30 lakh children in India are orphans, or have parents who cannot care for them. Of this number, 3.7 lakh reside in 9000 Child Care Institutions (CCIs).

"CCIs are the bedrock of child care in society, outside of the family unit", says Gloria.

A handful of CCIs, such as SOS Children's Village and Shishu Mandir provided high standards care. The rest were small, under-resourced and low-quality. In 2016, Gloria and Sujith set up Guardians of Dreams, to solve this problem. To do this at scale, they needed to build a model that could be adopted by small, independent CCIs.

So they went and tried to raise some funds, to do the development work. And hit a brick wall. No one knew what a CCI was. And no one cared. After meeting more than 70 potential funders and being turned down, Guardian of Dreams got connected to Ajit Isaac, through Rajesh Padmashali, editor of Outlook Business.

The meeting was just before the pandemic, and then, things went cold with Covid. Nevertheless, Gloria kept in touch with Ajit, keeping him updated about their work.

In 2021, she got a call from Ajit's office for a second meeting. He listened to their presentation, and how they proposed to solve the problem. And didn't say – great idea but this is too far-fetched or overambitious. In fact, Ajit agreed to fund the project by the end of that meeting.

Finally, there was a donor who understood, that to build capacity and scale, one needs to sit down, study a problem in-depth, design a solution, iterate and test it. Gloria and Sujith were young, passionate and persistent. They had given up corporate careers to take up a cause with no glamour, or financial incentive.

"Why don't we do some work with them and see," thought Ajit.

The upside – a potential transformation of the entire sector. The risk – the effort could fail. But that's how innovation happens.

In December 2021, Guardians of Dreams entered into three-year partnership with the newly set up Isaac Foundation and at Ajit's insistence, the MOU was signed in the Guardian of Dreams office with no media or photographers present. Ajit spent an hour talking with all the team members, including an intern, boosting their morale and already-high motivation.

JUSTICE FOR ALL

It was a chance meeting on a zoom call organised by Rohini

Nilekani during Covid that introduced Arghya Sengupta, founder of Vidhi Legal to Ajit Isaac.

"What struck me was that here was a philanthropist talking about criminal justice."

As a lawyer, Arghya Sengupta had seen most people shy from anything to do with 'criminals'.

When they met, Arghya realized that this was not a passing interest but a cause that Ajit truly believed in. Vidhi proposed a project called 'Crime and Punishment' which would study why there were so many undertrials in India. Ajit Isaac agreed to fund it.

"Politicians, when they play a constructive role, are tremendous changemakers in society."

Common sense says that we have too many undertrials because they cannot afford a good lawyer. But when you dig deeper, there is a more fundamental issue. Vidhi reviewed 882 laws and found that 370 out of those have criminal provisions.

To put it simply, a person may be committing a criminal act unwittingly.

"We documented 7,000 crimes: nearly 5,200 of them can end in a jail term," says Naveed Ahmad, Senior Resident Fellow and Lead, Crime and Punishment.

For example, if you don't give your dog sufficient exercise—the law does not define what 'sufficient exercise' is—there is a jail term attached to it. As per the Delhi Municipal Corporation Act, if a sweeper proceeds on leave without informing his commissioner, there is a criminal punishment attached to it. Shocking, isn't it?

The refrain from the government is: 'we don't have information'. Thanks to the Vidhi effort there is now a data set which shows all that needs to be decriminalised.

Another area of intervention is to understand how the system actually impacts people – for which Vidhi is working with a few journalists to document their stories. For example, a mentally ill person (in Jammu) spent 22 years in jail because the lawyers could not follow up on the case.

Ajit Isaac's suggestion was: "Why don't we go into all the districts and offer legal aid?"

For Vidhi, it was refreshing to see the passion with which he was looking at the issue. A second project funded by him is doing capacity building work for states. So that they can write better laws for the benefit of people. Work has started in Tamil Nadu, Ajit's home state, and there's been quite a lot of traction. As well as some startling discoveries.

For example, the Tamil Nadu state prison manual has 'A' and 'B' class prisoners. What this means in practical terms is that the labour that a prisoner does is explicitly dependent on their caste. Brahmin prisoners get to do the cooking, while the Dalit prisoners are assigned to clean latrines. Efforts are on to change such mindless practices, and more.

What the Vidhi team appreciates is that Ajit is not only a giver, but a learner.

"Ajit is a funder who completely lets you be", acknowledges Arghya Sengupta. There is no interference whatsoever, in terms of the work itself.

IN CONCLUSION

Construction for the CMC Paediatric Centre started on 22nd

July, 2024. The theme for the inauguration was the biblical story of Noah's Ark. As the animals were saved and the ark was no longer needed, its planks were dismantled and used to 'construct the hospital'. Signifying that the worst pain can lead to new hope and new beginnings.

"Somebody is giving us crores of money and he is so down to earth and normal," was the reaction of all those who interacted with him.

The CMC project will be completed by August 2026, around the same time as the Isaac Centre for Public Health becomes fully functional. The Tumkur Palliative Centre is still a work in progress, while Guardian of Dreams has completed its pilot program with 10 Child Care Institutions (CCIs). Based on the learnings from this pilot, the Capacity Accelerator Program has now been rolled out to 30 CCIs across Bangalore, Hyderabad, Chennai, and Ernakulam.

Meanwhile, the school project which is over a decade old now, is delivering measurable impact. Today, Quess Corp works with 75 government schools, and some of those who studied there are on their way to becoming doctors and engineers. Proving that the impossible can be made possible.

What's more, when multilateral agency officers come to Karnataka to see education levels, the government brings them to Quess Foundation Schools. Because they are now like lighthouses within the system. Ajit hopes that aspects of the program can be adopted as a standard across the state.

His own learnings included that for the work to succeed, you have to get people on your side. The local administration, the panchayat, even politicians. You need to understand the local milieu, local festivals, and 'make your way' into their lives. This takes time and patience.

"Development is like a big ship", says Ajit. "It takes time to turn."

Sarah and Tanya are co-passengers on this journey. Tanya is pursuing a PhD in public health from SRM University, studying the impact of heat stress and air pollution on pregnant women in India. She has no plans yet to join operations of any company but is very interested in working with the Foundation.

"But first, I need to develop as a public health professional," she says. "Only then will people respect me and listen to what I have to say."

Earning the stripes, so that she may
Carry this legacy, a long long way.

For more on Ajit Isaac Foundation scan:

ADVICE TO YOUNG PHILANTHROPISTS

Start before you hit the age of 50. It's the best time of your life. You have networks. You have some resources. Time is on your side.

You will have the satisfaction of seeing the results of some of this work in your lifetime.

Secondly, use every liquidity event to give away a little bit. Every five years or so, something will come. Give away a little bit. So you create a regular calendar of giving.

The third thing is that you must structure this in your mind. How much do you want to keep as your corpus? And do you want to give from your corpus, or from your revenue? Once you have this structure in your mind, it becomes a well-oiled machine at play.

Believe me, when you solve problems and impact lives, there's a sense of fulfilment and gratitude. It is a virtuous cycle that prompts you to do more and more and more.

"Scaling isn't just about numbers... it's about creating lasting impact."

Big is Beautiful

BINNY BANSAL

He made the playbook for unicorn startups in India.
Even in philanthropy, he believes in scale
and the power of market forces.

Binny Bansal was born in Chandigarh, back then, a sleepy, 'service class' town. Since both his parents were working, Binny would spend the afternoons with his cousins, who lived down the road. They were constantly being told, khelo mat, padhaai karo, whereas Binny's parents were easy going.

"My parents let me be independent...that had a big impact on me."

At St Anne's Convent, Binny was an avid sportsman but an average student. However, he was the class topper in computer science and learnt programming, on his own, from class five. Not in pursuit of marks, but because he liked it.

In class 11, Binny joined IIT coaching, where he aced physics but lagged behind in other subjects. This is when a streak of ambition surfaced; he put in the slog and made it to the top 5. With a JEE rank of 28, Binny joined IIT Delhi but went back to his easygoing ways. All he wanted after graduating was a job in computer science.

Despite an offer from D. E. Shaw, Binny joined Sarnoff, which was working on interesting problems in computer vision. Because he failed to finish his final year BTech project, Binny had to stay back on campus in the summer of 2005. Sachin Bansal, one year senior, was there for the same reason.

It was a case of 'jab we met' but not with his future business partner. Binny was too busy wooing his future wife Trisha, who was doing an internship in the same lab. But fate did bring Sachin and Binny together when they both moved to Bangalore. And, the rest is history.

When Walmart acquired a 77% controlling stake in Flipkart in 2018, Binny Bansal became the first unicorn founder in India to come into unimaginable wealth.

At 36, he was too young to retire. So, what were his options?

1. Launch another startup

2. Mentor other startups

3. Philanthropic giving

Binny has done all three, and that's what makes it a story worth telling.

It's safe to say that anything Binny does gets noticed, and sparks trends. In 2020, at age 38, Binny Bansal became the youngest person on the EdelGive Hurun India Philanthropy List. Four years later, the list features several names under 40, including startup founders. Why wait till your hair is silver, to start making a difference?

"Try some small experiments, support a few causes, get some learnings."

Build your personal balance sheet with good karma.
The only true, timeless wealth.

It was a second rejection from Google that really irked Binny. Thoda to ego hurt hua. "Apply to Amazon. I will refer you," said Sachin Bansal.

Sachin happened to live in the apartment next door. In Bangalore, the IIT crowd stuck together, even perpetuating hostel loyalties. Binny shared an apartment with chaps from Shivalik hostel while Sachin was staying with the Jwalamukhi guys. But they all hung out together on weekends and became friends.

Binny took Sachin's advice and got a job with Amazon. However, as it often happens in IT, he was not assigned to any team or project. So, each morning, Binny would go to the office, play table tennis, eat lunch, go to Barista and return home. In between, he would pass the time surfing the internet.

That's when he came across blogs like TechCrunch and Venture Beat. The energy around startups in Silicon Valley was exciting; Sachin got infected as well. Being from a business family, it was Sachin who proposed, yaar hum bhi kuch karte hain.

As coding was the only thing they knew how to do, it had to be some kind of tech idea.

The initial plan was to make a comparison shopping site, but the existing e-commerce platforms were poorly made. So, they ended up building one themselves. The Bansals decided to start with selling books, just as Amazon had, in its early years.

By August they had quit their jobs and in October 2007, Flipkart.com was launched.

Now came the tough part – talking to distributors and retailers, to procure books.

"Why are you leaving such a good job to get into this line?" was the constant refrain.

With little cooperation from the trade, the duo did what any self-respecting coder would – hacked their way to success. They crawled the websites of publishers, as well as amazon to list books on their own site. There was no inventory, the title was purchased after an order came in.

In the first four months, they got five orders a week. Then, they happened to meet Gaurav Singh Kushwaha, founder of Chakpak. A funded startup seeking to be the 'Indian IMDB'. The Chakpak team taught Sachin SEO and within six months, when someone searched for a book, Flipkart would show up on page one.

Till December 2008, they were still packing and dispatching orders with their own hands. Then, they shifted to an office in Koramangala with a small warehouse in the basement.

Binny's prospective father-in-law came to see, ladka karta kya hai. He left 'not quite sure' but thought the boy is from IIT, if this fails he will get a job. The marriage went ahead.

Things began looking up – in mid-2009, Accel Partners invested in Flipkart. Six months later, Tiger Global followed. By the end of 2010, the founders had done a small, secondary deal which brought $1.5 million in their bank accounts. Sachin bought a Mercedes, Binny now drove a BMW.

"But we were so busy growing the company, most of the money just lay in the bank".

For the true entrepreneur, money is a mere byproduct. The thrill lies in living the dream.

LET'S BUILD THIS CITY

In 2009, Mekin Maheshwari joined Flipkart as employee #2. An engineer from PESIT, he had worked with Yahoo for four years, felt it was 'too slow' and yearned to join a startup.

That didn't go as planned and he ended up running a technology centre for an American company, which was a decent enough job.

"But I was like, I can be building stuff for Indian users!"

So he quit and was in search of a co-founder when he happened to meet Binny and Sachin and decided, 'this could be my startup'. Mekin joined Flipkart as 'head of engineering' in August 2009, when they operated from a two bedroom house with four employees and two interns.

The tech built by the founders was good but it was not designed to operate at scale. That's what Mekin was hired for and the Bansals were happy to step aside and let him do the job. He built the tech team with raw talent, because no 'expert' can tell you how to reach a place which is not yet on the map.

Flipkart had to expand beyond books; they tried grocery, fashion, and then hit paydirt with mobile phones. Mekin stepped down as CTO to experiment with two startups within Flipkart – one in music and e-books, the other in payments.. Meanwhile, Flipkart started burning crazy amounts of money to compete with Amazon.

The founders were fighting multiple battles and one of them was hiring. Please take over the HR function, they said to Mekin. 'You are a people person'. But by mid-2015, Flipkart had grown to 35,000 people and Mekin was no longer having fun. He put in his papers. Like many early Flipkart employees, he was rich enough to 'no longer work for money'.

In 2016, in a historic deal, Flipkart was sold to Walmart for $16 billion. Binny stayed on as CEO for another year. And, then what?

"The greatest satisfaction comes from knowing we've inspired others to dream and build."

Sachin Bansal quickly launched another startup while Binny had other ambitions.

"I wanted to do interesting things, help others in the ecosystem."

But was that just a nice thing to say in press interviews, or would he actually do it?

ENABLING ENTREPRENEURS

With the Walmart acquisition, Flipkart had become what every startup aspired to be – a homegrown success story. But what would it take to create a hundred such startups?

"I knew that alone, I can possibly help 10-15 people... I wanted to do much more!"

Binny roped in his former Flipkart colleague Saikiran Krishnamurthy and together, they had breakfast conversations with a wide cross-section of founders. The idea was to pinpoint, what areas they were struggling with. It was a deeply personal project, with most of the breakfasts hosted by Binny, at his home.

The founders knew they could open up to someone who had seen it all, done it all. Through these conversations, 10 patterns emerged. And that's how xto10x was born.

In the early days, it was an 'academy' where eight company founders were invited to participate. Every other Friday, the group met for 4 hours and went into learning mode. The Flipkart experience anchored the program – what had worked for the company, what had not. With the deepest learnings emerging from their biggest mistakes.

Reflecting on his own journey, Binny knew that once you had product-market-fit (PMF) you were in new territory. Which was dangerous and uncharted. Even after Series C funding, an entrepreneur can still make catastrophic blunders. That's why only 1 in 10 such companies goes on to become a serious, long-term business.

Incubators and accelerators help early in the journey but at this stage, you are alone.

"So, my philosophy was to help growth startups in a sustainable way," says Binny.

xto10x is not structured as a non-profit, it is a viable, profit-making company. But it is anchored by a noble purpose. It is the rare founder who sets up a whole organisation and shares his learnings so honestly and generously. The time Binny spends is not transactional, it's in the spirit of being a coach to the next generation of founders.

Startups never have enough cash, so, instead of upfront fees, xto10x takes equity. Their belief is that there will be an upside. Five, seven, or even ten years down the line.

"Very few companies would be okay with this kind of delayed gratification," says Saikiran Krishnamurthy, CEO, xto10x.

In the last seven years, xto10x has worked with 450 founders, including almost every unicorn. It is now working with companies in Southeast Asia and Saudi Arabia. There is every likelihood that xto10x will be wildly profitable in the near future. But in Binny's own mental model it is a form of 'giving back'.

"For me, from the start, investing in startups was not about getting X% as a return."

Back in 2012, when Binny became an angel investor, it was with a purpose. To help more startups succeed, especially the ones whom the world might perceive as the 'crazy ones'. Among them – GreyOrange (warehouse robotics), Ather (electric vehicles), Pandorum (3-D printed corneas). All of them, at one time, were 'moonshots'.

Because when you've been to the moon, you know that nothing is impossible.

THE DILEMMA OF TWO INDIAS

At one end are the IIT-IIM educated, deep-funded entrepreneurs, pursuing larger-than-life ambitions. On the other is the average young person, who never learned to dream. When former Flipkart CTO Mekin Maheshwari started exploring the social impact space, he read the Annual State of Education (ASER) report. And, this reality hit him in the gut.

"I realised that entrepreneurial pedagogy is needed in our schools," says Mekin.

Learning cannot happen just sitting in the classroom, you need to 'do stuff' in the real world. So, in 2017, he set up Udhyam Learning Foundation. Using his own money, he began experimenting, building a model from first principles.18 months later, he knew that to achieve scale and impact, he would need to work with government schools.

While the number of children attending school has grown exponentially, the system has failed them. If you can do ratta and get marks, you are 'good'. While the vast majority of kids feels hopeless and useless, ki hamara toh kuch honey wala nahin. What if they could be instilled with a sense of agency, confidence and can-do spirit?

That was the proposition Mekin shared with Binny in 2018, when Udhyam was looking to scale. The idea resonated strongly with Binny, in principle it was not very different from xto10x. Except that Udhyam was working to sow seeds in soil which had never been cultivated. Having worked closely with Mekin, Binny believed in his vision.

"I see the problem, I see your passion" he said to Mekin. "How can I support you?"

In 2019, Udhyam started working with ITIs in Haryana, and in Delhi government schools, where entrepreneurship curriculum was incorporated into a program called 'Business Blasters'. The state gave every student Rs 2000 to team up, create and run an actual business, with teachers acting as mentors.

The top 145 Business Blasters teams were showcased at an exhibition where media and investors were invited. The enthusiasm and confidence with which kids made pitches and gave demos validated Mekin's hypothesis. Entrepreneurship is a mindset - it can be instilled.

Udhyam now partners with government schools in 10 states including Punjab, Uttarakhand, MP, Telangana, Andhra Pradesh, Maharashtra, Kerala and Karnataka.

From day 1, Mekin had decided not to take any money from the government. So Udhyam's annual budget of Rs 20 crore is funded by philanthropic donors, with Binny contributing a significant portion.

"We aren't vendors," says Mekin. "The government calls us 'noble people' from Bangalore".

Indeed, both the thinking and funding for Udhyam comes from the startup ecosystem of the city, in which Flipkart has played a huge role. It nurtured a bold new breed who leaped from employment to entrepreneurship in their twenties and thirties. PhonePe, CureFit, Jumbotail, Udaan, Groww, Slice... the list is ever-growing.

Business or social enterprise, the 'Flipkart Effect' is thinking at scale and placing trust in good people.

For Mekin, it's knowing he has a financial backer who will not question his model. Instead he will say – 'you solve this problem, I have your back'. As the one working in the field, you know what works best.

But whenever you need a sounding board, or someone to open doors for you, I'll be there.

In 2024, Mekin said to Binny, this year I want to do things differently. Let me push my team to raise as much money as possible. If there is a shortfall, I will come to you.

"Go for it!" said Binny.

With this approach, Udhyam was able to raise much larger sums of money than before. Mekin eventually asked Binny for only 50% of the money he had originally committed. That's the entrepreneurial mindset in action, even in non-profit mode.

CONNECTING WITH PROBLEMS

A decade ago, Atul Satija was Chief Business Officer of InMobi. Life was good. The company had received funding from Softbank and even became a unicorn. But all along, Atul had this junoon – before I turn 40, I am going to leave this space. So, in 2015, he quit InMobi to set up the Nudge Institute.

"How do we bring top talent in the country to solve social problems?" Atul asked himself.

The answer – you send out the right signals to young people with drive and ambition. You tell them, maximising wealth is not everything. Your talent can be harnessed to do something bigger than selling soaps or credit cards or being a coder. You won't be obnoxiously overpaid, but you'll be able to support your family comfortably.

> *"I define philanthropy as that which you are doing for others, rather than for yourself."*

In 2016, Atul launched NCore, to give incubation support and seed money to budding social entrepreneurs. A year later, NCore was looking for philanthropic money to expand its work. That's when Atul met Binny. It was a transitional phase, Walmart was on board but Binny was still the CEO of Flipkart.

Being part of the startup community, Atul had reached out to many founders, seeking support. He was prepared to spend a good deal of time answering questions. Like, what does the data say? Or, show me the evidence. It usually took long left-brain conversations over multiple meetings to get a buy-in.

"My model is - find the right people, right entrepreneurs and enable them."

Binny was different. Atul sensed a warm, high empathy personality. What was truly surprising was Binny's humility.

He simply said, "Look, I don't understand this space at all. I am here to listen and learn."

And, right away, he connected with the problem, asked some questions which made sense. But at the end of the day, it was about placing a bet on Atul Satija.

'I relate to you as a person, seems like you are doing something good, how can I help?'

By the end of the meeting Binny had said 'yes' and soon after, wrote a substantial cheque. How and where to use the money was completely up to to Atul - no conditions, no restrictions. Put it in your corpus, pay salary to employees, build an app. Whatever the organisation needs.

"I would call this 'high trust philanthropy', similar to the VC model for startups," says Atul.

Binny's funds were, in fact, used to support The Nudge Institute's office expenses that year, among other things. During Covid, Binny once again donated but this time to Give India, which, by then, was also under Atul's leadership.

In 2022, Binny made a five-year commitment to Nudge, re-affirming his belief in the team, and the progress it's made.

A NEW MISSION

One of the things that is never counted as 'impact' is job creation by startups. In its 10 years journey before acquisition, Flipkart created a million jobs, directly and indirectly. But it's only a drop in the ocean, when you see the number of jobs that a young and educated India actually needs.

"I have seen how boards and companies think of jobs. It's not a priority," says Binny.

Less than 10% of India's workforce is in formal jobs. The remaining 90% feel like failures. You are good for nothing, the system says to them. You will not be able to do anything. But the world is changing and so is the human capital ecosystem.

This is a huge opportunity for India's large, young workforce.

Binny sees a future where, say, an AI-trained Indian lawyer in a tier 2 city can be working for anybody, anywhere in the world. The challenge is how to create an army of AI-trained lawyers in India who can deliver it with better quality, speed, lower cost, consistently and in that, long term.

And to do this, across all sectors.

AI as a force for good is an idea that Binny is embracing wholeheartedly. In April 2025, he launched the 'Binny Bansal Institute for Inventing the Future' at Plaksha University. The vision is AI + X, where AI means frontier technologies and X could be healthcare, energy, agriculture — any sector at all.

Can AI solve real world problems? Create jobs, rather than destroy them? Binny strongly believes so.

"I am excited to see how this initiative will develop scalable solutions for global challenges and equip the next generation of innovators," he says.

The Institute for Inventing the Future aims to transform research findings into scalable, real world solutions. It will collaborate closely with UC Berkeley's world-renowned AI research laboratory.

Binny has committed Rs 70 crore towards the operating expense of the institute, as well as his time and mentorship.

At 42, Binny Bansal has time on his side, and is brimming with ideas and energy.

May more of our brightest and best
Keep striving to uplift the rest.

ADVICE TO YOUNG PHILANTHROPISTS

Everybody has some passion or the other. So try some small experiments, support some causes in a small way, get some learnings.

When you get an answer on how you can scale, double down on time and money.

Whether you put in time, or money, or both, what matters is the outcome.

"We are like venture capitalists but acting for the greater good."

Joy Capital

SUBROTO AND SUSMITA BAGCHI

The Bagchis believe in building institutions and then, walking away. No attachment to the money donated, nor to the outcome.

Subroto Bagchi was born in a government quarter with no water and no electricity but into a loving Bengali family which had made Odisha its home since four generations.

"My entire schooling was in Odia medium and in government schools."

One of Subroto's abiding memories is of his mother setting up her kitchen in the tiny quarters allotted to his father, after yet another transfer. As the youngest in the family, it was Subroto who was sent to next door houses with some curry, or a katori of kheer. And quickly, strangers would become familiar aunties and life-long friends.

The family had limited means, and yet, one summer his elder brother Amitav returned home from hostel without his sweater and only blanket. He had given them to a boy who had nothing. Oh, how Subroto longed to be like his boro dada!

Returning from New Delhi after being judged the 'Best NCC Cadet of India' at the Republic Day parade, Subroto felt magnanimous. He distributed NCC-issued blankets and sweaters to rikshaw-pullers, instead of returning them to his quarter master. Years later, he read a line from Mother Teresa – 'Before you give, you must have'.

Mother's words created remorse; he was giving away things that did not belong to him.

The urge to 'make something of himself' consumed Subroto Bagchi for the next four decades. A job as a lower division clerk was not enough. Qualifying as a management trainee in DCM was a turning point, opening the doors to a global career in IT.

After a stellar stint at Wipro, Subroto set up Mindtree with nine co-founders. And one day, Subroto and his wife Susmita realised that the 'Mother Teresa moment' had arrived – 'We have, now we must give'.

But who, how, when and where to give? That was the question which would consume them for the next several years.

Their two daughters were fully supportive – it's your money, do with it as you wish. They had just one request, please give all that you wish to give during your lifetime. This added urgency to the act of giving. It also fit in with the couple's philosophy of 'giving big' in order to lay the foundation for lasting institutions.

In this spirit, the Bagchis made eye-popping contributions to set up a world class cancer hospital and palliative care centre in Bhubaneswar and, to the Indian Institute of Science Medical School coming up in Bangalore.

Life came full circle when the Bagchis packed up their bags and moved to Bhubaneswar in 2016 to work full-time as public servants.

This feels apt, as Subroto feels that both Odisha and Karnataka are his 'motherlands'.

"Odisha gave me birth and Karnataka gave me identity."

Go kiss the world, glow like the sun
In the matrix of life, be The One.

It was a sunny April morning when Subroto Bagchi arrived at the Lok Sewa Bhawan in Bhubaneswar, to give a speech to a select audience. As he walked up to the podium, he had a spring in his step.

He had officially 'retired' from Mindtree, just two days earlier, on 31st March 2016.

"One last commitment, then Susmita and I will be free to travel," he thought to himself.

Two days later, there was a call from the Chief Minister's Office.

"Honourable CM would like to speak to you."

When he came on the line, the CM had an unusual request – help us in the area of skills development. What's more, he offered Subroto a post equivalent to 'cabinet minister'.

Subroto was taken aback. A man from the private sector working from inside the government? It was a daunting thought. That night, neither Subroto nor Susmita could sleep. By dawn, they had reached a consensus - when destiny calls, you do not turn away.

"You owe it to our state," said Susmita, to which Subroto agreed in principle. But while his heart said yes, the head was still undecided. The solution - to ask three people whose opinion he valued highly, before taking a final call. The first of them was Manish Sabharwal, founder of Team Lease.

"You must do it," said Manish, without hesitation. One down, two to go.

The second person he sought out was Nandan Nilekani, much admired for working with the government to set up Aadhar. Nandan listened patiently, then posed a question.

"Tell me one thing, can you speak Odia?"

"Yes," replied Subroto. "Better than most Odia people."

"Then, go ahead and do it!" said Nandan. Two down, one to go.

The last person Subroto consulted was his own brother, D. P. Bagchi, who had retired from the government as Chief Secretary in 2002.

"Who do you think you are?" he thundered over the phone. "You private sector guys, all the time you criticize the government. If you have got any capability and guts, go do it!"

Well, that sealed the deal. Subroto and Susmita packed four suitcases and landed in Bhubaneswar, thinking of this assignment as a two-year interim project. In the first meeting with the CM, it was clear that any and all support would be provided. Tell us, Mr Bagchi, any person, any consultant, anybody you need from anywhere.

Subroto smiled and said, "Sir I will not bring anybody. I will work with the system."

Did Gandhi take a bunch of strategy consultants to Champaran? No, you have to be the change you wish to see.

BACK TO BASICS

In the blazing heat of May, with temperatures touching 48 degrees, Subroto Bagchi headed out to the hinterland in a 'Government of Odisha' emblazoned Innova. His goal: to cover all 30 districts of Odisha in the next 30 days. Subroto's former boss, Azim Premji, had once made a remark, which stayed with him.

"The most successful US Presidents are those who, in the first 90 days... know what they are going to do," said Premji.

Subroto knew that his first 90 days were just as crucial. The 'system' was observing – was he just another casual, gyaan-giving outsider? Or did this man mean business?

The act of visiting an Industrial Training Institute (ITI) itself sent a signal. No one cared about school dropouts studying in a dilapidated building in the middle of nowhere. A visit by a government official with the rank of 'cabinet minister' was simply unheard of. There was a scramble to welcome, and to impress, the bada saheb.

"We have ten acres, four buildings, four lathe machines," said the principal of the first ITI.

"That's not what I want to know," Subroto replied. "Give me 10-6-4-2."

10 names of students you are proud of. Of these, 6 should be working outside Odisha - in BHEL Bangalore, Cochin Shipyard, DRDO, Tata Steel and the like. Of these 10, you have to tell me the names of 4 girls. And finally you have to tell me the names of 2 kids who have not taken a job, but set up a small shop or business of their own.

This strange request had the ITI in a frenzy. By the time he reached, the third ITI, 10-6 and 2 had been found. Only the 4 girls were missing, in fact they had been unable to locate even one. In fact the % of girls enrolled was an abysmal 6%, that too in trades like sewing and stenography.

Then came a voice from the back of the room. An old man who'd been with the ITI for several decades spoke up.

"Sir, there was a girl," he said. "An Adivasi girl."

She had lost her father at a young age, landed up in that ITI and studied Electronics for two years.

"Where is she now?" asked Subroto, barely able to contain his excitement.

"Sir, she is in the Indian Railways, working as a loco pilot."

Aha – this was the girl Subroto Bagchi had been searching for. In true ministerial fashion, he demanded to talk to the girl in 10 minutes. The power of government is such, that when it really wants to do something, it will get done. The girl came on the line, she had no idea who was calling or why. But she answered confidently.

"My name is Muni Tigga. Main Inter-City Express ko Bhubaneswar se kheench ke Palasa le ke jati hoon, aur wapas le ke aati hoon".

"To change the system from within, needs big picture thinking, urgency, and a narrative."

What Subroto Bagchi had been searching for was not four girls, but one Muni Tigga who could become an inspiration to thousands of girls, just like her. Muni Tigga was felicitated by the CM and covered extensively in the media. It changed the narrative around girl child enrolment in ITIs completely.

Now every third ITI Subroto Bagchi visited miraculously produced a hitherto forgotten girl student – working in DRDO, or some factory. Muni Tigga became a role model and inspiration for thousands of girls, just like her. Over the next couple of years, the girl child enrolment in ITIs would jump from 6% to 30%.

Once the 'system' was shaken, and awakened, there was no looking back.

LISTEN BEFORE YOU ACT

As he travelled across the state, meeting students and teachers at ITIs, Subroto Bagchi learnt a few home truths. The institutes were so shabby and inconsequential that the district collector's peon was considered to be more powerful than the principal of the local ITI.

An acquaintance even asked Subroto, with some concern, why he was endangering himself. He mentioned that in UP, no one dares to set foot in an ITI.

"Wo to raat mein hi chalte hain... They function only at night," he added.

"Why is that?" asked a puzzled Subroto.

"Wahan bandook banta hai," came the matter of fact reply. It's where the local goons assemble country-made guns.

The situation was not so bad in Odisha but clearly, the powers-that-be hardly cared. The kids of bureaucrats aspired for IITs, while ITIs were attended by kids who could not make it to college. The attitude of skills training providers was no better. For example, the government had given 42 acres of land to a leading engineering company, to train construction workers.

In the hostel set up for the trainees, there were no cots. When questioned, the company sheepishly said that it was training the kids to work on construction site, so they should not 'get used to' the luxury of a bed. This, Subroto said, was unacceptable. Would you do this for engineering or management trainees?

"I am coming back after 30 days," he said. "I want to see a good quality cot and mattress for each of these kids".

Wherever he went, people arranged for food in the circuit house.

"No, I will eat with the trainees of the institution that I visit," said Subroto.

At one such venue, he met a group of young women training to be nurses. After they heard his inspiring lecture on how important their service will be to the nation, a diminutive girl spoke up. In chaste Odia, she said - aap ek baat humein batayein. We study here in the morning, then go to the District Hospital for practicals.

"Sadak par log humein chhedte hain. They talk bad about us and say you have a poor character, that's why you are becoming a nurse."

The girl started sobbing, she was joined by the rest of the class. Listening to their anguish made Subroto feel like dirt. It made him realise a stark reality – as a nation, we do not give respect to skills. Being a carpenter in Germany or Switzerland or Korea is as respected as being an IT engineer.

Not so in India.

In Singapore, a young person educated at an ITE (equivalent to ITI) gets a starting salary of $34,000. A graduate of Singapore Polytechnique, which is globally benchmarked, will get $36,000. If you have an engineering degree, you will start at $37,000. However, in India, the salary differentials are enormous, from day 1.

Subroto pondered – how do we reform society? How do we make skilling aspirational?

One way to boost morale is to recognise and felicitate achievers. The biggest win possible was a gold medal at the 'Olympic of Skills' – the WorldSkill Competition. Forget Odisha, India had never won gold at this prestigious event.

At the national skills competition, Odisha was placed second after Maharashtra. The following year, they were #1 in the country but it was in 2019, at the WorldSkill Competition held at Kazan, Russia, that S. Aswatha Narayana struck gold for India. And yes, he was from Odisha.

Not only was he given a prize of Rs 1 crore, his institution received Rs 5 crore - an incentive to train more young men and women who would make the state proud.

THE VISION

Changing mindsets is not an easy task. But breaking down the problem, Subroto Bagchi articulated four visions. Number one — we will not just build skills, we are here to do human transformation. What does that mean? Human transformation has to get a brand and that brand will be 'Skilled in Odisha'.

"Inherently, ordinary people are capable of extraordinary things."

"Employers will ask, are you an ITI student or are you from one of the Odisha ITIs?"

Number two, in five years' time, corporate India must make a beeline to our technical institutions to 'lock in talent'. Like they go to engineering colleges and make offers to third year students, ITI students in Odisha must have an employment letter in hand before they finish their course.

The third vision – in five years' time, international employers will know where Odisha is and start hiring in Odisha. And last but not least, the state must become a sandbox of innovation. Any bright idea about skill development anywhere, we'll step forward and try it out here first.

It was not a two-year project, but a ten-year one. And luckily, Susmita was with him, all the way. Being an Odia, she too was deeply connected to her roots, as she travelled with Subroto across the length and breadth of the state. Then came an opportunity from the Chief Minister's office, to do her bit, independently.

"I was invited to take on the 'Mo School Abhiyan', which I gladly accepted."

Mo means my, and Mo School Abhiyan is a project conceived by the CM to connect the alumni of government schools with their alma mater. From police commissioners to famous doctors, to the prime minister's principal advisor P. K. Mishra – the who's who from the state of Odisha trace their education back to the government school system.

Many of them would contact the government and express a desire to 'do something'. However, there would invariably be questions about 'how our money would be used', or 'can we contribute in other ways'? And so, the CM decided it was time to set up an organisation to manage the program in a professional way.

Mo School Abhiyan was launched on Nov 14, 2017. In addition to channelising funds from donors, a matching contribution was provided by the state. So, if someone gives X to a particular school, the government matches it with 2X, and the district administration can decide what to use the money for.

Susmita joined as Chairperson in August 2019 and on a visit to Malkangiri district to conduct a review, the district education officer proudly shared a story.

"Ma'am, the smallest amount has come from my district," he said.

"I know," replied Susmita. She had seen 'Rs 200' highlighted in the annual report,

"No ma'am, you don't know the whole story," said the officer.

Pulla Palli Upper Primary School is located in one of the poorest parts of the district. The students were very diligent but so poor that they didn't even have a chataai.

People around the school saw these kids sitting on the bare floor for their lessons and decided to 'do something'. But a dari cost 600 rupees, which they could not afford…

Then someone said, "Arey, you don't need 600, just collect 200 rupees."

The government has a Mo School program, they will give the rest. Oh, they said, 200 rupees we can manage. Someone gave 5 rupees, someone gave 10 rupees, like that they gathered 200. Putting 20 names felt odd, so they put just one person's name and sent it to Mo School. 400 rupees was disbursed and the dari was purchased.

Susmita often uses the Pulla Palli story to demonstrate that no contribution is 'too small'.

"I went to the US..." she recalls. "I was talking to about 120 people from Odisha and at the end, they had tears in their eyes."

The emotional connect with individual schools has not only brought funding to the system but valuable academic inputs. The year before Covid, Subroto spent every Saturday for one full year mentoring the top 11 students of Class 10 at his former school. All of them got a first class, with one even joining medicine.

Serving the nation with their talent and intellect was indeed satisfying. But it was only one side of the story...

FINDING A PATH

When Mindtree started in 1999, Subroto Bagchi liquidated his provident fund, gratuity, and stock options, and put all the money into MindTree – Rs 56 lakh in total. The company went public in 2007, and it dawned on the Bagchis that they had come into significant wealth.

"Had it been 5X or 10X the original investment, I could safely say – this is my money."

When the multiple is, say, 1000X, the question arises, is it truly mine? The Bagchis were deeply inspired by a Rabindranath Tagore poem, which contained this idea:

Your breath is not yours, your speech is not yours, your wealth is not yours.

When you came out of your mother's womb, the nurse held you upside down, patted your back, and then, you start breathing. So, breath is given to you, as a loan. You have to leave it behind, one day. If I have to return my breath, then what about wealth?

Am I the owner, or am I just a custodian, with a duty to use it for the greater good?

The Bagchis sat down with their daughters to discuss, as a family, what should we do with our money? The girls responded – it's your money, give it to whomever you want.

"But please do it in your lifetime," was their request. "Don't leave the job for us."

It was also important to keep enough for the Bagchis to live comfortably, till the very end. Accordingly, 1/3rd of Subroto's holdings in Mindtree were kept aside for this purpose – to be managed by Susmita – while 2/3rd was their corpus for philanthropic work, to be managed jointly.

Now there was an important decision to make – do we get directly involved in solving problems, or, support organisations who are doing good work? The Bagchis decided that it was more prudent to support existing organisations. In that spirit, they looked for causes and vehicles to contribute to.

Over the years, the Bagchis supported many worthy organisations working in education and health (cancer, vision and geriatric care being the focus). Then came Covid, and everything changed. Sitting in their government bungalow with expansive gardens, the couple had plenty of time, and the urge to 'do something' in that time of crisis.

Odisha is a state which supplies migrant labour to all parts of India. As wave after wave of workers returned, the government did its best to help - setting up quarantine centres, running kitchens.

But these people suddenly had no income, no means of sustenance. This is where the Bagchis stepped in.

"We met the administration and said, here is some money to take care of them."

This act of generosity was inspired by ideas put forth by Nobel Laureate Abhijit Banerjee. The Bagchis chose two districts – the first being Bolangir, where Subroto was born. An extremely backward district, with a large agricultural migrant population. The second was Puri, a pilgrim town whose economy was shattered during Covid.

The most affected were women, particularly widows, who make a living by selling diyas, or wash utensils in roadside eateries. So, the moment a woman came to the quarantine centre, she received a cash transfer of Rs 2500 in her Aadhar-linked bank account. On the advice of the district collector of Puri, each beneficiary received cash for 6 months.

While it was the need of the hour, the Bagchis were well aware that it would not create a permanent impact.

What more can we do, was the Big Question.

CREATING INSTITUTIONS

As they struggled with this dilemma, the Bagchis had a surprising realisation. Over the years, they had spent most of their philanthropic corpus, but the Mindtree shares kept aside for personal use had appreciated significantly. So, once again, they sat down with their daughters to figure out – iska kya hoga?

"The decision was that 90% of this money will be given away in our lifetime, as well."

This realisation gave a kind of urgency to making a decision. If the additional corpus had to put to good use – within the next few years – the Bagchis would need to find a large project.

They were both gung-ho about doing 'something big' but, deciding what to do was a dance between emotion and reason.

Subroto is impulse-driven, he comes up with 20 ideas. Susmita is the pragmatist who shoots down 10 of them (and rightly so, says her spouse). But when there is an 'aha' moment, where emotion and reason come together, there is no looking back.

"We walk away after making our contribution to an institution."

The cause that the Bagchis were most drawn to was health. However, they were unable to find an NGO with good governance – and a scalable model – in the sector. Finally, they realised, a large corpus could be best used to fund a hospital. A traditional choice, perhaps, but one which was sure to benefit the state.

So, they walked into the chief secretary's office and shared this idea.

Without hesitation, he said, "Do something for cancer patients."

There was just one government cancer hospital in the state, in Cuttack, and it could not handle the rush of cases. Most patients therefore went to Kolkata, or even as far as Mumbai, in search of treatment. The entire family faced great hardship and often ended up going bankrupt.

The Bagchis readily agreed. Yes, we will find an organisation doing good work and provide funds to set up a specialist cancer hospital in Odisha. So, they reached out to Tata Memorial Centre, and a few other institutions. But either there was no connect, or it didn't work out for technical reasons.

One of the organisations that the Bagchis greatly admired was Karunashraya, an institution which provides end-of-life care to terminally ill cancer patients. When you walk into their campus in

Bangalore, you don't feel that you are in a medical establishment. There is an air of peace, of acceptance, and of divinity.

"It made me realise that even death can be a sublime experience," says Subroto.

The Bagchis requested Karunashraya to come to Bhubaneswar and set up a palliative care centre. However, they still hadn't found a partner to set up the hospital itself and expressed their frustration in this matter. That's when Kishore Rao, founder, Karunashraya, made an excellent suggestion.

"Why don't you look at the work of Shankara Cancer Research Foundation?" he said.

The Bagchis met Dr. B. S. Srinath, the man behind the Sri Shankara Cancer Hospital, and were impressed by his body of work. A celebrated cancer surgeon, the good doctor had returned to India and set up several hospitals. Then, he had the desire to create a charitable institution.

To build a world-class cancer hospital one needs Rs 2 crore per bed. Dr. Srinath did not have the means. However, he was an ardent devotee of Shankaracharya. When he met his guru, His Holiness said – our muth has 5 acres of land in Bangalore, take it for your hospital. Then, bit by bit, Dr. Srinath raised enough money to put up 650 beds.

"Will you help us set up a hospital in Bhubaneswar?" the Bagchis asked him.

Dr. Srinath was more than happy to share his expertise but Subroto said, no, we want you to give you the money to set up the hospital. Susmita and Subroto were inspired by philanthropist Alfred P Sloan and engineer Charles F Kettering who signed a cheque, and walked away.

Creating the renowned Memorial Sloan Kettering Institute.

When Dr. Srinath consulted the Shankaracharya, who said that Bhubaneswar is actually one of the many names of Lord Shiva. Go ahead, what are you waiting for? The government was extremely supportive. 22 acres of prime land with all clearances was sanctioned in quick time.

"Lasting inter-generational institutions get built when people come together."

From day one, this hospital would be one of the largest in India for cancer treatment, with 750 in-patient beds and 300 beds for people who have been operated on and need to come back for further treatment.

But then, Susmita wondered, what about patients who cannot be cured? We also need to offer palliative care.

So the Bagchis went to the government and they gave an adjacent 20 acres of land, completely free. This would be the site of the Bagchi-Karunashraya Palliative Care centre. The Bagchis donated Rs 370 crore, of which 240 crore was for the cancer hospital, 130 crores was for palliative care.

But to build a world-class hospital it takes Rs 2 crores per bed... where would the rest of the money come from?

TAKING THE LEAD

From the outset, Subroto was clear that there would be no Bagchi Trust and neither would they be members of the board. In fact, he was even hesitant at first about the hospital being named 'Bagchi Shankara', until Susmita convinced him otherwise.

It is important to lend our name, she said, in order to build trust and donate, as well.

"We want other people to say – 'I can outdo that'. That's a very powerful idea."

So, if your name is attached to an institution but you are not going to interfere, anything can happen once you have given the money. The institution can become a great success, or an abject failure. It's a high risk model with no guarantees. So the key is to identify people with the competence and the integrity, and place a bet on them.

This is a venture capital mindset, applied to philanthropy. A mindset that some initiatives may fail, but one or two will become wildly successful. In case of a VC, there is a desire, to get financial returns on the money invested. That's not the case with philanthropic money, of course. Here, the returns come to you in a different form.

"I call it 'joy capital'... Money which will relieve some pain and suffering in this world," says Subroto.

He also believes in the 'power of good'. When you start something in the spirit of service and operate with integrity, it attracts like-minded people. A gentleman based in London who lost his wife to cancer heard about the Bagchi Karunashraya Centre and wrote a cheque for Rs 40 lakh. And this is just one of many such people coming forward.

The money donated by the Bagchis created a critical mass, the momentum will come from both the government and civil society. As time goes by, paying patients subsidise the poor patients, the insurance model kicks in, and there will be CSR money and government schemes for low-income households.

Another case in point is the Indian Institute of Science project, which is envisaged as a super-speciality hospital but will also have a medical school attached. N.S. Parthasarathy (a co-founder of Mindtree), and his wife Radha, were keen to be a part of the IISc project. He heard about what the Bagchis had done in Odisha and reached out.

"We were looking for another project at that point of time," says Susmita. "It clicked."

Together, the two Mindtree founders and their wives committed Rs 425 crore to the IISc hospital. Sounds like a lot of money, but it's nowhere near what is needed to build an institution in the league of Harvard or Stanford Medical School. That would need an outlay of about Rs 2000 crore.

"But when Partha, Radha, Susmita and I came together, it opened the floodgates."

In fact, says Subroto, the idea of 'how much is enough' is slowly getting redefined.

Paying your taxes – good, but not enough.

Donating a little here and there – great, but not enough.

If you have made big money, you need to sign up for bigger things and make bigger commitments. The collective power of 'individual social responsibility' will then kick in.

THE IMPACT

The brief given to the architect designing the cancer hospital was simple. Build a beautiful space which represents not just treatment but healing. That vision became a reality when The Bagchi Sri Shankara Cancer Centre and Research Institute was formally inaugurated on February 15, 2024.

By this time Karunashraya was already providing pain management and counselling services to patients and their families through home visits. The 110-bed Bagchi Karunashraya Palliative Care Centre followed on January 21, 2025. Both centres are attracting patients from West Bengal, Jharkhand, Chhattisgarh, and beyond.

As for the public service stint, Subroto Bagchi stepped down as Chairman of the Odisha Skill Development Authority after putting in eight years of sweat, spirit and strategy. Odisha's ITIs now send students to Singapore for internships, as well as job placements.

"My task was making people believe in themselves, to go beyond their self-perception."

Susmita's journey with Mo School Abhiyaan was equally satisfying. By the time her term ended, more than Rs 700 crore contributed by the alumni had been channelised to Odisha's government schools. The overall infrastructure and quality of teaching thus improved vastly, improving the odds for its students.

It's not how much we give, but how much love we put into giving, Mother Teresa used to say.

So, give all you can, with all your love...
That's the best anyone can do, in this earthly life.

Post Script:

In his new book, 'The Day the Chariot Moved: How India Grows at the Grassroots', Subroto Bagchi has shared his reflections on his eight-year long tenure as Chairman of the Odisha Skill Development Authority. A must-read for anyone working in policy, development, or change management.

For more on the Bagchis' philanthropic work :

ADVICE TO YOUNG PHILANTHROPISTS

Susmita: I would say a very simple thing, don't procrastinate. Just do it. Do it now.

Subroto: Make sure that you work hard, pay your taxes, don't cut corners, build some really solid economic power - however large or small it may be - and put it to good use.

Corollary to that is, I think it is important to be engaged but not attached. As a principle in whatever work we do, we guide ourselves on the basis of three things:

1. We will not have anything to do with the supply chain of your organization.
2. We will not come and tell you whom to employ.
3. We will never ever be part of your trust or board.

So, we do our pre-work and then take a risk, on the basis of shared vision, competence, scalability and governance.

There are so many problems, intervention is required now. Don't start doing a business case analysis and long-term planning, human misery does not wait. Find someone who is capable of making an impact and give them a free hand, tell them to 'think big'. Put your resources behind them. Then, the result is magical.

Concluding Reflections

India has always had a very strong tradition of giving. In the past, the purpose of giving was usually to uplift the less fortunate. While this remains a strong motivator for philanthropists today, India's philanthropic landscape is undergoing a transformation.

Today, wealth creators are engaging with causes not just emotionally but systemically.

They are building institutions, backing changemakers, and investing in population-scale solutions that will help shape India's future. Today, a strong sense of purpose and a desire for lasting impact sit side-by-side with the existing impulses of generosity, seva and daan.

This book — 'Live to Give' — showcases this change. It brings together sixteen stories of Indian philanthropists who have embraced giving not as a side project, but as a second calling.

Some lead with their hearts and work hands-on to uplift lives. Others bring strategic clarity to build systems and scale solutions. Still others give with quiet trust, enabling those closest to the ground, while yet others build lasting institutions.

Whether Prana, Gyaan, or Daan — each path is purposeful, and each story is a reflection of what it means to give with intent and what it means to experience the joy of giving.

Each story embodies a wonderful fusion of Gandhiji's mantra — 'Be the change you want to see in the world' — and Mother Teresa's gentle belief — 'It's not how much we give but how much love we put into giving'.

We are deeply grateful to these 16 philanthropists for generously sharing their time and their work, thus enabling Rashmi Bansal to capture their journeys with nuance, authenticity, and emotional depth. Rashmi's storytelling reminds us that behind every act of giving is a human journey — of reflection, courage, and commitment.

At AIP, we strive every day to enable philanthropists at every step of their giving journey — in every way, for every cause. We are able to do this due to the generous support of our Core Founders and Founders, who passionately believe in the transformative power of strategic philanthropy and in the need to encourage it in every way possible.

As we celebrate philanthropy through this book, we hope it also inspires many more to join the philanthropic movement and to give more, give sooner, and give better. The future we dream of for all begins with us. Let us live to give.

Amitabh Jaipuria

CEO, Accelerate Indian Philanthropy

For more on AIP scan:

Acknowledgments

I wish to express my deep gratitude to Ashish Dhawan and Accelerate Indian Philanthropy (AIP) for this wonderful idea and the support in connecting me to these 16 amazing philanthropists.

Thank you, Piyush Doshi, Amitabh Jaipuria, and Aditi Ray, for your guidance, vision, and unwavering belief in this project.

To Radhika Jain, Preethi Jain, Vishal Dutta, Supriya Shukla, and Shayan Ahmad, for keeping up the momentum.

Bhavi Mehta for delivering against all odds, and ever-cheerful Madan, for never complaining about making one more pdf.

Varsha Shah, who is the backbone of Bushfire Publishing.

My friend Prosenjit Datta for his valuable early feedback.

Sapna Nair for conducting supporting interviews.

Dipanita Chatterji, Sobhana Menon, and Goonja Tanna from Eklavya School, Ahmedabad; Shireen Sultana, Dhanashree Joglekar, Arshia Mulla and Samyukta Prabhu from WIIM Book Club; and Nandini Bhaskaran – for vetting the copy.

My four-legged babies Maya and Buttercup; dearest Nivi; Lata; my parents; and Yatin – for keeping me grounded.

To all the philanthropists who let me into their hearts and homes. You have energised me, inspired me.

I am hopeful about the future. Of our country, of our world.

Resource List

To connect with the foundations in this book, write to:

The Shibulal Family Philanthropic Initiatives: info@sfpi.org

Rekhta Foundation: contact@rekhta.org

Parivartan Bihar: info@parivartanbihar.org

Natco Trust: trust@natcopharma.com

Telerad Foundation: info@teleradfoundation.org

Veddis Foundation: info@veddis.org.

Wadhwani Institute of AI: contact@wadhwaniai.org

Simply Sport: darshan@simplysport.in

Aparajita Foundation: pbhasin3@gmail.com

Mariwala Health Initiative:
contact@mariwalahealthinitiative.org

Koita Foundation: info@koitafoundation.org

Faizal Shabana Foundation: faizal@kefholdings.com

Rare Foundation (Jhunjhunwala Family):
rarefamilyfoundation@gmail.com

Ajit Isaac Foundation: aif@iecorp.in

Accelerate Indian Philanthropy (AIP) :
info@indianphilanthropy.org

Notes